LAUTNER

THE STONE VALLEY PACK
BOOK ONE

ELIZABETH JONES

CONTENTS

1. Dani — 1
2. Lautner — 9
3. Dani — 15
4. Lautner — 21
5. Dani — 26
6. Lautner — 33
7. Lautner — 36
8. Dani — 41
9. Lautner — 45
10. Dani — 53
11. Lautner — 56
12. Lautner — 61
13. Dani — 63
14. Lautner — 69
15. Lautner — 72
16. Lautner — 79
17. Lautner — 86
18. Dani — 89
19. Lautner — 97
20. Lautner — 105
21. Dani — 110
22. Lautner — 115
23. Dani — 120
24. Lautner — 123
25. Lautner — 131
26. Dani — 138
27. Lautner — 142
28. Dani — 147
29. Lautner — 150
30. Lautner — 156
31. Lautner — 162

32. Lautner	165
33. Dani	169
34. Lautner	176
35. Dani	181
36. Lautner	187
37. Lautner	196
38. Lautner	202
39. Dani	205
40. Lautner	211
41. Lautner	216
42. Dani	219
43. Lautner	223
44. Lautner	228
45. Lautner	233
46. Lautner	235
47. Dani	239
48. Lautner	245
49. Dani	250
50. Lautner	257
51. Dani	261
52. Lautner	264
53. Dani	268
Seth Coming Soon	273
About the Author	275

www.AuthorElizabethJones@gmail.com

Elizabeth Jones
Lautner: The Stone Valley Pack Book One
Copyright © Elizabeth Jones 2020
All rights reserved.

This is a work of fiction. Names, characters, places, events, locales, and incidents are either the author's imagination or used in a fictitious manner. Any resemblance to actual persons, living or dead, or actual events is purely coincidental. This book requires written permission from the author before it is reproduced in any form, except for brief quotations for a book review. This book contains mature themes and graphic sexual descriptions. If such things bother you, please do not continue reading past this point.

ISBN: 9798746741752

For Enquiries contact me at authorelizabethjones@gmail.com

Cover design: vikncharlie
Formatting: Bookish Author Services
Proofread: Heart Full of Reads Editing Services

This book is dedicated to my family. I have dreamed about being an author since I was in my teens, but it took me a long time to get here. I want my kids to know that with hard work and dedication, dreams can come true. To always follow their passion and let nothing stand in their way. And last but not least, to my husband, Lee. Not only has he put up with my endless amount of crazy for the past ten years, but for always believing in me. He has been my rock writing this book and never once gave up on my ability to see it through to the end. I love you all, always.

CHAPTER 1
DANI

Contract. Marriage. Drake. My father watches me from behind his desk, his crow black eyes boring into mine, just waiting for me to break. This is how he enjoys it, playing me, knowing damn well there isn't anything I can do about it.

"I mean, you're lucky that Drake would even want to marry you, considering the disappointment you turned out to be. After all, you can't shift. I suppose you did get your mother's looks, and, well ... Drake; he just loves a virgin." He leers with a sadistic glint in his eye.

I remain still. No matter how much I want to shout and scream at my father, I know it would be futile. There are only two ways this can play out. I can refuse, which would probably end me up in the hospital for a few days and still marrying Drake. Or I can remain stoic, hoping my walls stay in place just long enough to get me the hell out of here. I choose the latter. I wouldn't give him the satisfaction of seeing just how repulsed I am at the thought of Drake getting his hands or dick anywhere near me.

"You disappoint me, Danika," he spits. "I was hoping you would put up some sort of fight at least." His eyes continue to bore into mine as I start to feel the brush of his power against my skin. The power of the alpha. It feels like a thousand spiders racing over my body as I shudder at the intrusion, but he doesn't stop. His power rises, slamming into me until I fall to my knees, gasping for breath. My eyes lower in submission of their own accord, staring at the Persian rug beneath me. My mind searches for anything to help keep me from losing consciousness.

On my twelfth birthday, my father had caught me and my best friend, Lacey, in here, sampling his expensive scotch. The way his soulless black eyes had glanced at my friend had turned my stomach, and I had vomited all over it. He had backhanded me so hard across the face I thought I was going to pass out from the pain. I remember screaming at Lacey to run, to save herself. But like the true friend she is, she remained and watched as my father beat me, not being able to do a damn thing but letting me know that she wouldn't abandon me.

I would never forget that day. It's the day my seizures had started. I'd curled into a ball in the middle of the floor, trying to protect my fragile body from my father's vicious assault. White light flashed behind my closed eyelids, and a growl resounded around the room. It was the last thing I remember. The next day, I woke up in my room to my father handing me my medication.

The high-pitched shrill of his office phone pulls me from my memories as I hear my father curse, his power slowly leaving me. I slowly lift my eyes, watching him answer the call.

"Very well," he mutters as if he isn't vaguely interested in whoever is on the other side of the phone. But I can see the way his shoulders tense up. Whoever it is, has my father rattled, and I can't help but smile. "I will be there tonight as requested," he barks, slamming the receiver back into its cradle. I watch as he brings his fingers to his forehead, rubbing them back and forth rhythmically, deep in thought.

This is my chance.

Climbing to my feet, I head toward the big oak doors of his office, wanting far away from this room and the nightmares they hold.

"Danika," he calls out just as I reach the handle.

With a sigh, I turn around, meeting his cruel crow black eyes once more.

"Your fate is sealed." He smiles, holding the contract high up in the air, waving it around like a victory flag. "There's nothing you can do about it now."

I turn away, hoping he doesn't notice the uncontrollable shudder running down my spine at his words.

※

"Your father is going to kill you one of these days, Dani," Lacey warns me.

I pick up the concealer off my dressing table, applying it under my tired eyes. After leaving my father's office, I had come straight up to my bedroom calling her. She had come straight 'round after hearing about my father's latest news.

"I mean, what is he thinking, ordering you to marry Drake. He's like what, thirty," she continues, undeterred by my silence. "You deserve so much better than that sadistic asshole."

I lift my eyes up to meet hers in the mirror, and I can tell she means every word. I loved Lacey dearly, but she's still too innocent when it comes to my father. I honestly believe that deep down, she believes my father will change and let me lead my own life one day. It's all lies, and yet, it's one of the reasons I love her. She always believes in the good in people, even those who can't be saved.

Sighing, I place the concealer down. "Have you met my father. He doesn't give a damn what I want; he never has."

"But surely, there must be something we can do to get you out of this? You're only nineteen and haven't even shifted yet. How can he expect you to marry!" she snaps, pacing the floor.

"I have no doubt my father has something invested in this marriage, which means he can't kill me. Not yet, so stop worrying."

"Ugh, why are you accepting this?"

Groaning loudly, I pinch the bridge of my nose in a feeble attempt to stop the migraine I can feel coming on. "I'm not. I just need time to think," I reply as my phone beeps loudly beside me. I quickly pick it up, grateful for the distraction.

Daniel: *Everything okay? I haven't heard from you in days*
D x

I smile as I read Daniel's text. We had met six weeks ago on an app created by the Shifter Council, designed to encourage communication between the packs. As a rule, packs didn't get along. Too much testosterone is my guess. Most of the alphas were opposed to it, mine included. Luckily, I had a secret burner phone that Lacey had sneaked in for me after my father confiscated my last one.

Me: *Not really. I could use a drink x*

I place my phone back on the dressing table continuing to get ready.

"So, what's the plan. Where are you going tonight?" Lacey asks, finally dropping down on my bed.

"I don't know," I reply honestly. My father and Drake left about an hour ago. I'd overheard him explaining to Terry, our pack's tracker, that they wouldn't be back until at least the early hours of the morning. That meant for the next few hours, I am free.

"Anywhere that isn't here," I answer as my phone beeps again.

Daniel: *Meet me tonight? D x*
Me: *Where? x*
Daniel: *The Warehouse D x*

I can feel the goosebumps rising on my arm—the Warehouse. The one place forbidden by my father. Situated on the outskirts of Stone Valley, it's home to the Sun Sinners Motorcycle Club. A group of vampires that ran most of the businesses in the area, legal and otherwise. The Warehouse clientele isn't your everyday club full of underage teens. It's home to the dark underworld of the Valley. There are many rumors about the place, from illegal fights to the death, to the selling of black-market body parts. I nervously nip at my bottom lip, wondering just how pissed I am at my father to risk taking such a chance. That's easy. I'm super pissed.

Me: *See you at 8 x*

Placing my phone down, I head over to my closet, searching for something to wear.

"I'm going to the Warehouse," I say to Lacey as I pull out a short black dress that leaves little to the imagination.

"The Warehouse. Are you Insane? It-it's not safe," she stammers, looking at me as if I've clearly lost my mind. Maybe I had.

"No, but it's the perfect place," I answer. "Who's going to see me?" I head into the bathroom, not waiting for her reply. She knows better than to try and talk me out of it.

The dress clings to my body like a second skin as I carefully pull up the zip at the side. Turning around, I check out my reflection in the full-length mirror. My silver-blonde hair hung in loose waves down my back, and the sultry dark makeup I'd added earlier completed the look. I was almost unrecognizable even to myself. Lacey was right. If my father could see me now, he probably would kill me.

"Wow, you look amazing," Lacey says as I stride back into the room.

"Are you sure you don't want to come?" I ask, although I know she would never betray an order from her alpha. He terrified her, and she had every right to fear him. I'd always tried my hardest to keep Lacey away from him. Away from trouble. I was only offering her to come along to be kind. If I thought for a minute she would have agreed, I would never have asked. My father had never used her against me, but I wouldn't put it past him.

"No, I'll stay. Someone needs to deal with your father's spies," she warns me.

"Remember, if my father or Drake rings, I'm in the shower or—"

"Gone to bed early, I know," she finishes for me. "It's not

the first time. I still don't like the thought of you going alone, though." She braids her hair nervously from where she sits on the bed.

"I won't be going alone," I say, as I slip my feet into a pair of four-inch stilettoes with a frown. I hated wearing heels. At 5ft 2, I was relatively short, and if the Warehouse clientele were as bad as I'd heard, I didn't want to look small and weak any more than necessary. "I'm meeting Daniel."

Lacey knew all about Daniel and our texts, but judging by the tense look on her face, I can tell she doesn't approve of me running off to meet a stranger. I don't blame her, but as strange as it sounds, I trust him.

"Don't worry," I say, smiling confidently to ease her nerves. "I promise I won't be late."

"Fine, just promise me if he gives you any serial killer vibes, you'll get the hell out of there. I don't want to see you on one of those murder documentaries you love so much," she grumbles, and I laugh. I did have an unhealthy obsession with murder porn as I liked to call it. Maybe it's the fact that my whole life was one big mess of violence and despair. I could relate to why half of these people became murderers. After all, in most cases, it was their upbringing, their parents' fault. And I can so relate to that. Lacey, on the other hand, fainted at the slightest hint of blood.

"I promise," I say, going over and giving her a hug before heading for the door. "Don't worry, Lace. I'll see you later."

I practically jog my way downstairs as I head for the exit through the kitchen, leading into the underground garage. My old 1964 red Ford Mustang greets me as I climb inside. I start the engine, hearing her purr as I nervously shiver in anticipation of what lies ahead. Waiting for the garage door to open, I quickly check my phone—one new text.

Daniel: *See you at the bar at 8 D x*

My smile widens as I slip my phone back into my purse. Exiting the garage, I ease down the road, following the signs for Stone Valley.

CHAPTER 2
LAUTNER

My eyes scan the room from where I sit at the pack's usual table, nestled in the back corner of the Warehouse. Destiny, one of the Sun Sinners' whores, astride my lap, whispers her dirty fantasies in my ear. I grip Destiny's hips roughly, and she eagerly grinds against me, begging for my attention. Usually, I hate being touched. Prolonged touching was reserved for fucking or fighting, and this is neither. This is business.

"Are you ready for tonight?" Seth asks, dropping down in the booth beside me. Destiny stops her gyrating just long enough to throw him a dirty look before continuing to rub herself against me. Seth is the closest thing I have for a best friend; he's also my pack brother. He's looking rather happy tonight, which makes a change from his usual brooding.

"I'm always ready," I reply as Destiny ups her game, stroking me through my jeans with deft fingers. She can try all she wants, but I'm not getting hard. Not yet. Business first, pleasure later. The Warehouse on a Friday night meant only one thing, fight night. The illegal cage fights hosted by the Club brought in a shit ton of money, and as the undefeated champion, Cal paid me five grand a fight. Don't get me wrong, his choice of fighters were getting better, but I'd grown up fighting. Fighting to survive. It was second nature. Violence ran in my blood, and I didn't get my reputation as the youngest pack enforcer for nothing.

Relieved at Seth's interruption, I remove Destiny's eager hand, nudging her off my lap. "Leave us."

"But Lautner," she whines, her long fake nails clawing their way down my naked chest, leaving little red streaks in their wake as if staking her claim. "I thought you wanted to play?" She raises her eyebrow suggestively.

"Later," I say, forcing a smile on my face, even though I want nothing more than to throw her off me. "Right now, we got business."

She reluctantly moves from my lap, taking extra time to rub herself against me in all the right places, before heading back to her pole in the middle of the dance floor.

"You do realize we're supposed to be looking for signs of the hunters, not getting our dick wet," Seth reminds me with a laugh.

"You know as well as I do, Destiny has very loose lips," I remind him, pulling my black wifebeater back over my head.

"And even looser hips by the looks of it," he remarks as we watch her perform a crazy move on the pole.

Tearing my eyes away from Destiny, I glance around the room. "Where's Daniel?" I ask, hoping he's keeping out of trouble. Daniel is nineteen, the youngest member of our pack and our alpha's only son. He's your typical technology-obsessed teen. Always with his head in his iPhone or iPad.

"Off meeting some female he's been chatting to on that

shifter app he's been so obsessed with lately," Seth replies, clearly bored.

Great, that's all we need—a lovesick teenager hanging around the place. Don't get me wrong, I have nothing against love; it's just not for me. I fight, and I fuck; and depending on the night, not necessarily in that order.

"Anyways," he continues regaining my attention, "did you find out anything useful from Destiny? Or just her fees for tonight."

"Ha-ha," I reply at his dry humor. Destiny may be a Club whore, but she is damn good at getting men to talk. It's one of the reasons the Sun Sinners paid her so generously.

"A few days ago, two members of the South River Pack came in. Cal sent her over with a couple of free beers as she worked her magic. It wasn't long before they started talking. According to the men, they were running an errand for their alpha and were a little late for their weekly meet. By the time they got back, it was already too late. They said it looked like a massacre had taken place."

"That must be what the meeting is about tonight. I take it there were no other survivors?" Seth asks, raising his brow.

I shake my head. "One person is missing, though, who they claim would have been in attendance. Tai, their pack's enforcer."

"You think they took him?"

I nod. "From what I've heard about Tai, he doesn't seem the type to betray his pack."

"You think he could still be alive?"

"Doubt it. They've had more than enough time to torture him for information."

"So, we're back to square one," he replies defeatedly, slumping back in the booth.

"Not necessarily. We know they're close. It won't be long before they come looking for us. Hopefully, Mick and Ryan are having better luck than we are."

Mick is our alpha, and Ryan, our beta. The Shifter Council had called this afternoon for an emergency meeting. As shifters, we've always had our enemies, usually strays—lone shifters who prefer to follow their animal instincts rather than their human ones. It was Seth's job to track them, and I, as the enforcer, to take them out. It was a tedious job, but one we had gotten used to doing over the years. But none had ever come close to being an actual threat as these new hunters.

It started about a year ago. Single pack members going missing, only to be found tortured and mutilated a few days later. Now, entire packs were being wiped out, and no one had even come close to finding out who they were.

"Lautner." At the sound of my name, I turn my head, finding Thane, Vice President of the Sun Sinners, heading toward us. Tonight, Thane is dressed from head to toe in black leather, his long black hair flowing freely down his back. He's the easiest to place amongst the vampires, always adoring a flair for the dramatics. "Cal wants to see you in his office before the fight," he says, coming to a stop before me.

"Why?" I ask, instantly on edge. Cal is the President of the Sun Sinners MC and owner of the Warehouse, and he had never called me in before a fight.

Thane shrugs his shoulders, picking at his black-painted nails. "Do I look like his personal assistant," he replies sarcastically.

"You're his VP, aren't you," I quip.

"Yeah, VP, not PA," Thane snaps. "Now I suggest you go and ask him."

I extend my middle finger, flipping him off. Standing, I

nod to Seth before making my way down to Cal's office in the basement. It's cold and dark down here with no windows, but luckily, I can see perfectly well with my heightened eyesight. Coming to a stop outside Cal's office, I rap my knuckles against the door.

"Come in," Cal's gruff voice calls out.

I enter the room, which is a lot more pleasant than the dingy dark corridor I had walked down to get here. Cal might be an old vampire, but the man has expensive taste. If it weren't for the lack of windows, it might easily be mistaken for a fancy New York office.

"Lautner." His smile widens as he sees me, ushering me in with a wave of his hand as if he's motherfucking royalty or some shit.

"What's going on, Cal?" I ask, dropping into the black executive leather chair across from him.

I watch as he leans back in his chair, placing his legs on the table. Picking up his cigarettes, he taps one out before offering me one. I shake my head as he shrugs his shoulders before lighting one up.

"The Stone Valley Pack and the Sun Sinners have always had an understanding, yes. You leave us to our business, and we leave you to yours," he says on an exhale, sending a waft of smoke my way.

I nod.

"Good, then let's not fuck about. I was approached yesterday by Tommy West. It looks like he, and his brother, Brandon, are back in town."

I tighten my hold on the leather armrests as I feel my anger rise. That asshole had raped and killed two humans in our territory two years ago. If it hadn't been for Seth screwing up and getting his ass kidnapped, he would be dead by now, him and his brother.

"What does he want?" I ask, wondering what the hell would bring them back here. It was suicide, and they knew it.

"You. He paid me ten thousand dollars so he can get in the ring with you tonight."

I can feel the brush of my wolf beneath my skin, excited at the prospect of finally getting our revenge on one of the West brothers. "Good. I've been waiting to get my hands on Tommy," I say as I watch Cal smile, taking another drag of his cigarette. "But I have one condition."

"And what's that?" Cal asks, dropping his feet from the desk and leaning forward toward me.

"He doesn't leave the ring alive."

CHAPTER 3
DANI

I cautiously make my way through the Warehouse as my eyes search out the bar. I'd promised Lacey that I would stay out of trouble, and I'd meant it. But I wasn't naïve. An alpha like my father didn't get to keep his position for so many years without making enemies along the way. I've no doubt there would be many here tonight who would love to use me against my father. Luckily, I wasn't worried about being recognized. My father had kept me hidden for most of my life, probably embarrassed by the disappointment I turned out to be. Keeping my head high, I can feel their eyes penetrate at my back, but I'm not worried. I know they will smell wolf. I may not have shifted yet, but I've no doubt she's in there, somewhere. Besides, according to rumor, shifting is forbidden inside the club, so I should be safe for tonight. I continue walking straight ahead, coming to a set of four steel steps leading down. As people brush past me in both directions, I make my way over to the bar I spot in the far corner.

"What can I get you?" a man asks as I sit down on an old, battered bar stool that had seen better days.

"Beer," I shout to be heard over the loud music. He nods, turning away to retrieve my order. I catch sight of the Sun Sinners emblem on the back of his leather kutte. It's a picture of a flaming skull with the word "prospect" underneath.

"Dani," a male voice calls out behind me.

I slowly turn around, my eyes widening as I take in the man before me. He's gorgeous. His dark wavy brown hair hanging just over his right eye as he smiles shyly, revealing two perfect dimples at his cheeks.

"Daniel?" I ask, although somehow, I already know it's him.

He nods. "Wow, you look incredible." His eyes shamelessly rake up and down my body as I feel the rush of heat in my cheeks. I'm not used to compliments, and I'd been worried that I wouldn't blend in tonight. But by the look Daniel is throwing my way, I had definitely succeeded.

"Is everything alright? I'm kind of surprised you agreed to meet me," he replies, taking the empty seat next to me as his leg brushes against mine.

"Yeah, everything's fine," I assure him. "I just wanted to get out of the house and experience this place for myself." Although Daniel and I had been chatting for weeks now, I had never told him who my father is. There were some things better kept to yourself. I also have no intention of telling him about my upcoming engagement to Drake. My friendship with Daniel is like an alternate universe in which I can pretend to be normal.

"Yeah, this place is something alright," he laughs, "and you couldn't have picked a better night than fight night. My pack brother, Lautner, is the champion here, if you want to watch?" he asks eagerly, pride evident in his voice.

I nod before taking a quick drink of my beer.

"By the way, sorry I'm a little late. With all this hunter business going on, I've been trying to find possible locations for the pack to stake out in case they turn up here next."

"What hunter business?" I ask, confused.

"Damn, you weren't lying, were you. Your alpha really does keep you in the dark. I'm sorry, I shouldn't have said anything," he says, averting his eyes.

"Please, tell me. If it concerns shifters, then I deserve to know," I plead, wondering what my father is hiding. He had always kept his pack on a tight leash and everyone on a need-to-know basis.

After a moment's silence, he nods before continuing, "A small pack a few towns over were massacred at their meet. It's not the first one either, it's been going on for the past year now. The numbers started small, but now they seem to be getting bolder, and it looks like they are heading this way," he responds nervously, looking away as if he is wondering whether or not he is going to get into trouble for telling me.

"Is that why my father was called away tonight?"

"Yeah. All the alphas were summoned by the Council to try and work out a way of identifying them before they hit us. My alpha has me tracking abandoned locations online, looking for any signs of recent activity."

"Should we be worried?"

"I haven't found any trace of them yet. I think we're good for now." He smiles.

Picking up my beer, I drink up, finishing the remainder of the bottle. I don't drink much, and I can already feel the effects of the alcohol calming my nerves.

Daniel turns toward the bar ordering us another two drinks. Turning to me, he hands over another beer to me. "So, are you ready to head upstairs and witness your first infamous Warehouse fight?"

Smiling, I nod, accepting the drink from his hand as we both stand. Daniel places his hand low on my back, leading the way. "Is it always so busy here?" I ask as we wait behind a row of people waiting to climb the stairs.

"Only on fight night. Shifters, humans, vampires, the gene pool doesn't matter. Most people pretend that they detest violence, but they can't help but be enamored when it all comes down to it. The women," he suddenly whispers in my ear, causing me to shiver, "they get off on it. You can smell their arousal in the air. And the men ... they feel a need to prove their worth. It brings their dominant side out to play. After a fight, you can feel the sexual tension in the air." He moves away slightly, and I feel dizzy at his words. I'm certainly feeling something in the air tonight.

As the crowd starts moving, I find myself eager to make my way to the second floor.

"There's my other pack brother, Seth," he points toward the left side of the cage.

Wow. The man he is referring to is huge. He stands, leaning back against the cage, thick tattooed arms folded across his chest. His eyes taking in everything around him, scowling at anybody who dares get too close.

"He doesn't look like he's having a good time," I say.

"Seth's a recovering addict. He's been clean for just over a year now, but this place ... well, Thane is the biggest drug dealer in the Valley. You can get anything and everything in this place. Usually, Lautner and I take turns keeping an eye on him just in case he slips off the wagon."

"What happened to him?" I ask curiously.

"Two years ago, there were a few attacks in Stone Valley. Women found raped and beaten in the woods. You might've heard about it, considering you're just the next town over."

I shake my head as he continues, "Well, the pack went out and caught the scent of two new strays in the area. Brothers, Brandon and Tommy West. I was only seventeen back then, so I wasn't allowed to go. One night, the pack got separated in their search, and when they returned home, Seth was missing. Lautner spent the next forty-eight hours searching every square inch of the Valley. Eventually, he found him alone in the cellar of an old cabin down by smokey's creek, bound, naked to a chair, covered in blood. Some of it was his own, the rest ... we don't know. Seth wouldn't talk about it, and we just let it go. That's when it started."

"The drugs?" I inquire.

"Yeah, and the nightmares."

"That's awful. I'm so sorry," I say, placing my hand on Daniel's arm in comfort.

"Yeah, well, as I say, we don't talk about it," he grumbles.

"Did you ever find them?"

"No, and the attacks stopped after that. The scent was never picked up again. Come on," he says, taking my hand and entwining our fingers together. "We better keep him company."

"Seth," Daniel calls out as we draw nearer. The man looks up, his scowl slowly easing as a smile takes its place.

"Hey man, you having a good night?" Seth asks as we approach, but his eyes remain fixed on me.

"Yeah. This is my friend Dani. Dani, this is Seth."

"It's nice to meet you." I hold out my hand, half

expecting him to refuse it. Instead, his warm palm connects with mine.

"You know, Daniel here has been talking about you for weeks now. It's great to finally put a face to the name." He winks.

"Thanks, Seth," Daniel mutters, his cheeks reddening as he turns away. "Where's Lautner?" he asks, quickly changing the subject.

Seth shrugs his shoulders. "Cal wanted a word with him before the fight. He should be here soon." As the words leave his mouth, the lights around us begin to dim. A tall man with long black hair, dressed from head to toe in black leather, starts walking toward the cage.

Suddenly nervous, I lick my lips, wondering what I'm letting myself in for.

Fight night is about to begin.

CHAPTER 4
LAUTNER

I remain hidden in the shadows, waiting for Thane to make his way down into the cage, ready to introduce the fight. My eyes glance around the room, knowing Tommy is up here somewhere. I spot Seth easily in the crowd, but I quickly turn away. I know I should have come straight up here and warned him off Tommy's reappearance, but I couldn't do it. He would have wanted to take my place, and he isn't ready to face his demons yet. Whatever had happened to him at their hands still plagues him, and I can't risk Tommy escaping a second time.

"Ladies and gentlemen," Thane's voice calls out loudly through a microphone. "Introducing to you your undefeated champion from the Stone Valley Pack, Lautner."

The crowd cheers loudly, but I pay them little attention. My eyes are firmly glued to the far corner where I now see Tommy smirking, leaning against the far wall. I casually stroll toward the ring, letting him know I'm not intimidated by his reappearance. In fact, I'm looking forward to it.

"And now introducing his opponent, Tommy West," Thane continues. This time the crowd reacts around me with a mixture of cheers and boos.

I watch him saunter toward the cage, his eyes never leaving mine. He had obviously been working out since the last time we met, looking to have gained at least twenty pounds of muscle. As if reading my mind, he smiles, a nervous tick working at the corner of his mouth.

"So, you're the old champion of this place." He smirks cockily, coming to a stop a few feet away from me.

"Tommy West. The way you and your brother left the Valley, I'm surprised you've got the balls to get in the ring with me. It must be my lucky day."

"You're dead, Lautner," he sneers, looking me up and down, obviously unimpressed by what he sees.

I return his sneer. The man before me was nothing more than a rapist and murderer. "You honestly think you can beat me in a fight, Tommy. You're crazier than I thought. You and your brother couldn't take me out. Where the hell is he, anyway? Don't tell me he's finally gotten sick of your bullshit." I watch his hands curl into fists, knowing I've hit a nerve. I can hear the chains behind me as a padlock clicks into place. This is it. Only one of us is leaving here tonight, alive, and there's no doubt in my mind that that person will be me.

"You leave him out of this," Tommy snaps, cracking his knuckles.

"It's a shame he's not going to be here to witness your death."

"You think you're untouchable, don't you," he snickers. "You've got no idea what you're up against."

The bell rings, cutting him off. We circle one another, looking for an opening. I carefully lower the barrier between my wolf as I feel Tommy do the same. I watch as his fist lashes out, but I quickly see it coming, ducking out of the way. He keeps pushing forward, feigning left and right, trying to catch me off guard. I watch as his breathing increases with every punch. He might be a big guy, but he tires easily.

Tommy lunges once more, this time catching me off guard with a hard right hook to the face. The son of a bitch is stronger than I thought. I quickly respond, punching him in the ribs until he drops his guard, and I hit his nose, hearing the satisfying crack of it breaking. Changing my tactics, I fake a left as he moves to block me. Turning swiftly, I catch him in the head with a roundhouse kick.

"That all you got," he snarls, advancing again. We continue to trade blows, and it isn't long before the scent of blood permeates the air. I can feel it trickle down the side of my face, but Tommy is bleeding just as badly. He catches me with a kick to the midsection, sending me crashing against the cage wall. My wolf growls underneath my skin, but it has nothing to do with the hit from Tommy. My wolf is drawn to the scent of vanilla that envelops us, coming from outside the cage. Turning, I focus my attention on the crowd, trying to trace its source. Tommy uses the distraction to his own advantage, landing three hard punches to the side of my head that I fail to block. *Fuck*. My head is spinning. I need to focus. The scent continues to torture me as I struggle to concentrate.

Pulling myself back to my feet, I turn to Tommy. The smirk on his face says it all. He thinks he's won. Unable to control my distracted wolf, I pull my shields back into place, blocking him out. This fight, I'm on my own. With the delicious scent no longer at the forefront of my mind, I plan my advance.

I throw a left that he easily blocks before catching him in the Adam's apple with my right. Caught off guard, he stumbles back, clutching at his throat. His mouth a wide O in shock as I quickly hook my leg behind his, forcing him to his knees. He lands hard as I grab his arm, twisting it behind his back.

"Your good pal Seth liked it rough too," he growls out as I pull tighter. "He fought a good fight, but we fucked him good."

"You're a fucking liar," I growl back, pulling on his arm until I hear the satisfying pop of his shoulder dislocating.

"Why don't you ask him," he groans, turning his eyes toward the outside of the cage, searching for Seth. I grip his hair with my free hand, twisting his head back at an odd angle, forcing his eyes back to me. "You don't get to look at him. You will look at me as you die."

Blocking out the noise from the crowd, I circle my hands around his throat, increasing the pressure. "This is it motherfucker," I whisper in his ear. "Say your last goodbyes. I'm going after your brother next, and I promise he won't get off as easy as you."

"You leave Brandon alone," he gasps, trying to claw at my hold with his one good hand.

"I don't think so. You can't imagine the things I'm planning on doing to him in the pit." I tighten my hold as I feel him start to weaken. "I'm going to take my sweet time skinning that bastard alive for what you both did. And when he begs for death, I'm going to let him heal and start all over again."

With a final burst of adrenaline, Tommy struggles wildly against my hold, panic taking over, furiously tapping at my shoulder as if in submission.

"This isn't the fucking UFC," I spit. "The rules are to the death. I'll see you in hell, Tommy."

With a sharp twist, the sound of his neck snapping reverberates around the room. I let his body fall to the floor—the crowd cheering wildly, chanting my name.

I instantly look up, finding Seth in the crowd. He's pressed against the cage, his eyes watching Tommy's unmoving body at my feet. I think back to Tommy's words, not wanting to believe them. As if reading my mind, Seth quickly looks up, and I can see the war raging within him. He's pissed. Whether at Tommy or me, it's hard to tell. I'm guessing it's both. Seth turns away, vanishing into the crowd. I can hear Thane behind me entering the ring, ordering his men to take Tommy's body out back and drain him. Never one to miss out on an opportunity, I knew he would make a hefty profit tonight selling shifter blood.

"Seth," I hear Daniel call out as I turn my head to look at him, instantly noticing the blonde at his side. As if sensing me looking, she lifts her head. She has the palest blue eyes that I've ever seen, but it isn't her eyes that hold me captive; it's my wolf. *Mate.*

CHAPTER 5
DANI

"Seth," Daniel calls out beside me after his friend, but I don't turn around. I'm too focused on the man in the cage whose amber eyes hold mine captive. My body trembling under the unfamiliar rush of power, burning its way under my skin.

He exits the cage like a natural-born predator. His muscles rippling under a multitude of scars scattered across his chest like a magnificent piece of art. *Had it only been moments ago that I watched him kill a man with his bare hands.* Yet as he strides toward me with purpose, I feel no fear but a sense of belonging.

"You need to leave. Now." He stops before me, my eyes dropping to his perfect mouth. "Can you hear me?" he growls, clearly irritated, and yet my breath catches in my throat as I close my eyes, feeling that growl right between my legs.

"No." It's the only word I can think to say. This close, his scent wraps around me, and he smells like the woods on a rainy fall day. The rush of power beneath my skin burns, as if seeking a way out to scent him for herself.

"It's not going to happen, you hear me."

Confused, I raise my head, opening my eyes. I'm surprised to find his eyes are no longer a beautiful burning amber but a deep black that sends a nervous shiver up my spine. There is nothing gentle about his gaze. It's hard and unforgiving. As if he wants nothing more than to kill me himself.

"Lautner," Daniel calls out as I hear him coming to a stop behind me.

"Where did Seth go?" Lautner asks, tearing his gaze from mine, leaving me cold.

"Don't worry, he's alright. He just needs a little time. I see you've met my friend Dani. Dani, this is Lautner."

"We've met. Now get her out of here, Daniel. She doesn't belong here," he spits maliciously.

"She's here with me," Daniel continues, undeterred by the look of hatred on Lautner's face.

"Fine, then take your whore, but keep her out of my way," he snaps.

I don't know what I had been expecting when he finally came over, but this open hostility wasn't it. "I'm no whore," I hear myself say, finally finding my voice. "My name is Dani Court, asshole," I snap back.

He smirks at my words as if I'd dared to speak to him that way. "Well, listen here, Dani Court. I don't know what the hell you're doing here, and I honestly don't care. Just stay the hell out of my way. We clear?"

"There you are." A scantily clad brunette comes up behind him, wrapping her arms around his waist and pressing herself tightly against his back. "Are you ready to play with me yet?" she asks, her voice husky as her hands roam over the taut muscles at his chest.

His eyes continue to watch me as if waiting for my response—a cruel smile on his face. I have the sudden urge to rip her hands away from him and replace them with my own. That man belonged to me, not her. I wait, glaring daggers at him, hoping he will cast her aside. Instead, he places his arm over her shoulder, pulling her close. "Let's go, babe," he replies, turning away with a sneer and taking whatever power I had been feeling beneath my skin along with him.

I watch until he vanishes into the crowd, immediately feeling the loss of his presence. A migraine comes out of nowhere as I gasp aloud, holding my head. The intense pain feels like it's splitting my brain in two as I start to panic. The last thing I want to do is have a seizure in the middle of the Warehouse.

"Dani, what's wrong?" Daniel asks, immediately rushing to my side.

"Pills. I need my pills." I frantically search my purse. "I know I put them in here somewhere," I mutter, finally grasping the pill bottle. I shake two out in the palm of my hand, swallowing them down with a drink of my beer as I wait for them to take effect.

"Come over here." Daniel takes my arm, leading me over to a seat on the outside of the cage.

We sit in silence for a few minutes, until finally, my heart stops pounding against my chest, and my breathing returns to normal.

"I'm okay," I finally say, breaking the awkward silence between us.

"Are you sure?" he asks, obviously still worried by my episode. "What was that?"

"Migraine," I say quietly, not wanting anyone else to hear. "The migraines come on first as a warning. If I don't take my pills in time, I end up having a seizure."

"Seizure," he repeats, looking confused. "You're a shifter, aren't you. Is that even possible?"

"I'm just special, I guess," I reply sarcastically, irritated by his response. He isn't the first shifter to look at me as if I were crazy. Shifters were supposed to be pretty much immune to everything except silver.

"Shit. I'm sorry, Dani. I didn't mean it to sound like that," he apologizes, bouncing on the balls of his feet, clearly uncomfortable. "It's just, well … I've never known a shifter to suffer any form of illness. Except for Lautner, that is, but his is more mental," he tries to joke before turning serious once more. "Look, I'm sorry, I should have warned you about him. He's not the most pleasant person to be around. In fact, he's a total asshole," he mutters angrily.

"It's okay, Daniel, really." I smile, hoping to ease some of the tension from the past few minutes.

"No, it's not."

"How about another drink, maybe something stronger this time?" I ask, trying to change the subject. The truth is, I didn't want to talk about Lautner, not with Daniel. He'd gotten under my skin, and I'm not sure why. I didn't know the man, and frankly, I'm not sure I wanted to after the way he'd acted.

"Sure. I can get us another drink," he says, jumping to his feet. "Stay here."

As Daniel heads back down to the bar, I start to think maybe Lacey had been right all along. I should never have come here. The last thing I want to do is stick around and risk running into Lautner and his girlfriend again. With my mind made up, I collect my purse off the floor, rushing down the stairs, hoping to hit the exit before Daniel returns.

As I fight my way through the crowded dance floor, a voice behind me stops me in my tracks.

"We need to talk."

His voice is like a gentle caress across my skin as I turn around, finding Lautner behind me. I feel like a deer caught in the headlights of his sparkling amber eyes as my heart starts beating erratically within my chest. He takes a step closer as I hear Daniel call out my name. Lautner scowls, turning to Daniel. Free from his gaze, I turn away, walking in the opposite direction. I see another staircase just to the right leading down and I hurry toward it, making my way down into its cold depths below.

"Dani," Lautner calls out right behind me now. I keep my head down, trying to ignore him. "Wait." His hand catches my shoulder, and I gasp at the electric charge, now humming through my body.

"You don't get to run from me," he growls in my ear. "Not unless you want me to chase you."

His words send a delicious shiver up my spine that has nothing to do with the cold and everything to do with his proximity behind me.

"I'm only doing what you asked, remember," I say, surprised at how husky my voice sounds. "I'm staying out of your way. I suggest you take your own advice and do the same. Go back to your girlfriend. I'm sure she'll be looking for you."

"Are you jealous, Dani?" he teases, bringing his chest tight against my back, brushing his stubbled cheek against mine.

"No," I lie as my breath catches in my throat, and I shudder at the pleasure of his touch.

"I think you're lying," he whispers. His hand trails down my arm, leaving goosebumps in their wake, and I moan at the sensation.

"What do you want from me?" I ask breathlessly.

"I ask the questions. Now, why did you run from me?" His hand continues to stroke little intricate patterns on my arm as if prepared to keep me here if I try to run again.

"I wasn't running; I was avoiding you. There's a difference." I close my eyes, trying to control the unfamiliar sensations raging through my body, making me feel alive for the very first time in my life.

"You shouldn't be down here. This is the Sun Sinners' private quarters. Unless you're invited, it's not safe."

"Something tells me I'd be safer with the vampires than you," I state, meaning every word.

He chuckles against my back, and I feel it vibrate all the way to my toes. "Your instincts are right," he replies, his hand moving across the plains of my stomach, pinning me against him. He towers over my petite frame, his body on fire as I lean back, desperate to capture its heat.

"Why are you doing this?" I whisper, wondering where the sudden rush of confidence is coming from.

"I don't know. I should be running as far away as possible from you right now, and yet here I am."

"That's not an answer," I say, opening my eyes and taking a step away from him. I feel the loss of his heat immediately, wrapping my arms over my chest for warmth.

"It's the only one I can give you."

His attitude is really starting to piss me off as I turn around to face him. My eyes darting over to the stairs behind him, wishing I'd never come down here in the first place. *Would he even let me leave?* I know Daniel will be looking for me.

"What ... are you hoping Daniel will come to your rescue," he sneers as if reading my mind. "No one can save you from me, Dani. Not unless I choose to let you go."

I shiver under the intensity of his gaze, sensing the truth in his words.

He's right. I'm completely at his mercy. I should be afraid. I'd just witnessed him kill a man with his bare hand's only moments ago, and yet with complete certainty, I know he would never hurt me. My feet move of their own accord as if pulled by an invisible string, until I'm standing before him, staring into his amber eyes. "What makes you think I need saving?" I ask, my hands reaching out until my palms connect with his muscled chest. He had yet to put on a shirt, and my fingertips trace the delicate white lines of his scars as I revel in the intense pleasure that fills my body at the contact of our skin.

"You're playing with fire Dani ... walk away," he growls.

His words sound like a threat.

A warning.

I should listen.

I should walk away and go back to Daniel, but I can't.

This close, I'm suffocating in his scent and burning in the heat of his body.

I can smell the faint hint of whiskey on his breath, and more than anything, I want a taste.

Before I realize what I'm doing, I close the gap ... kissing him.

CHAPTER 6
LAUTNER

Her lips are soft as she takes me by surprise, but I respond instantly. Gripping her hips, I pull her tight against my body, deepening the kiss. She moans softly against my lips. Her hands clutching my forearms so tightly I know I will have little half-moon indents from her fingernails. I growl in approval. Usually, I hated it when a female tried to leave her mark on me. I had enough scars from a violent past. But with Dani, here, now, I want her to mark every available inch of flesh on my body, and when it heals, I want her to do it all over again. "Harder," I say, breaking the kiss. I ruthlessly push her against the back wall, claiming her lips once more. I can't keep my hands still as they travel down her body, gliding over her breasts. Her nipples are like stiff peaks as I pinch one over her dress, rolling it between my fingers as she whimpers in pleasure.

I force my thigh between her warm legs as she rocks herself against me, and I know she needs this just as much as I do. Her teeth nip my bottom lip, driving me crazy as her hands weave their way into my hair, gripping it tight.

I remove my knee, desperate to feel her for myself. "Don't stop," she begs against my mouth as if fearing my rejection. I couldn't stop now, even if I wanted to. My hands want to caress every inch of her body as I imprint it to memory. I glide my hand down until it reaches the hem of her dress, teasing the bare skin at her thigh. I can smell her arousal. It's vanilla and passion rolled into one. I want nothing more than to drag her into the nearest empty room, strip her naked, and worship her body from head to toe. But I know I wouldn't make it. I can't take my hands or mouth away from her for a damn second.

"Tell me you want this, Dani." I whisper against her throat, slipping my hand under her panties. She gasps against my mouth at the feel of my hand against her swollen clit.

"I want this," she replies breathlessly. I run my fingers teasingly through her soaking wet heat as she shudders in pleasure. I want nothing more than to slide my dick deep inside her as she comes apart around me, but I need to make sure she is ready for me first. I'm a big guy, and as I slip my finger inside her, she's so damn tight it's taking every bit of my control to keep it slow. I work her over, my finger slowly gliding in and out as I brush my thumb against her clit. She tips her head back as if in submission, biting her lip. *One bite. One bite, that's all it would take, and she'd be ours. Claim her,* my wolf begs.

Ignoring the cries within, I insert another finger, playing her body like a goddamn instrument. My body is on fire in its need for her. I'm harder than I ever thought possible.

"Lautner," she pleads.

"Come for me, Dani. Let go." I nuzzle at her neck,

needing to feel her release around me more than I needed to breathe. To know she is satisfied.

I bring my thumb against her clit once more, increasing the pressure until she cries out, coming hard around my fingers.

"What the ..."

With a growl, I force my lips from Dani's throat, turning to find Daniel standing at the bottom of the stairs. If looks could kill, we would both be dead by now, but the interruption is the awakening I need. I slowly release her, pushing myself away. My wolf growling within, demanding we go back and take what is rightfully ours.

"Fuck," I mutter, readjusting my hard length that would not get the release it wanted. *How the hell did this happen? One minute I'm in the back room with Destiny, ready to forget all about this damn female, and the next minute, I'm out here searching for her.*

I take another step back, hoping the distance will clear my head. It doesn't. I sneak a glance over to Dani. Her eyes are dilated, cheeks flushed, lips swollen from my kisses. She looks damn near perfect, which only pisses me off more.

"Goddammit, Daniel, didn't I tell you to get her out of here." I shake my head.

"Fuck you, Lautner. What the hell is wrong with you?" Daniel seethes, clenching his fists.

"Don't push me." I take a step toward him. I don't want to hurt Daniel; he's like my brother. But right now, my wolf just sees him as competition, and he'd kill him; I have no doubt.

"Lautner," Seth calls out. I hold Daniel's stare, waiting until his eyes drop to the floor in submission before looking to Seth behind him.

"We got trouble."

CHAPTER 7
LAUTNER

I follow Seth back up the stairs, refusing to look back. "What is it?" I snap, looking in the direction Seth is pointing, but thinking Daniel has just had a lucky escape.

At first, I have no idea what Seth is talking about, until the lone man standing at the bar takes another drink, his coat riding up, revealing the guns at his waist.

"Shit. We need to move." I turn my back on Seth, not waiting for Daniel to reappear. Hopefully, he's taking my advice and getting Dani the hell out of here because this guy is about to light up the Warehouse, by the looks of it.

I advance closer, noting the faint bead of sweat as it drips down his forehead. He's nervous. I slow my pace, not wanting to spook him. Frowning, the man turns to look at me, pulling the gun free from his waist and opening fire.

"Get down," I cry out, throwing my body to the floor. But my voice goes unheard over the music. I see a few bodies drop dead to the floor, and it isn't long before the screaming starts. I push myself up as I stalk toward him. It's like a goddamn obstacle course as I fight my way through the crowds hurrying toward the exits. The hunter smiles at my approach as if waiting for me, pulling the trigger. I dodge to the right, the bullet embedding itself into the wooden beam by my head, missing me by inches.

"What the fuck do you think you're doing? You're in a Vampire bar, asshole. Do you really think you're going to get out alive?" Seth shouts from where he is taking cover on the other side of the room.

The distraction is just what I need as I dive behind an overturned table. It was going to turn into a bloodbath soon if we didn't disarm him.

A scream echoes loudly across the room that has my wolf clawing to get out. *Dani*. I try to fight the change, but my wolf isn't messing around. His mate needs him. Within seconds, my wolf's howl echoes loudly throughout the room. I can hear Seth curse, but I'm too far gone. It's suicide to shift, given the Sun Sinners' rules, but my need to protect Dani consumes me. I hear the empty click of the barrel as I jump out from behind the table. The man is sweating profusely now as he tries to refill his weapon, his hands trembling as the bullets miss the chamber, landing in a pool at his feet. I growl in satisfaction as he backs up, hitting the wall behind him. I crouch low, snapping my teeth, preparing to attack.

"What the fuck is going on here?" Cal shouts from above. The distraction is enough for the shooter to turn and smash through a window into the night. *Dani*. I quickly scan the room. It's pretty much empty now, everyone having already left after hearing the gunshots. I find Daniel dragging a reluctant Dani toward the back exit.

"Nothing to do with us," Seth says, appearing from a

darkened corner, holding up his hands as he walks toward the Sun Sinners President.

Ignoring him, Cal turns his full attention to me.

"Shift," he demands, his voice cutting through the air around me like ice.

I close my eyes as my body distorts and cracks until I'm human once more. Naked, I stand, ready to face my punishment.

The rest of the Sun Sinners are now gathered around us, and I watch Cal survey the damage around him. "Find the shooter," he commands as the vampires race off into the night. "I'm disappointed in you, Lautner. You, more than anyone, know the rules here."

I remain silent. I'm not going to try and defend myself. I can't. I made a stupid move, and I deserve whatever came next.

"Here's the deal. You don't get paid for the fight here tonight," Cal says, walking toward me.

"Deal," I respond quickly, wondering why I'm getting let off so easily.

"Not so fast. I can't have rumors spreading that the Sun Sinners have gone soft, can I?" He laughs. "Now, I could gather the Sun Sinners to give you a good kicking, but where's the fun in that. We both know you would enjoy it." He smirks, circling me. "What I need is more shifter blood. And a champion's blood, such as yours ... well, that could be worth a lot more."

"You want my blood. How much are we talking about?" I ask cautiously.

"Don't worry. You're one of my top incomes. Just enough that you might be slightly weak for a few days."

"Fine. Let's get this over with," I say between gritted teeth.

"Not now. I have plenty after tonight's fight. I'll call you. Now, if you'll excuse me, I have a human to kill." In the blink of an eye, he's gone.

"Motherfucker," Seth says, turning toward me. "What the hell were you thinking shifting in here. That could have gone a hell of a lot worse," he growls, clearly irritated at my stupidity.

Ignoring him, I turn to find Daniel storming toward us. His eyes are dark. The power of his wolf seeping out under his anger and lack of control.

"Why? She was with me. Why her?" Daniel growls, coming to a stop before me.

Without thinking, I grab him by the neck, pinning him against the wall. "What the hell do you think you're playing at, bringing her here. You nearly got us all killed!"

"Me," Daniel gasps, struggling for air. *Shit*. I loosen my hold around his neck just enough to let him speak. "What did I do? She was my date."

"Your date. You know nothing, kid, do you."

"Let him go, Lautner," Seth calls out.

"Is she safe?" I ask Daniel, ignoring him.

"Yeah, I watched her get into her car and drive off," he replies. I loosen my hold, letting him fall to the floor before me, clutching his reddened throat.

"She? Who's she? Do you mean Dani?" Seth demands, grabbing my arm. Wrong move. I swing, catching him with a right hook.

"She is none of your damn business," I hiss.

"Shit," he mutters, rubbing his jaw. "Is Dani your mate?"

"No."

"Shifting just now. That wasn't a mistake. You had no

control over it. Your wolf was protecting his mate, no matter the cost."

"I have no intention of taking a mate, Seth. You know that better than anyone."

"Sometimes we don't get to make that choice," Seth states, rubbing his jaw.

"I do. All I have to do is get the next seventy-two hours over with, and then I'm free from this damn mating curse."

"That easy, huh," Seth replies sarcastically.

"Yeah, it is," I snap, turning around to meet the eyes of a distraught Daniel.

"Your mate?" he asks sadly. The question rolls off his lips with such desperation I almost feel bad for him. Almost. But the thought of any man touching Dani like I just did fills me with rage.

Dani would never belong to him. She belongs to me. The other half of my soul. My mate. Mine.

"I'm sorry, Daniel."

I storm from the Warehouse, jumping on my bike. The familiar thrum of the engine between my thighs doing little to ease any of the built-up tension. My wolf is too damn close to the surface right now, and I have to keep him under control. If I shifted now, I would search all damn night until I found her, burying myself between her legs. Now that I'd had a taste, I wasn't sure how I was going to resist. The next seventy-two hours were going to be a bitch. I just hoped that I was strong enough to resist.

CHAPTER 8
DANI

I slam the car door behind me, making my way toward my house. My body still on fire from Lautner's touch, I swear I can still feel his hands caressing my skin. *What is it about him that calls to me?* After Lautner left, Daniel wouldn't even look at me. I could feel the pain radiating from him, yet I couldn't say anything. I had never wanted to hurt Daniel; that was never my intention. But with Lautner, it's like I had no control over my body. I was inextricably drawn to him. I had followed Daniel back upstairs just as the gunshots went off. I remember screaming before Daniel threw me to the ground, practically dragging me out the back door.

"How did it go?" Lacey asks tiredly from her sleeping bag on the floor as I enter my bedroom.

"Fine." I sigh, stripping out of my dress and curling up in bed. I knew Lacey would want to know everything that happened tonight, but I was having a hard time understanding it myself.

"Just fine? You're the only one of our pack to have ever ventured to the Warehouse, and that's all I get. Fine," she huffs, crossing her arms across her chest.

"It's just a bar, Lacey," I reply. "You know ... alcohol, music, illegal cage fights to the death. Oh, and a sexy shifter that looked like he wanted to kill me."

"Daniel?" she quickly jumps in, concern lacing her voice. "I knew he was a serial killer. Didn't I tell you not to go?"

"It wasn't Daniel. It was his pack brother, Lautner."

"Tell me everything," she says, turning on the bedside light.

I sit up with another sigh, trying to piece the past few hours together in my mind. "Well, when I got there, I met Daniel, and he was great. We had a drink, and then we ...."

"Was he hot?" she interrupted.

"Who?"

"Daniel. Lautner. Both?"

"Yes. For the sake of this conversation, I'm going to tell you right now, they were both hot. It was going well at first. Daniel and I had a drink, and then we went to watch the fight. That's when it got weird. Lautner, their pack's enforcer, was fighting this guy called Tommy West. Turns out the Stone Valley Pack has a bad history with him and his brother. Lautner snapped his neck inside the cage," I shiver, replaying it back in my mind.

"That's awful."

"Not really. From what I hear, he deserved it; but that's not the weird part. As soon as Lautner looked over, our eyes met, and it's like we were instantly connected. There was a deep rush of power under my skin, and everything became different around me. Magnified. I ... I think it was my wolf."

"Wow, and you start off with, fine."

Taking a deep breath, I continue, "He came straight over after the fight acting weird and telling me to leave. Then he called me a whore, before actually leaving with a woman who looked like a whore," I mutter jealously.

"A whore," she retorts. "Who the hell does he think he is, calling you that. You're a virgin, aren't you."

"Gee, thanks. I wasn't exactly going to stop and tell him that."

"You know what I mean. Asshole," she mutters.

"That's what I called him, but that's not the end of it. He found me later as I was leaving, wanting to talk. He touched my arm, and it was like an electric current ran through my body. I don't know what came over me, but I ... I kissed him."

"You kissed Lautner," she shrieks excitedly.

Blushing, I look away. It had gone a lot farther than kissing, but I wasn't about to tell Lacey that. The man had given me my very first orgasm, well ... one that wasn't produced by my own hand. Clearing my throat, I continue, "Then some crazy man with a gun started firing blindly. It was a pretty wild night, really."

"I wish I'd gone with you now," she says excitedly. "But back to the kiss. Please tell me it was good. And what about Drake? What about Daniel? Are you going to see Lautner again?" she asks, bombarding me with her questions.

"I don't think so. Lautner kept telling me to leave. I don't think he would be too happy to see me again," I respond. Although, by the way his hands had been touching me, I think he was fooling himself more than me. "Besides, my father has a contract, remember. I'm Drake's."

"But what if Lautner is your fated mate?" she asks quietly.

"Don't be crazy, Lace. There's no such thing as fated

mates. Besides, even if there is, I still haven't shifted properly. Just because I think I may have felt my wolf earlier tonight doesn't change a thing. I don't think I could mate, even if I wanted to."

"I'm telling you; all the signs are there. The instant connection. Couldn't take your eyes off him. Lautner might be the one."

I lie back down, nestling myself under the safety of my comforter, wishing that Lacey were right. There was just something about Lautner that called to me. He had made me feel alive for the very first time in my life.

"Earth to Dani, you still awake?" Lacey whispers.

"Yeah, I'm just tired. It's been a long night," I reply.

"If he is your fated mate, he might be exactly what you need to get out of your engagement to Drake. He's an enforcer, isn't he? If there is anyone capable of standing up to your father, it would be him."

"Maybe," I reply with a yawn, struggling to keep my eyes open. I'd been wide awake on the drive home, but now the adrenaline is leaving my system, I feel more tired than I'd ever been before. "Right now, I need to sleep. We have that pack meeting early in the morning, and I don't need another reason for my father to be pissed at me," I say, setting the alarm on my phone. "Did anyone call?"

"Just Drake, but don't worry, you're in the clear. I told him you were in the shower. He said he would see you at tomorrow's meet."

Breathing a sigh of relief, I close my eyes, my mind instantly picturing the gorgeous shifter with the beautiful amber eyes. Deep down, I know that I will probably never see him again, but for the briefest moment, I imagine that Lacey is right. That Lautner is my fated mate, and there is a chance of better future for me, after all.

CHAPTER 9
LAUTNER

There's no sign of Mick's Escalade by the time we get home. Our alpha owned an old hotel on the outskirts of the Valley. It isn't huge by any standards, but we all have a room here. The first floor held two reception rooms, a fully equipped bar, and a kitchen. While the remaining two floors have our private rooms and spares for Council members or allies that need a safe place when passing through.

As I dismount from my bike, Daniel tries his best to ignore me as he brushes past.

"Don't mention any of this to your father," I call out to his retreating form.

He stops, turning around to face me. "You mean our alpha, right," he snaps.

"This is my business, Daniel, not pack business. I will handle it how I see fit. Unless you want to take me on, I suggest you walk away now and keep your goddamn mouth shut."

"Whatever, Lautner. Unlike you, we can't lie to our alpha," he states.

"I'm not asking you to lie. I'm asking you not to mention it. There's a difference," I snap.

"Whatever," he mutters. "This is going to bring you down, and it will take all of us down with it."

I wince at his words, hating that he is right, that I was dragging them both into my mess. I had no intention of lying to my alpha forever, just long enough for the mate bond to be over. I know if Mick found out, he would only try to dissuade me. He would tell me I wasn't my father, but they have no idea of the darkness that simmers inside me. My father had made me a cold-blooded killer by the age of eight. And now, at twenty-six, I used my skills to its full advantage, torturing and killing for the pack. If I didn't let the monster loose inside of me now and again, I'd just be another stray on the street killing for fun.

"You should take it easy on him," Seth says as we watch Daniel retreat indoors. "You did just steal his girlfriend, after all."

"I didn't do shit."

"I get it. You're pissed, but maybe you should talk about it."

"And what about you, Seth. Are you ready to talk? Tommy's dead now. I killed him." I know I'm goading him, waiting for a response. I hate that he hadn't screamed at me yet. I had just taken away the one thing he's wanted since we'd gotten him back two years ago—the chance at revenge.

Seth stares daggers at me as the silence stretches out between us, neither of us wanting to give in.

"I know you're looking for a fight, Lautner, but you're not going to get one from me. Not tonight. Just tell me you're alright, and I'll drop it," Seth finally replies.

I wanted to say yes. That the moment we left the Warehouse, and I had gotten some distance from Dani, the lava that ran through my veins had instantly cooled. But the truth is, I felt empty. No longer whole. Not like when I had first left tonight. Somewhere over the past few hours, she had taken a part of me with her, and the only way to get it back would be to hunt her down and claim her, but there is no way I'm admitting defeat. The man is stronger than the wolf.

Not trusting my words, I nod.

"Good. I'm going for a drink. You coming?" Seth asks, walking past me, not waiting for an answer.

No sooner had we walked through the door when Seth's phone rings.

"Where?" he commands down the phone. "I got it, Thane. Send over the coordinates and stay there. We're on the way."

"The Sun Sinners found a body," Seth says, turning toward me, pushing the phone back into his jean pocket.

"So let their asses deal with it. What's it got to do with us?"

"The body is mutilated and partially changed. We need to get out there now before it gets light. This could be the sign we've been waiting for."

"Fine, I'll get the keys. We're taking your car, though. I'm not getting blood in my trunk like last time. It took me forever to get that shit out," I grumble, heading toward the kitchen.

Seth is waiting by his black chevy when I return, tossing him the keys.

"I tried phoning Mick and Ryan to let them know, but their phones are still switched off. Daniel's going to stay here and fill them in when they get back," Seth informs me unlocking the car. I climb into the passenger seat, wondering what else can go wrong tonight.

Seth quickly types the coordinates Thane sent over into the GPS, and we head out.

"What now," I ask Seth as he finally pulls over at our destination.

"This way." Thane bangs against the side of the car, causing me to jump at his sudden appearance. This mate shit must have me more off my game than usual.

"Fucker," I snarl, knowing he can hear me just as well as if I were shouting it at him.

Thane just grins as he raises his middle finger, flipping me off. "I'm the one doing you guys a favor, remember that. Now let's go!"

Exiting the car, I wait as Seth gathers our supplies from the trunk. We follow Thane down an old trail leading toward the creek. The sound of water sloshing against the rocks getting louder as we continue, and it's not long before the faint scent of death hits me.

"The head and arm were found here, and Kai found his torso about a mile east," Thane points out.

"What about the rest?" I ask, wrinkling my nose.

"Well, that's for you to find, isn't it. This is clearly pack business, nothing to do with the vampires."

"What about the shooter. Did you get him?"

Thane shakes his head. "That fucker vanished as soon as he left the Warehouse. We followed his scent, and it passes through here. However, considering how weak it is, he probably came this way before, not after. We'll find him," he replies. "Nobody hits the Club and gets away with it. I'll see you both next Friday." And just like that, the vampires are gone.

Seth walks over with the plastic carrier bags in his hand. They weren't ideal, but they would do the job of transporting the body. As he opens one of the bags, I pick up the partially shifted arm in front of me. It's cold and almost frozen. "It looks like they tried to freeze the body to preserve it," I say to Seth, my eyes taking in the numerous track marks also present. No doubt they'd been injecting him during the torture to keep him awake and in pain. I bring it closer to my nose, catching the faint scent of ammonia and acetone. "Crank," I say to Seth as I place it in the bag.

Once we'd bagged up the head, it was clear that one of us would have to shift and sniff out the other parts of our John Doe.

Seth pulls a quarter out of his back pocket. "Call it?"

"Heads," I say as he flips the coin into the air.

"Shit," he grumbles, placing the quarter back in his pocket.

I smile, letting out a sigh of relief. Don't get me wrong, I love to shift. But sniffing out decomposed flesh wasn't the best part; that smell stayed in your nose for days. There is also the problem that my wolf desperately wanted to find his mate. I would have a hard time keeping focused on the matter at hand.

I collect Seth's discarded clothes, placing them in a clean bag as he prepares to shift. I wait until I hear him snorting behind me before turning around. It doesn't take long for Seth to catch the scent as I quietly follow behind him. We find the torso to the east, where Thane said it would be, and his legs shortly after. It must have taken us about two hours before we have all our John Doe bagged up and in the back of the trunk. Looking at the lightning sky, we had made it just in time.

Seth re-emerges from behind a tree, fully clothed with his cell phone in hand. "Alpha's orders are to dispose of the body a few miles out if we can."

"Great. Let's get this over with," I mutter sliding into the driver's seat.

"You better let me drive. The last thing we need is to get pulled over. If this is the work of the hunters, leaving bodies out in the open, I wouldn't put it past them to try and frame us, and with your driving, we'd be pulled over instantly," Seth quips.

Disgruntled and too tired to put up a fight, I do as he says. I know he's right. I just want to get this over with, so I can go back home and drink myself into oblivion until I pass out. Hopefully, taking a few more hours off this goddamn mate bond.

Seth chooses a spot well out of the way of the usual trails, and we quickly get to work.

Mick and Ryan are already waiting in the office by the time we get back.

"You look like shit," Mick says, glancing up at my face as we enter.

"Finding and burying a body in the middle of the night will do that to you," I quip.

"That's not what I'm talking about, and you know it." Mick shakes his head in amusement before turning his eyes to Seth. "Who hit you?"

"My own stupidity," he grumbles.

"Do I even want to know?" Mick asks, rubbing his tired eyes.

I shake my head. "It's not important."

"Alright then, tell me something that is. How did the fight go?" Mick asks, instantly all business.

"Did you speak to Daniel yet?"

"Yeah, now I'm talking to you."

"Cal called me into the office before the fight. Tommy West put down a lot of money to get in the cage with me tonight."

"No sign of Brandon?" he asks.

"No, and from the sounds of it, I don't think Brandon even knows he was there."

"Is he dead?" Mick asks, his eyes traveling over to Seth. I can see the pain on my alpha's face, no doubt wondering just how well Seth is coping after seeing Tommy again.

"I snapped his neck," I reply coldly.

"You do realize when Brandon finds out his younger brother is dead, he's going to come straight here."

"Brandon's a dead man," Seth spits out angrily behind me.

"We will deal with him when the time comes in the—"

"No, he's mine," Seth cuts in, his voice shaking with rage. "After everything that happened, I want to be the one to take him out. I need this," he says, looking directly at me. I know he is waiting for me to acknowledge his request. I had already taken Tommy from him. He needed Brandon to himself.

In the silence of the room, Tommy's words once again plague me. If he and Brandon had done to Seth what he'd hinted at, I didn't know if I'd be able to sit back and let Seth kill him. I wanted to do it myself in the pit, just like I promised Tommy before he died. But I wasn't about to let Seth down. I give him a nod, quickly turning away.

"Very well," Mick states, "when the time comes, he's yours. Now, what about the body?"

"I didn't recognize him, so he's not local. Whoever took him kept him alive for several days. There's plenty of damage done to the body. Fingernails ripped off, missing teeth, burn marks. They worked him over pretty good before they eventually killed him. My bet is it's Tai. The time frame fits. I sent Daniel a couple of photos before we buried him to see if he can make a positive ID."

"What about the attack on the Warehouse?" Mick continues.

"Cal seemed to think it was a hit against the Club, but after finding the body, my gut says it's the hunters, and they were well prepared. Once the shooter got out of the Warehouse, none of the vampires could find him. I think that was the plan all along, to lure us to the body."

Mick nods, accepting my theory. "I'll wake Daniel and see if he can make a formal identification. I'll also ring the Council and send them a copy, find out what our next move is."

"You sure that's everything," he asks, looking me dead in the eye. "Nothing else to report?"

"That's it," I reply, holding his gaze. I'm not ready to admit what else had happened tonight. There's already too much going on without adding a fated mate, I have no intention of claiming, into this shitstorm.

"Alright, we'll reconvene in a few hours. Both of you go get some rest. If the hunters are here, you're going to need it."

CHAPTER 10
DANI

"Danika!" my father shouts.

"Yes, Father." I jump, mentally kicking myself for not paying attention. We were sitting around the kitchen table as my father held our pack's weekly meet.

"Did you hear what I just said?"

I lower my eyes in submission, remaining quiet. The meeting had started at nine am sharp and had been underway for the past half-hour. Unfortunately for me, my mind was still in bed, replaying last night's events.

"No, Father. Sorry," I mumble, wishing he would hurry up and get this over with.

"What I was saying to the pack, is that the hunters are here. The Council have agreed that neighboring packs should pull their resources together and find them before they can kill any more of us. Which means we are to work closely with the Stone Valley Pack," he spits the words out in obvious disgust. "Their alpha, Mick, wants us to convene at his place in Stone Valley. He has more than enough rooms to accommodate us for a few days while dealing with this mess. The quicker we find and destroy these hunters, the quicker we can get back on with our lives. We leave for Stone Valley this afternoon."

I can feel the blood draining from my face as I look over to my father. *Go to Stone Valley and meet the pack. They would recognize me. What if they told my father about last night?*

"I-I think I should stay here," I stammer in panic. "I'm not going to be much help."

"Don't be a fool, Danika. You will not be searching for the hunters. Drake has requested your presence. Would you deny your fiancé the chance to spend some time together?"

I turn to see Drake leering at me from across the table, and I quickly turn away.

"You will be attending. Is that clear?" my father commands.

"Yes, Father. How long will we be there?"

"A few days at most. Long enough for us to gather intel. If that's everything ..." he asks, pausing as he looks around the room. Everyone remains silent as my father stands up, his chair scraping loudly against the floor. "Good. Meeting adjourned."

My eyes dart to Lacey as I take her hand, making for a quick exit. I pull her up the stairs, and I don't stop until I have my bedroom door shut firmly behind us. I go straight over to the CD player, turning it on and letting the sound of AC/DC flood the room.

"What am I going to do?" I whisper anxiously, pacing the floor.

"Dani, calm down. Listen to me. Everyone knows that the Ridgeway Pack is forbidden to attend the Warehouse. I doubt they would rat you out in front of your alpha," she whispers back.

"They won't be expecting me, though; they don't know I'm Ridgeway," I explain. "I told them my name was Dani Court, not Cortez." I head over to the bed, forcing my restless body to sit down beside her. "Oh my God, Lacey, I kissed him. He really is going to think I'm a whore when I turn up engaged to Drake."

"I hate to say it, but you've got bigger problems than that. If Lautner really is your fated mate, it won't be long until your father and Drake find out. These guys turn totally possessive when they find their mates. He won't take well to you turning up with another man."

My stomach goes into overdrive at the thought. One false move on my part, and I would likely be signing his death warrant. When my father wanted something, he didn't let anyone or anything stand in his way, especially fate.

CHAPTER 11
LAUTNER

"Glad you could finally join us." Mick looks at me pointedly as I enter his office, where my brothers are already in attendance.

I don't say a word as I take my seat next to Seth. I'd barely slept last night. My wolf kept me awake half the damn night, demanding we find Dani. If last night's kill is the work of the hunters, it meant that no shifter in the Valley or surrounding area was safe.

"Any news from the Council about our John Doe?" I ask.

"We got a positive ID. You were right. The victim was Tai Jacobson. As you all know, he was badly tortured. Whoever these hunters are, it's clear they know what they're doing."

"Well, I say we let Daniel work his magic on the computer, and we can be rid of these hunters within the next few hours."

Mick holds up his hand. "Not so fast, Lautner. The

Council has decided that the best way to eradicate the hunters is to team up with another pack. I know a lot of you don't like working with others." He pauses, looking directly at me. "But that's their decision to make."

"Bullshit. We can easily find the hunters without getting another pack involved." I shift in my seat, unable to sit still due to the raging fire still burning within. The cold shower earlier, having made no effect.

"The Council wants the matter dealt with quickly, and it's the best way. The Ridgeway Pack will be arriving this afternoon. I don't like it either, that's why I invited them here. This is our territory, and they will respect our rules. Until then, I suggest you sort out whatever the hells got you in such a bad mood, so I don't need to worry about your ass this afternoon. Meeting adjourned."

I quickly stand, ready to make a hasty retreat.

"Lautner," Mick calls out as I watch my pack brothers leave the room, wishing I could flee with them.

"What's going on? And don't lie to me," he says sternly.

"Nothing, I'm just worried about Seth." It's not a lie, not completely. I knew seeing Tommy again after all these years would bring back unwanted memories, but so far, he'd been acting like a goddamn robot. It's not healthy. Sure, I was acting the same, running away from my own demons, but Seth isn't like me. He's the smart one.

"Look, I know something went down last night between you and Seth. I'm not an idiot. Sort it out now. I will not have us looking weak in front of the Ridgeway Pack. The Council is just looking to replace me, and I won't give them the satisfaction. You're one of my best men, and I need you on board."

Shit. I knew Mick was having a hard time with the Council, but I hadn't realized it was that bad.

"I won't make the situation worse. You have my word." Holding Mick's gaze, I bow my head in a show of respect before leaving the room. I'm not surprised to see Seth already outside, waiting for me.

"What?" I snap.

"You should have told him."

"There's nothing to tell," I say as I go to walk past him.

"You know, Daniel and Dani have been talking for weeks now. Do you really think he's just going to stop talking to her after last night? Maybe after your bond breaks, Daniel and Dani might ...."

My hands grip his shirt as I pull him close, not letting him finish. "Don't even go there, Seth," I spit. The idea of Daniel being around Dani kills me, and I had no intention of letting him continue his friendship. As far as I'm concerned, Daniel would never see her again.

"What about Dani? Doesn't she get a say in this? Think about how selfish you're being," Seth pleads as I let him go.

"What? Selfish to whom. She will find another, someone who wants her. I may not get a second chance, but females do."

"You know there's no turning back."

"I know," I growl, my wolf starting to get on edge. "Leave it, Seth, or should we continue where we left off last night."

"I don't want you to make a mistake, Lautner. You're my best friend."

"If you were really my friend, Seth, you would tell me what the fuck went down when Tommy and Brandon took you. Who was the one that stayed up all night going hunting after you would wake the whole house up screaming. Who was the one who sat up all night when you were coming off the smack, making sure you didn't choke on your own vomit. It was me, that's who. Don't talk to me about being selfish."

His eyes drop to the floor in defeat as I stomp away, taking my small victory into the bar.

Daniel is already perched on a bar stool as I enter.

"Hey man," Daniel starts, looking up from his phone, catching me coming in. "I just wanted to say, look, I'm sorry about last night, about Dani. I know we were there on pack business, and I shouldn't have arranged to meet her. My mistake."

Daniel's phone beeps in his hand, and I recall Seth's words. *He's been talking to Dani for weeks.*

Anger rips through me, and before I can stop myself, I snatch the phone from his hand, staring down at the screen. The name on the top of the text read Teresa as I let out a ragged breath.

"I want you to cut all ties with Dani, you hear me?"

"No. She's my friend."

"Not anymore. Teresa is," I say, returning his phone before I end up doing something stupid like finding her number.

I needed to get out of here. To go for a run, anything to get rid of this excess energy pumping through my veins. But I know if I shifted, I would only end up searching for her. My wolf wants nothing more than to follow the sweet scent of vanilla until we found her. Forcing her to submit beneath us, claiming her mind, body, and soul. With a groan, I leave the bar, heading back upstairs to my room.

As soon as I enter, I pull open my bedside drawer, gripping the emergency bottle of whiskey. My throat burns, and my eyes water as I drink deep, waiting for the comfortably numb feeling to take hold. I know Mick's right about teaming up with another pack, but it's the last thing I want to do when my wolf is on edge. He's itching for a fight, and I'm a ticking time bomb right now. I just hope we get a lead on the hunters soon.

Rubbing my tired eyes, I place the bottle of whiskey back on the table by my bed. I lie down atop the cool sheets, my cock aching, begging me for release. I'd been hard since last night. Since I'd first laid eyes on Dani Court. And I know, without a doubt, it will only get worse over the next few days. Shoving my joggers down my thighs, I grip my cock, hissing at the contact as I stroke its long length. Images of Dani's tight body against mine has my hand working overtime, and it isn't long before I come hard, ejaculating over my stomach.

Shit. I tip my head back, drawing in ragged breaths. I have no idea how I'm going to survive the next few days. I'm still fucking hard. Picking up my phone, I scroll through my contacts until I come across the one name that might be able to help me forget all about Dani fucking Court. I quickly send a text before crashing back on the bed, closing my eyes and waiting for sleep to drag me under.

CHAPTER 12
LAUTNER

Eighteen years ago

"Do it," my father screams from the sidelines of the ring. The boy in front of me smiles as if sensing my fear. He could only be about ten, but the confidence with which he held himself makes me think of him as older. His fist smashes into my face once more as I fall to the floor. It's not so bad. His punches were no way near as hard as my father's after a night of heavy drinking. Pulling myself up, I put my fists up once more, just like my father had taught me the night before. I don't want to be here, it's my eighth birthday, but my father had told me I would get a surprise if I won. I'm not used to surprises. Birthdays were usually spent quietly locked away as my father hid, crying over my mom.

The boy advances again, and I throw out a kick, nearly losing my footing. The boy snickers, obviously enjoying my feeble attempt at an attack. I'm no good at this. My father keeps telling me that I will be a strong wolf one day, and I will need to fight to control the power within me. There would be no room for weakness. The boy comes at me again, only this time I remember the blocking technique, and I manage to catch him with a punch of my own. I can hear my father cheering wildly, and I can't stop the smile that lights up my face. I do it again and again, each hit feeling better than the last as my father calls out my name. As the boy lands on the ground in front of me, I straddle his hips, my punches continuing to land. The small crowd screaming in a chorus to finish him off.

The boy below me goes still, but I don't stop, even when little drops of water land on his cheek. Had it started raining? I had no idea. Hands gripped my shoulders, pulling me away as I'm announced the winner. My father's smile turns into a frown when he notices the tears on my face. I quickly wipe them away, straightening my shoulders.

"You did good, Lautner." My father claps a hand to my back as we head out the door of the abandoned barn, back to his car.

"Will the boy be alright?" I ask.

My father stops abruptly, turning me to face him, and I shudder under the intensity of his gaze.

"There are two types of people in this world, Lautner. Those who are strong and those who are weak. Which do you want to be?"

"Strong," I say as my father nods in approval.

"Then it doesn't matter about your opponent. You live to fight another day."

CHAPTER 13
DANI

It's late in the afternoon, and Lacey had stayed with me all day as I packed my bag, ready for my trip to Stone Valley. "You should definitely take these with you," she says with a smile, producing the black lace and silk underwear she had bought me last Christmas.

I snatch them from her hands. "Lace, I have no intention of giving Drake the wrong idea."

"I meant in case anything happens with Lautner." She raises her eyebrow suggestively, biting her lip.

"Yeah, like that's going to happen with my father and Drake around. I probably won't even get the chance to speak with him," I reply, placing them in my bag, just in case.

"Promise you will call me tonight and let me know how it goes?" she asks worriedly.

"I promise. I plan to hide out in my room as much as possible over the next few days."

"Danika," my father's voice carries up the stairs. "It's time to go."

I quickly check my phone, hoping to see a text back from Daniel. I'd texted him earlier, warning him of my arrival. The last thing I need is for Lautner to cause a scene and start shouting at me to leave again. Disappointed, I turn my phone off, hiding it at the bottom of my bag.

I rush over to Lacey, giving her one last hug before leaving the room. The butterflies that had plagued me all afternoon go into overdrive as I descend the stairs. I have no idea what will happen over the next few days, and I dread not having my best friend by my side.

There's a total of six of us heading to Stone Valley, and no one is looking forward to it. There are many reasons why packs keep themselves isolated from others of their kind. Bitter rivalries and distrust are only the start. The idea of putting two packs under one roof screams like a bad idea, but the Council's orders cannot be broken.

My father smirks up at me from where he stands at the bottom of the stairs. He had something up his sleeve, and I knew it would be something I wouldn't like. It's at that moment I notice Drake waiting by his side, wearing the same expression.

"Danika," Drake greets me coldly. A shiver of unease running down my spine as I wonder just what they have planned for me. "As we are heading into enemy territory as it were, I feel it only right that you wear my ring to let everyone know to whom you belong."

I scoff silently at his words. *To whom I belong. Is he fucking kidding me?* But I know he isn't. That's all I am to him. An item to use and discard as he chooses.

As my foot hits the bottom stair, he holds out the gaudiest ring I have ever seen. It screams money and possession.

"Take it," my father growls, his mouth turning into a cruel smile at my obvious discomfort.

I reach out to take the ring from Drake's hand, but he pulls back.

"Allow me," he replies, taking my left hand in his. I remain frozen as he slides the ring onto my finger.

"There you are now." My father chuckles, no doubt enjoying the uncomfortable position he'd thrown me into.

Drake watches me warily. He must've been expecting me to put up more of a fight over the ring. Usually, he would have been right, but I wasn't in the mood to piss my father off any more than necessary. I'm heading into the unknown in Stone Valley, and I can't take the risk.

I follow Drake outside as he climbs straight into the passenger seat of my father's Lincoln Navigator. I would be traveling with my father, Drake, and Sid, while Terry and Logan would follow in Terry's Jeep. Following his lead, I climb into the backseat, putting my headphones in and randomly selecting one of my Spotify playlists on my iPod.

As the sound of a random rock song begins to play, I look down at the hideous ring adorning my finger—Lacey's words replaying in my mind. *"If Lautner is your fated mate, he isn't going to take well to you turning up with another man. These guys turn totally possessive. It won't be long until your father and Drake find out."*

I close my eyes, praying that Daniel had received my text and told his pack brothers the truth about me. If not, the Stone Valley Pack were going to be in for one hell of a surprise when I walked through their door.

I turn my attention to the window as my father navigates a path down an old dirt track through the woods that would lead us into Stone Valley. The sun had set about thirty minutes ago, and it's getting harder to make out the road ahead of us. The car dips suddenly as my father slams on the brakes. "Bloody potholes," he mutters before starting forward again.

"What?" I snap, irritated, catching Drake staring at me from the corner of my eye.

"Nothing, just picturing you tied up naked in my bed. It won't be long now." He leers.

"We're not married yet. I suggest you get rid of that thought, right—" The back window shatters behind me as I put my hands over my head in protection.

"Get down!" my father shouts as I quickly unclip my seatbelt and huddle in a ball on the floor. I can hear the bullets pounding against the side of the car. Sid is beside me, and I hear his door open as he rolls out the door preparing to protect his alpha. At the sound of howling, I realize the others must have followed suit. The gunshots fade as my pack brothers race off into the night, preparing to attack their prey.

A blood-curdling scream in the distance is the only sound as I close my eyes, wishing I weren't so defenseless. It seemed like forever until I finally hear Terry's voice call out, "You're safe now, Dani."

My legs feel like jelly as I shakily climb out of the car, holding onto the door for support.

"How many?" my father demands as he comes to stand beside me.

"At least five that we counted," Terry replies.

"Where's Drake?" my father asks, looking around as if just noticing he is a man down.

"Over here." Drake strolls down the hill, naked, a big smile on his face. Behind him, he drags the body of a man. He stops before us, bowing his head to his alpha. "I managed to catch this one before he got away."

I stare down at the dead man at his feet, fresh blood still pumping from the severed artery at his neck where Drake had gone in for the kill.

The man is young, younger than I expected. He must only be early twenties, if that.

"You should have kept him alive," my father scolds. "The enforcers could have gotten more information out of him."

"With all due respect, Alpha, he tried to kill you and your daughter. We are one less hunter down. Once the packs convene, I'm sure we can capture a live one," he responds, throwing me a wink.

"You just better hope Lautner doesn't send you to the pit," Terry jibes behind him as Sid snickers. *Lautner*. Just the sound of his name has my heart beating faster. It wouldn't be long now before I saw him again. I'm just not sure if I'm excited or scared.

Drake scowls as he stares Terry down. "You dare talk to your Beta that way?" he snarls, Terry and Sid both dropping their heads, remaining quiet.

Satisfied at their submission, Drake storms off as I turn to Terry. "What's the pit?" I ask, eager to hear of anything that involves Lautner.

"It's just a rumor I've heard. Lautner is the Stone Valley Pack enforcer and a mean son of a bitch, from what I hear. Apparently, he has an underground chamber where he tortures and kills strays. But don't worry, Dani, I'm sure it's just that, a rumor." He smiles as he goes to follow the rest of the pack.

Terry, Drake, and Sid get to work burying the body, while Logan changes the blown-out tire. The car is a mess, but it worked. It would get us the rest of the way to Stone Valley.

I draw closer to my father. I can hear him shouting down the phone from inside his car—no doubt speaking to the Stone Valley Pack alpha, letting him know what happened. Nervously I look around, hoping the hunters won't show up again.

"They're long gone," Drake says, coming to stand by me as I look up, grateful to see he is now fully clothed.

"I wasn't looking," I snap, hating that he'd noticed. I hated to feel weak, and the worst part is, he knows it. "Why did you ask that I come?" I change the subject.

"Why wouldn't I. You're my fiancé, after all. A man needs to know his female is safe. Who knows where they could be sneaking off too." His hand trails up my arm to my throat, but there is nothing gentle in his gesture. "Because that's what you are, Dani, mine."

I look up, meeting his harsh stare head-on. The bastard knew all about my visit to the Warehouse. I should have known one of them would have had someone following me.

"I'm a big girl. I can take care of myself," I say, hoping he can't see the panic rising within me.

"Let's go," my father interrupts as Drake's hand falls from my throat, and I breathe a sigh of relief.

CHAPTER 14
LAUTNER

"Lautner. Wake up!" Seth bangs against my door, waking me from a restless slumber for the second time that day. Groaning, I roll out of bed.

Rubbing the sleep from my eyes, I open the door. "What is it?"

"The Ridgeway Pack were attacked on their way here."

"Any casualties?" I ask, instantly awake, my body craving some action—anything to take my mind off of her.

"Not on our side, but one of them killed a hunter," he replies, shrugging his shoulders.

"Idiot. We need one alive, at least for now," I reply, irritated.

"Mick wants everyone downstairs now before they arrive."

"Yeah, alright, I'll be down in a minute."

Closing the door, I quickly change into a black wifebeater and jeans before going into the bathroom and throwing some cold water on my face.

Fuck, I silently growl, wishing they'd caught one alive. A bit of violence would have sated the monster within, if only for a little while. *You know what else would sate your monster, that pretty little blonde,* my wolf perks up. "Shut up," I mutter out loud. The sooner these seventy-two fours were up, the sooner I could get my life back on track.

Everyone is already waiting in the bar when I enter. Mick looks up, giving me a quick glance before resuming his conversation with Ryan. Good. The last thing I need is another lecture on my tardiness.

After a few minutes, Mick stands up, clearing his throat. "I'm sure you've heard the Ridgeway Pack were attacked on their way here. No casualties on our side, but we are one less hunter down."

"How many hunters?" I ask.

"Five."

I nod. That's no big deal.

"Their alpha's pissed; his only daughter is with them."

"His daughter," Seth chimes in. "What the hell is he bringing her for? Surely he would want to keep her out of danger."

"That's his business, not ours," Mick states. "They should be here in the next few minutes. I don't have to tell you, but I'm going to, anyway. We need to play nice. That means no fighting, and for fuck's sake, stay the hell away from his daughter."

I pretend not to notice that his words are directed at me. He needn't have to be worried. I've no intention of sleeping with the alpha's daughter. My wolf and I are already too preoccupied with the feisty blonde Dani, who is already screwing up my life for the foreseeable future.

I nod along with everyone else needing another drink. I head over to the bar where Seth is already there, waiting.

"You planning on playing nice," he quips as I sit down next to him.

"That depends. Are you planning on leaving the mate shit alone?"

He chuckles. "We'll call it a truce for tonight."

"Lautner," Daniel calls out. His eyes are wild as he looks around the room, striding over, his phone in his hand. "I really need to talk to you."

"Not now, Daniel," I snap.

"Look, it's important. It's about last night," he continues.

"What is it?" I ask, pissed that he would even bring this up.

"Dani ... she ..."

"Don't you talk about her. Not here," I seethe.

"You don't understand," he shouts, shaking in frustration.

"Spit it out, Daniel," Ryan interjects, coming over.

"Last night, at the Warehouse, she told everyone her name was Dani Court, but her real name is Danika Cortez. As in daughter to the alpha of the Ridgeway Pack, and she is on her way here."

"Shit," mutters Seth beside me as I stare Daniel down.

"What did you do, Lautner?" Ryan demands.

"I—"

Mick clears his throat. "They're here."

CHAPTER 15
LAUTNER

Dani. Here. My heart begins beating precariously in my chest as I rub my sweaty palms against the side of my jeans. My wolf is doing goddamn somersaults inside of me as I wait, holding my breath.

An older man is first through the door. This must be the Alpha Cortez. His reputation is almost as bad as mine. Almost. I sneer as his eyes scan the room, distaste evident on his face. He is everything I imagined, from his expensive suit and shiny shoes to the look of superiority he wore on his face. It's well known he never got his hands dirty. He had enough money to sit back and let everyone else do the dirty work for him.

I wait impatiently as a few others file in, but I pay them little attention. Usually, I would be able to give a play-by-play account of their age, height, weight, and clothes, but they were not who I was interested in. No, the one I was waiting for hadn't shown up yet. I didn't know whether to be relieved or pissed at Daniel for getting our hopes up. *Mate.*

"Leave it. I don't need any help," her voice snaps out angrily as the door pushes open, and Dani walks in. I grip the countertop in front of me, forcing myself to remain seated. The mating heat slams back into me with such force I feel as though I'm suffocating, and she is my only source of oxygen. I know if I could just take her into my arms, she would burn with me like the sweetest sin, fighting fire with fire. She looks just as good as I remember from last night. Her clothing more casual, this time in jeans and a tight sweater, looked just as good on her as any dress.

My eyes stalk her every move as she heads straight over to stand beside her father. I want to look away, but the magnetic pull from last night won't let me. I watch her face soften, her anger leaving her as she introduces herself to Mick and Ryan. My hands are aching from their death grip against the countertop as I wait for her to look over. Finally, she looks my way, her eyes wary as if she doesn't know how to respond to seeing me again, and I feel the same way.

She nervously nibbles the bottom of her lip as her eyes leave mine, and I notice the man standing by her side. I watch frozen as he throws his arm around her shoulders, pulling her tight against his body.

"Lautner," I hear someone call out, but I can't focus. All I can think about is removing the man's hand from her body.

"And finally," Cortez resumes, "may I introduce my daughter, Danika, and her fiancé, Drake."

Fiancé. What the fuck. My wolf demands we go to her. One bite at the base of her throat, and no man would ever touch her again. Not without the promise of certain death by my hand.

"Don't," Seth whispers in a voice so low I can barely hear him, his hand encircling my wrist.

I turn to look at him, finding myself halfway across the room, not even realizing I'd moved.

"Not now," I hear him say under his breath, his fingers increasing their pressure. Out of the corner of my eye, I catch a few of the Ridgeway Pack take a few steps back. *Good.* I never played well with others, and right now, I would gladly show them just what I'm capable of. Growling, I slowly back up with Seth keeping his hand firmly on my wrist. I would kick his ass if I weren't so grateful for the distraction.

I can feel the suspicious stares of everyone in the room watching me as I sit down. I turn around, meeting Mick's intense gaze head-on. There was going to be hell to pay once the introductions were over. I had never really lied to my alpha before, and now I would have to admit to not just one mistake, but two.

Fiancé. How can this be? She belonged to me. My mate. Mine alone. Whether I want to accept it or not.

I force my head down, refusing to look in her direction until Ryan approaches me.

"Mick wants to see you. Now!"

Seth instantly stands by my side, ready to join me.

"Just Lautner," Ryan orders.

Seth looks to Ryan as if ready to argue, but now isn't the time, not with a room full of enemy pack. Mick would already be pissed, and I didn't want to escalate the situation.

"Stay here, Seth. I got this."

I follow Ryan as he leads me out back through the kitchen and into the office where Mick is already waiting. It's the only place we can talk freely without being overheard in a house full of shifters. The walls are soundproofed, and for what I'm about to tell Mick, it's a damn good thing too, or this treaty would be over in a matter of minutes.

I wait for Ryan to close the door before finally looking up.

"Sit," Mick orders.

"I'd rather stand."

"It's not a request. Sit down," he repeats.

I drop down into the seat across from him. His piercing gaze doing little to relieve the tension that has bubbled under my skin. I feel as if I'm about to explode, and I can't help but wonder just how badly I've fucked up this time. Although technically, it's not my fault.

"Lautner," Ryan snaps, and I realize I must have missed my alpha speaking.

"What the fuck is going on with you?" Mick demands.

"It's not my fault ..." I begin until I realize just how pathetic I sounded. I might be fucked right now, but I'm no coward. It's time to take responsibility for my shit.

"During my fight with Tommy, something caught my wolf's attention ... a female. I couldn't focus, and Tommy started getting the better of me. I thought he had me at one point until I managed to reign in my wolf and take control. After the fight, I sought her out."

I watch his face waiting for my words to register.

"Danika Cortez ... is my fated mate." The words tumble out of my mouth, and I wish I could take them back. Saying it out loud just made it too damn real. I'd never been a man that had to deal with emotions; it's what made me good at my job. My father sought to create a monster, and he'd succeeded.

"Your mate," he seethes, clearly pissed at just finding out the news.

I watch as he closes his eyes, probably thinking about how badly I've screwed up again. He wouldn't be wrong.

"I thought the Ridgeway Pack were forbidden from attending the Warehouse?" Ryan asks.

"Well, it looks like someone forgot to tell Dani that because she was there. She told me her name was Dani Court, not Cortez."

"Do you realize what this means? She is already spoken for. Fated mate or not, it won't matter in the eyes of the Council. If you act on this, your actions will start a war between the two packs."

"I have no intention of claiming her. I give you my word. I have this under control."

"Under control!" he shouts, slamming his hands down on the desk with such force, it moves a few inches toward me. "You couldn't even last five minutes once she entered the room. You don't get it, Lautner, do you. The choice has already been taken from you. It's never been heard of for a man to reject his mate."

"Like you said, she is already spoken for," I reply vehemently, clenching my fists. "Besides, I only found out seconds before she entered that she's Ridgeway. If I'd had time to prepare, it would have been different."

"It's an arranged marriage, you know. She never had a say in it and never will. Her father saw to that."

"It doesn't make a difference to me whether she wants him or not. It doesn't change anything," I reply coldly, keeping my emotions at bay. Which is relatively easy, considering I didn't have any until yesterday when she walked into my life.

Mick studies me intently as I fidget in my seat. "You have to promise me that if you can't handle it, you'll get the hell out. Go for a run, go to the Warehouse. I don't give a shit. She is here under our protection, as is her fiancé."

I wince at his words, my mind drifting back to only a few minutes before and the idiot that dared place his hands on her. I could guarantee Dani's safety, but her fiancé's, well, that's a different story. I'd be lying if I said I hadn't already planned his death fifty times since the moment I'd laid eyes on him.

"I promise to leave if it gets to that. I can handle this," I reply. "The man is stronger than the wolf," I repeat the words of my father.

Mick's face softens as he once again sits down. "You're not your father, Lautner. You are not bound to the same mistakes."

I ignore his comment, wishing everyone would back the fuck off about my father issues. They didn't know the true extent of the monster he became and the hate he'd instilled in me. I was worse than my father. I'm selfish and uncontrollable, bringing me to lie number two. "There's another thing I need to tell you. When the shooter started firing at the Warehouse, I shifted."

"You shifted," Ryan cut in, shocked at my carelessness. "What the hell were you thinking?"

"That's the problem, I wasn't," I say between gritted teeth. "He started shooting wildly, and I heard Dani scream. It was instinct."

"Cal was lenient, I take it?" Mick asks.

I nod. "We came to an agreement over my punishment."

"What does he want?"

"My blood, to sell. Not yet though. He will call me when it's time."

Mick opens the bottom drawer of his desk, bringing out two glasses and a bottle of whiskey. He pours a good measure into both glasses before handing me one, waiting until I'd taken a drink.

"Did I ever tell you what happened with Evie?" he asks, leaning back in his chair.

I shake my head. I knew Evie was Daniel's mom, but she'd left before I got here.

"I loved her, you know. We were childhood sweethearts. When Daniel came along, we couldn't have been happier. Then she met her fated mate, Blaine," Mick says sadly.

"She betrayed you," I say, pissed.

"No, she didn't betray me; she couldn't help it. I knew she loved me, but he was her mate. She hated the thought of hurting me, but it wasn't meant to be. We agreed to part ways, and Daniel stayed here with me."

"Why are you telling me this?"

"Because Lautner, some things just aren't in our control. I made a promise to the Council that the two packs could work together."

"You know I won't let you or my pack down. The man is stronger than the wolf," I say, looking him dead in the eye.

He nods once before taking another drink. "Only time will tell. But for now, I can't have you around everyone, not tonight. I won't take that risk."

CHAPTER 16
LAUTNER

The cool night air is a welcome relief on my overheated skin as I lean back against the wall. I had left Mick's office, passing straight through the kitchen and out the back door.

"Thought I might find you out here," Seth says as I open my eyes. "Alpha's orders, I take it."

"Yeah, can't have me fucking up the Council's plans," I quip, "besides, it's for the best. Look, about before ... in there. I just wanted to say thanks for having my back."

"Wow, an apology. I think it's the first I've ever gotten from you."

"And it'll be the last," I state with a smile.

"You're my brother, Lautner. I've always got your back, even when I disagree with you."

"Oh, I'm sorry. I didn't realize anyone was out here," Dani's voice floats over me, caressing my skin.

"No worries." Seth smiles. "Danika, isn't it. Are you lost?"

"No. I just needed some air. Look, I can go somewhere else," she offers, looking between us.

"No, stay. I was just leaving. Lautner, you coming?"

I know he is giving me an out, a chance to escape, but I can't do it. I stay where I am, listening to the sounds of his heavy boots retreating.

"Mind if I join you?" she asks, moving closer.

"It's a free country," I mutter. This close, I can hear her heart beating in her chest as her vanilla scent envelops me.

"About last night," she begins nervously, biting her bottom lip. "Can you please not say a word about the Warehouse. It's just our pack is forbidden to attend."

I smile, but it's not a friendly smile. It's the smile of a predator. "Afraid your father will find out you've been hanging out with the lower-class wolves," I reply sarcastically.

"That's not it," she replies, putting her head down, although we both know she is lying. She brings her hand up to her face, pushing back a few loose strands of silver-blonde hair, the moonlight catching the diamond on her finger.

"I forgot that congratulations are in order," I spit out, trying to contain the raging jealousy within.

"My father arranged the marriage," she mumbles, keeping her eyes away from me.

"So, I've heard. Doesn't surprise me. Your alpha is a control freak."

"Can I ask you something," she says, boldly stepping closer to me. "Why do you look at me like that?"

"Like what?"

"Like you hate me. Last night you wanted nothing to do with me, then ..."

"Then what?" I say, needing to hear her words.

"Then I ... we ..." Her face blushes crimson as she inadvertently looks down at my hand, no doubt remembering the orgasm that had ripped through her body. I know I am.

"You kissed me, remember. Not the other way around," I say as if it were nothing.

"You didn't put up much of a fight."

I shrug my shoulders. "You threw yourself at me. I wasn't going to say no. What's the matter, your fiancé not giving it to you," I spit, hating the thought of any man's hands touching her skin or feeling her silken heat around him.

She scowls at my words, probably expecting me to be nicer just because I fingered her last night. Well, she's got the wrong guy for that. I'm a predator, and everything about her screams prey, but damn it if that didn't turn me on even more.

"No ... I ... thought we had a connection."

"And now?" I ask, watching as her tongue swipes enticingly across her bottom lip—that little innocent move calling to my wolf. I lower my shield, letting my wolf's power caress the air around us. I watch, fascinated as her breathing remains the same. Unlike me, she is shivering in the frigid air, not overcome with the mating heat. Before I have a chance to stop myself, I grab her arm, pulling her flush against my body, spinning and trapping her between my body and the wall.

"My turn," I growl, sounding somewhere stuck between man and wolf.

The pulse point at her throat beats rapidly as I stroke my thumb across it.

My wolf calls out to hers, yet she remains dormant to our call. I push harder, letting my power caress her skin.

Shit. I shouldn't be doing this. If I gave my wolf too much power, he would claim her, and there wouldn't be a damn thing I could do about it. But I have to know for sure if she really is my mate.

"How do you do that?" I growl, lowering my head to her throat, gently nipping at the delicate area above her collarbone. She moans at the contact, encouraging me to bite harder. I do. My wolf surges forward, demanding I finish this. That I push her jeans down her thighs and seat myself deep inside her, taking her hard and fast as I bite down, claiming her. I loosen my bite, fighting back some control. I need to back off before I did something I would regret, yet I'm lost in the moment, in the scent of her.

"I don't know what you're talking about," she moans, my lips kissing their way across her throat, soothing my playful bites. Her hands grip my hips roughly until finally, I feel the power of her wolf within, pushing against my own.

"There she is." A fine sheen of sweat breaks out across her skin, answering our call. Her cheeks no longer pale but blushed crimson as she tries to look away.

"Eyes on me, Dani," I command, feeling the rush of our combined power. There is no doubt about it. Danika Cortez is our mate. Her eyes are dilated as she moans at the searing heat she now feels flowing under her skin. It's like an addiction. The longer it burns, the more aroused she became. The smell of her arousal is like a fine wine, and I want nothing more than to drink at the pool between her legs. My lips instantly find hers, coaxing her to open to me as she whimpers against my lips. It takes every bit of my resolve not to shred the clothes from her body and take her against the wall, emptying myself into her again and again, until the fire evaporates, or consumes us entirely, whichever comes first.

"What are you doing to me?" she pants angrily, her lust quickly turning to fear, fighting me. The panic in her voice is enough for me to let her go. I watch as she dives straight into her pocket, taking out a pill bottle. She quickly pops the lid, taking out two pills and placing them in her mouth.

"What are those?" I demand, taking the bottle from her hand.

"Hey," she snatches them back. "I need those."

"Why?"

"I suffer from seizures," she replies, turning away.

"Says who? Where do you get them?"

"My father gets them for me, and the rest is none of your business. Can we please not talk about this," she snaps.

I watch her take a few deep breaths, composing herself. Her breathing once again returning to normal, and her wolf hidden, taking her mating heat with it.

"You need to leave, Dani. There's nothing for you here," I lie, taking a step back, wishing I'd followed Seth back inside earlier when I had the chance.

"I—"

"Dani," a voice bellows angrily, cutting her off before she can continue. "There you are," Drake says, coming around the corner, his eyes traveling between the two of us, with a mixture of mistrust and disgust. "You shouldn't be out here alone." He goes straight over to Dani, putting his arm around her shoulders as Dani tenses up.

"I'm not alone," she replies, clearly pissed at the intrusion.

"Your alpha's orders were clear. You are to stay with a member of your own pack. It's not safe." He throws me a look of pure hatred, which I meet with one of my own.

"We were just talking," Dani replies, moving away from him as his hand slides off her shoulder.

"Lautner, isn't it?" he asks, his tone trying to sound threatening, but only resulting in making him look weak.

I nod. "And if I'm not mistaken, you're Deacon, aren't you?" His face flushes red in anger at my disrespect.

"The name's Drake," he spits between clenched teeth. "Beta to the Ridgeway Pack, and future mate to the Alpha's daughter. You are what, nothing but an enforcer," he dismisses with a wave of his hand.

My smile widens at his description. The man before me couldn't stomach the job I do.

"That's right." I smirk, determined to make fun of him. "I heard it was you that messed up today, killing the hunter."

"We are one hunter down, thanks to me," he sneers, just as I feel the brush of his power in the air, knowing his wolf is scoping me out.

My wolf snarls within at the lesser wolf before us. He's no match for us. "No, you slowed us down. If you'd caught him alive, I would have been able to do my job, and you could have all gone back home and lived happily ever after," I snap.

Drake's hand lashes out, gripping Dani's arm tightly, as I catch her wincing in pain. With lightning speed, I pry his wrist from her arm, twisting it back. "You don't fucking touch her," I growl, hating the sight of another man's hands on her skin.

"I am her protector, her fiancé, her mate," he snarls, but I refuse to ease my grip.

"She doesn't need protecting from me." I let go of his hand, but the promise in my tone is real. If he did anything like that again, I will take him down.

"Dani, let's go," Drake snaps.

I can see the war that is playing out inside of her. It's written all over her face. She wants to stay, but that would be a big mistake for both of us. Making the decision for her, I turn my back on them, walking away.

CHAPTER 17
LAUTNER

Eight years ago

"You ready?" my father asks.

I'm more than ready. I'm sixteen and newly shifted. The power that flows just beneath my skin is intoxicating. My father had been right. It's a power unlike any other, and I'm looking forward to testing out my newfound strength. It didn't matter all these fights were fought in human form. The secret is to open yourself up just enough to let your wolf's predatory instincts guide you.

I'd come to love the fights I once hated. The blood, the destruction, they opened up a darkness in me that my father encouraged wholeheartedly. It's my driving force in the pitiful world of the strays. I'm revered here for my skills.

My eyes glance over to the adoring females on the outside of the makeshift ring as my father follows my gaze, chuckling.

"You can have it all, Lautner. Whoever you desire. But first, you must prove yourself worthy."

The bell rings, and my father backs away as I smile at my opponent, cracking my knuckles. My opponent is a few years older than me, but we matched each other well in height and weight. His thick biceps promised a deadly hit, but I didn't plan on letting him get close enough to test my theory. We circle one another, sizing each other up, waiting for the other to strike first. I lunge forward, hitting hard and fast anywhere I can land. My opponent follows my movements, blocking my every attempt. This guy's good, but I'm better. He goes to throw a left as I catch his arm, stepping behind him, landing two blows just below his ribcage at his kidney. He goes down hard on his knees, doubling over. I swiftly deliver a punch to the back of his head as he goes down, knowing he isn't about to get back up.

My body is on fire, hungry for something else as I greedily eye the females outside the ring.

"Go pick one, or two." My father chuckles, obviously pleased by my performance.

"I thought it wasn't allowed?" I ask cautiously.

"Trust me, you will know when you find the one. Your mate. She will call out to you until you bleed on the inside," he spits. "It will take everything in you to fight it, but that's what you'll do. You'll fight against the lust and false promises that she'll undoubtedly make."

"John mated, and he—"

His fist catches me mid-sentence as my head snaps back. It's my own fault; I should have been more prepared, more ready.

"That's what it will be like," my father states. I can feel the blood from my nose trickle into my mouth. "It catches you unaware, until you can't escape. Others are weak. John is *weak. He may look happy now, but just you wait, he will end up like me, broken. They all do. Promise me you won't let a mate ruin what I've created. The monster inside that feeds on the pain and destruction of lesser men. If you do, others will know your weakness. They will destroy you. The man is stronger than the wolf."*

"The man is stronger than the wolf," I repeat after him. *It had become our mantra now. Words to live by. I wouldn't let the wolf inside me dictate my future. I'm capable of anything. I didn't need anybody else. If I ever did meet my mate, she better run as far away from me as she possibly could. She would be nothing to me, no matter what my wolf craved. I'm in charge.*

I turn toward the females now with a sneer on my lips. They were nothing to me—just holes to fill for my satisfaction. My prize, for a win I earned in the blood, sweat, and tears of my opponents.

A female shyly advances my way, coming to a stop before me. I recognize her immediately, but I forget her name. She is the same age as me and had been watching me for a while.

I scent the air cautiously, catching nothing more than the overpowering scent of her perfume. I relax my shoulders, knowing she is no threat to my wolf and me. Smiling, I take her hand, leading her to the trailers on the outskirts of the park.

CHAPTER 18
DANI

I glance at the clock above the bar. It had been thirty minutes since I'd followed Drake back inside, and so far, Lautner had been a no show.

"I just hope their alpha has plans about keeping him in check while we're here. He's clearly unstable. His alpha should have him on a leash," Drake snaps, his arm tightening around my shoulders, pulling me closer. He had been like this since finding me outside. I'd wanted nothing more than to vanish upstairs and call Lacey, but the way Drake is acting, I wouldn't be surprised if he tried to follow me, and that's the last thing I want to happen.

"Don't worry about Lautner," my father replies, stretching back in his chair. He looked as if he didn't have a care in the world, even though his eyes are scanning the room, no doubt looking for the man in question. "Lautner has his own demons."

I wanted to pry further, demand to know what dirt my father had on him, but it's pointless. He would never tell me. This is my father's specialty. He's not stupid. Before he'd walked through the door, he would have had every member of the Stone Valley Pack checked thoroughly. Looking for anything incriminating that might give him the upper hand should he need it.

The sound of the door opening has me eagerly looking up, only to be disappointed at the sight of Seth. As if sensing who I'm looking for, he makes his way over to our table.

"Alpha Cortez," he greets, "Drake, Danika. Mind if I join you?"

"Not at all," I say before my father or Drake can protest. I gesture to the chair across from me, grateful for a change in conversation.

"I'm sorry to hear about the attack on your way here."

"I—"

"She's fine," Drake cuts me off coldly. "I was there to look out for her."

"I'm talking to Dani," Seth dismisses him with a shake of his head. "Will you be helping in the search?" he continues, looking directly at me.

"Me. Oh no. I'm not much good at tracking. To be honest, I'm not entirely sure why I'm here."

"Well, I'm glad you are." He smiles, causing Drake to shift uncomfortably beside me.

"I'm sure your alpha has already stated that Danika is mine. And your pack are to leave her alone," he spits disdainfully,

"Of course," Seth replies, "I'm only being friendly."

It's at that moment Lautner decides to return. His presence sucking the air out of the room as he heads over to the bar for a drink. I watch him converse with Daniel, keeping his back ramrod straight as if determined not to seek me out.

I know he wants to. He can deny it all he wants, but the connection between us is undeniable. It's like an invisible string that binds us together.

My father's phone rings as he scowls, looking down at the screen. "I need to take this," he says, standing. "Drake." He ushers with a tip of his head. I can see the anger on Drake's face; he didn't want to leave me alone with Seth. His eyes bore holes into my skull in warning before following my father from the room.

"Well, he's friendly, isn't he." Seth chuckles, but I continue to watch Lautner as his alpha approaches him.

"Don't give up on him," Seth says, breaking my focus.

"Excuse me?"

"Your mate. You can't keep your eyes off him while Drake, here, is practically dripping his claim for all to see. You only have eyes for one man."

I shrug my shoulders, unable to put into words whatever I feel for Lautner. "That's none of your business," I state. "My pack doesn't believe in fated mates."

"And you?"

"Does it matter. I'm engaged," I say.

He leans forward, the seriousness on his face instantly making me uneasy. "Lautner is my best friend, but right now, he's a loaded gun ... and you, Dani, hold the trigger."

"Why are you telling me this?" I ask.

"Because he doesn't know how to help himself. Lautner's complicated and refuses to let people in. If you are his mate, he won't accept this easily. You will need to fight for him."

"Why should I? If that's what he wants."

"His father, Drew, was a weak man. After Lautner's mom died, he vanished from the pack taking Lautner with him. Lautner grew up amongst the strays, fighting for survival. Watching as his father descended into madness. He doesn't trust people, and the thought of being mated after what happened to his father, well, he's too strong for that, too stubborn. He believes that in order to be strong, he must be alone. There's only one person in this world that Lautner fears. You."

"That's insane," I start.

His eyes roam over my tiny stature, and with a laugh, he replies, "Fine, maybe not you exactly, but what you represent."

"So, what should I do?"

"That's the million-dollar question, isn't it," he replies, leaning back in his seat. "So, tell me, why is it that Lautner's running around enraged with the mating heat, and yet, here you sit, calmly, with another man's arm around your shoulders?"

"I don't understand."

He scents the air around me. "Is she immune to Lautner? Or is there something else we should know about?"

I turn away from him. There's no way I'm about to discuss my inability to shift with this man. "That's damn personal. I think it's time for you to leave."

"I was just—"

"She asked you to leave." Lautner appears as if out of nowhere like my dark guardian angel, his eyes black, directed at Seth.

"Whatever you say," he replies, placing his hands up, and slowly getting out of the chair as if not to provoke him. By the looks of it, Seth had dealt with Lautner and his anger long enough to know how to deal with him.

"Thank you," I say to Lautner, but he doesn't respond. To be honest, I didn't expect him to. Instead, he walks from the room, taking a bottle of whiskey with him. I glance at the clock on the wall to see it's well past midnight now. Taking a final look around the room, I'm surprised to find neither my father nor Drake had returned. I quickly bid goodnight to Terry as I pass, looking to make a quick escape to my room on the third floor.

"Danika," my father's stern voice calls out from behind me just as I reach the safety of my room.

"Can it wait till tomorrow, Father? I'm tired after everything that happened today."

"Now," he replies sternly, looking at me as if I were some petulant child.

Raising my shoulders, I enter his room, noticing Drake already settled into the armchair by the old fireplace, his signature smirk in place.

"Drake was just informing me that you and Lautner," he spits out the name in disgust, "were looking rather close outside."

"I was just getting some air. Lautner was already outside; it's hardly close," I say in my defense.

"Don't take me for a fool, Danika. You think anyone from this pack will help you? You are bound to Drake."

"Don't worry, Father, nothing will ruin your plans. I'm not plotting against you if that's what you think. I will marry Drake, and you can inherit whatever it is you deem more important than your daughter's happiness."

He stalks toward me, raising his fist, and I realize I've gone too far.

"You dare to speak to your alpha this way." His clenched fist lashes out, catching me in my midsection as I double over, winded. His hand reaches down as it clutches my face, raising it to his.

"Do you think you're above talking to me with respect?" He twists my face around to look at Drake. "I have kept him from your bed till your wedding night, but I can easily change that arrangement."

Gasping for air, I try to hold back the fear that threatens to consume me, but I'm too late. Drake watches me carefully before cupping himself and throwing me a wink. I close my eyes to block him out.

"I'm sorry," I hear myself saying. "My nerves are still frayed after today's attack. I'll stay away from Lautner." His eyes stare into mine as if seeking the truth in my words. I hold his gaze until finally, satisfied, he drops me to the ground.

"Get cleaned up," he replies, walking away, clearly finished with me for now.

I nod, pulling myself up off the floor, clutching my stomach. I exit the room as quickly as I can while my hand fumbles in my pocket for my key.

As soon as the door opens, I quickly enter, locking it behind me. I head straight into the small bathroom, turning on the light to see what damage my father had done to my ribs. He'd gone easy with his punch tonight. The area is red, but he hadn't broken a rib this time. I go over to the bed and lie down, my hand automatically dialing Lacey's number.

"It took you long enough to ring me," she answers excitedly. "I've been waiting all day."

"Well, sorry, it's not all about you," I snap, instantly regretting it. It's not Lacey's fault. "I'm sorry, Lace. I've just been with my father. My nerves are a little on edge."

"It's alright. So come on, spill, what am I missing. Have you seen Lautner yet?"

For the first time that night, I finally relax. I tell her all about the hunters and the attack on our way here. "Shit. Are you okay?" she asks, concerned.

"I'm fine now," I assure her, "just exhausted."

"What about Lautner, did any of them mention last night in front of your father?"

I shake my head before realizing she can't see me. "No, everyone's been great about the whole thing, but Drake mentioned it before."

"Asshole," she mutters. "I knew he would have had someone watching. What about Lautner?"

"That's complicated," I start. "I think we had a moment before."

"Now this, I want to hear."

"I went outside to get some air, and he was there. He knows something's wrong with me. He kept asking me about my wolf."

"What did you say?"

"Nothing. He used his power against me, and ... I don't know, it was nothing like my father's. It was powerful, but instead of fear, it lit a fire deep inside of me. She's there, Lacey ... my wolf."

"I told you he was your mate, didn't I? She's responding to him. What happened next?"

"We kissed."

"And?"

"Nothing. Drake showed up, and Lautner left. That's it."

"That's it! Girl, you're killing me. Go find him. You deserve a true mate, not some sadist like Drake that your father picked out for you."

"Maybe," I say, just to shut her up. "Anyway, Lace, I'm exhausted. I'll ring you tomorrow, okay."

"You better. Night, Dani."

"Night, Lace," I reply, hanging up.

Were Seth and Lacey right? Is Lautner my fated mate? I wanted to believe it, and yet from the old stories I'd heard, a male couldn't resist his mate, and Lautner looked like I was the last thing he wanted. I think back to our encounter outside. The way his voice and power caressed over my skin, burning me from the inside out. No man had ever caused my body to respond in such a way. I needed to see him again, to catch him alone and demand he tell me the truth.

My phone beeps beside me.

Daniel: *Just wanted to make sure you were alright after today D x*

I smile, happy that Daniel still wanted to be friends after everything that happened last night.

Me: *I can't sleep,* I reply.
Daniel: *Me either. Everyone's gone to bed. Meet me downstairs for a drink D x*

The text is accompanied by a photo of Daniel, all alone, holding a bottle of tequila.

Daniel: *Join me?????? please D x*

Smiling, I climb off the bed, grateful that I hadn't bothered getting changed into my pajamas as I quietly slip out of the room.

CHAPTER 19
LAUTNER

The heat on my skin is unbearable. Groaning, I climb out of bed, heading once again into the bathroom and running the cold water. Stepping into the shower, I expected my skin to sizzle under the cold water. It didn't, but it did nothing to penetrate the raging heat that consumed me, either. Closing my eyes, I remember her body pressed against mine outside. Never had anyone felt so right pressed against my body. Her scent still lingers on my skin, no matter how many times I washed it. My cock, almost painfully full, rocks forward of its own accord. I grasp it firmly, imagining her delicate fingers as they explored the tip before her mouth carefully encased me, tasting my precum. I come hard, not once but twice. Images of her mouth against me, assaulting my mind. Finally, somewhat sated, I step out of the shower, throwing my joggers back on. I need a plan, and I need her out of my life before it's too late.

"Wrong way, Dani, for God's sake, are you trying to get

us into trouble," I hear Daniel whisper loudly, somewhere outside my door.

What the hell is Daniel doing, creeping about in the middle of the night with Dani? I quickly open my door, finding Dani leaning against the wall, her eyes glassy, a half-empty bottle of tequila in her hands.

"What the hell. Are you drunk?" I demand, my hands clenching into fists, itching to kill Daniel.

"Shh, maybe a little." She laughs as Daniel comes round the corner behind her.

Unable to stop myself, I slam him back against the wall. "What the fuck is wrong with you, letting her get like that," I growl.

"We were just having a little fun," he slurs, completely oblivious to the danger he is in right now.

Fun. If he so much as kissed her, I would kill him, pack or not. "What did you do?" I hiss.

"Nothing, we just—" My fist lashes out, catching him in the face and taking him down.

"Take the hint, Daniel. She. Is. Not. Yours. She will never be yours." I go to hit him again.

"Lautner, stop," Mick commands as I turn to see him and Ryan standing in the hallway.

"What's this, a party we weren't invited to," Ryan quips.

"Daniel, get out of here and sober up. You know better than this," Mick commands as he helps his son off the floor.

"I was just trying to help her," Daniel tries to explain, touching the blood at his lip.

Dani doubles over. "I think I'm going to be sick."

Damn it. I quickly hurry over to her side, guiding her back into my room and to the bathroom inside.

I sit on the floor beside her as she leans back against the cold tile, closing her eyes. Even drunk, she looks perfect.

"She alright?" Ryan asks, catching me by surprise.

"Yeah, I think she just needs to sleep it off."

"Good. You need to get her back to her room now before her father or Drake realizes she's gone. To be honest, I'm surprised. I thought if anyone were going to fuck this treaty up, it would have been you, but it's not over yet, is it," he replies coldly, stalking out of the room.

As I watch him disappear, I'm surprised to find that there is actually something we can both agree on. I suppose there's always a first time for everything.

"He doesn't like you much, does he?" Dani asks as I turn around to find her watching me curiously.

"What do you want, Dani?" I ask, ignoring her question. I'm not about to get into the hatred between Ryan and me. "I know you didn't just happen to turn up outside my room by accident. A hotel this size, and you end up at my door."

She closes her eyes as we sit in silence. "This is all your fault, you know," she says, finally opening her eyes.

"Mine. I was just minding my own business. You're the one running around in the middle of the night with Daniel."

"I'm not talking about that." She shakes her head in frustration. "I'm talking about you showing up in my life and making me realize what I can never have," she replies sadly, and I hate how much it hurts me inside, seeing her sad. She looks miserable, and there's not a damn thing I can do about it. Scratch that, I could, but I won't. It's time Dani realized that she is wasting her time.

"What do you see when you look at me, Dani? I'm no knight in shining armor. You think you can use me to end your contract with Drake, is that it?" I shake my head, pissed. "I fight, and I fuck. You're nothing to me. I would never start a war between the two packs over you."

"What are you so afraid of?"

"Nothing."

"Then admit it. Just once, for me," she snaps angrily.

"Admit what?" I ask, although I already know what she is going to ask.

"That you're my mate. That this connection I feel is real." Our eyes lock, and I hate that she has this hold over me. I need to lie. To crush whatever fantasy she may be holding on to.

"Does it matter. You're engaged, remember," I throw her words back at her.

I can see her anger and frustration brimming beneath her skin, but she remains calm, reigning it all in. I'm impressed. It takes practice to control emotions. I'd had years of practice honing it as a skill, a weapon, but in that moment, she has more control than me. "Just answer the question, Lautner. What do you have to lose?" she replies sadly.

I think over her words, she's right. There's nothing to lose between us. She is already spoken for, and even if she wasn't, I have no intention of taking a mate.

I nod. "Fine. You are my mate, Danika Cortez."

She closes her eyes as if the words mean more to her than she cared to admit. "Was that so hard." She smiles sadly.

I watch as she sits there, her eyes closed. She'd no idea how hard that was for me to admit out loud. Physically, I can't deny my attraction to her. Hell, I'm hard right now, but mentally, I'm broken.

"Don't look so worried. I couldn't mate with you even if I wanted to," she replies sadly, opening her eyes. "I get Drake. There will never be anyone else for me."

I can see it in her eyes; she speaks the truth. I know she wants me. Even now, I can sense how nervous she is, just the two of us. The way her tongue snakes out and wets her bottom lip, gives her away too easily.

"What does your father have over you?" I ask, knowing without a doubt her father would be behind this.

She laughs, looking away, but it's a sad laugh. I watch as she climbs to her feet, heading toward the door.

I quickly jump up. "Where do you think you're going?" I growl, not ready for her to leave just yet.

"I shouldn't be here, Lautner. It was a selfish moment."

Her sad eyes turn toward me, calling forth a protectiveness inside me I'd never known before.

"If my father knew for even a second that I was here, he would kill you."

"I'm not afraid of your father, Dani."

"You should be," she says. "I'm sorry. I can't be here."

She goes to rush past me, but I catch her forearm tightly. She gasps at the contact, no doubt feeling the same rush of desire at our connection. This is how it's supposed to be—her and me. Together. Touching. She turns to face me, bringing her lips just inches from mine. I have no idea why the mating heat affects her so differently, but I know she can still feel it.

"You know ... I thought I was going to die today when the hunters attacked. It's the first time in my life I'd ever really feared death. I'd never had anything to live for until I met you, yesterday," she whispers, her words penetrating somewhere deep inside of me. "Make me feel again, Lautner." She moves closer until her breasts push up against my chest, and I can smell her arousal. "Touch me. Make me feel alive again." Her hands glide up to my face, brushing her fingers across my stubbled cheek.

My lips attack hers with a ferocious need. She thought she was selfish, but I'm the selfish one. I don't give a shit about her father, and neither should she. She would only have to say the word, and I would kill him. I would do anything for her.

Her moans turn into a desperate need as she climbs up my body. I grip her hips, lifting her up so she can wrap her legs firmly around my waist. I'm rock-hard as I growl, feeling her heat and wishing there were no barriers between us. Her hands roam over my arms and chest as if she can't get enough of touching me. She feels like my lifeline at that moment. My hands gliding under her hoodie, feeling the bare skin at her back as I trail my hands up. *Fuck.* Her skin is all bare, and I know she isn't wearing a bra. I feel pissed for a minute, thinking why the hell she is out with Daniel without a bra, but no, now's not the time. I want to erase every bad memory from her mind, if only for a little while. I break the kiss just long enough to remove her top, pulling it over her head and throwing it to the floor. I bring my mouth down to her nipple, flicking my tongue over her hardened peak before sucking it hard as she arches her back.

"Tell me what you need, Dani." I carry her over to the bed, laying her down as my body covers hers. My hand slides down to undo the button on her jeans as I quickly push them down her thighs, desperate to feel her once more. My fingers finally brushing against her folds as she moans, shuddering beneath me.

"My mate," she whispers.

It's the only answer I need. My fingers slowly penetrate her as she shudders at the intrusion.

"More," she moans, moving against my fingers. Unable to control myself, I shimmy down the bed, removing the rest of her clothing before settling between her thighs.

One taste. Just one, I promise myself.

I place my free hand over her stomach, holding her in

place as I lean forward, sliding my tongue through her heat. I take my time savoring every lick and suck. Her moans the only sound in the quiet of the night.

I lower my barrier, letting the power of my wolf caress her skin as I continue to feast between her legs. This is how it's supposed to be.

"Lautner." Her hands tangle in my hair, holding me to her as I growl against her pussy. She stiffens below me before coming hard against my mouth.

My mouth clamps down on her thigh, my wolf within demanding control. I shudder at the feel of her flesh between my teeth. *Do it.* I close my eyes, trying to force the barrier back into place, but it's no good. We want her. With a growl, I pull away.

"Get out." I dare not move. I'm losing control. If she didn't leave now, I would claim her, whether she wanted it or not.

"Lautner," her voice is timid as if she's unsure of what's come over me.

"Get out, Dani." I wipe my hands down my face, and I realize that I'm shaking. I need to get rid of her. If I didn't, there would be no stopping what happened next. Marriage contract, the Council, none of it would matter.

As if sensing the tension in the room, she quickly climbs off my bed. I can hear her rustling to get ready, but I don't watch. It's taking every ounce of my control to stay frozen and not go to her.

I can feel her eyes bore into my back as I grit my teeth. "What are you waiting for? Another rejection." I force the words out, hating myself more than I ever thought possible —my father's words replaying on a loop in my mind. *The man is stronger than the wolf.* He was wrong. For the first time in my life, the words didn't bring me comfort. They were nothing but a lie. I turn to face Dani, her eyes shining with the unshed tears she is fighting to hold back. "If you're so desperate for a fuck, remember, your fiancé is just next door to you."

"I hate you, Lautner," she replies, her voice full of conflicting emotions as she storms from the room.

Free from my wolf's hold, I finally move, slamming the door shut behind her. I want nothing more than to follow her and take back every goddamn word I said, but I know I can't. It wouldn't do neither of us any good. Picking up the empty bottle of whiskey, I throw it against the wall where it shatters, scattering glass all over the floor, as if it were the shards of ice breaking around my heart.

CHAPTER 20
LAUTNER

"What the ..." I glance over my shoulder, finding Ryan and Daniel both standing in the kitchen doorway, looking as if they'd seen a ghost.

As soon as I woke up this morning, I'd come straight down, starting breakfast. I'd barely slept last night after she left. My mind trying to think of ways to get her out of here before we both made a mistake. But the only way to get rid of Dani is to deal with the hunters so she can go back home.

"Since when do you get up early?" Ryan starts as Daniel goes straight for the food I'd already prepared and laid out.

"Since we got hunters in our territory. And I can't do what I do best until all you motherfuckers have eaten," I grumble, piling bacon onto a plate.

I look over to Daniel. He looked alright, considering how hard I punched him last night. A split lip wasn't so bad, given it would have been a hell of a lot worse if Mick and Ryan hadn't shown up when they did.

"About last night," he mutters as if sensing me staring. "I'm sorry."

I hear his words, but I still can't help the jealousy that rises within. I hated the way Dani looked happy around him.

"She doesn't need you to take care of her; She has a fiancé for that," I say, wondering if I'm saying it more to myself than him.

"Are we good?" he asks, finally looking over at me.

I want to say no, but I've no right to say that to him. Dani is nothing to me, and I need to keep it that way. "Yeah, we're good. Just don't do it again." I turn back to the rest of the bacon sizzling in the pan, not wanting to talk anymore.

It isn't long before both packs are up and ready. Dani had been a no show, not that I'm bothered, or at least that's what I keep telling myself. Considering how upset she'd been last night, I wouldn't be surprised if I didn't see her at all this morning, which is probably for the best. I need to keep as much distance as I can from her. The clock is ticking, and the less I saw of her from now on, the better.

Ryan informed me that Mick and Cortez held a private meeting last night. The plan is to split into two groups and head out to where the Ridgeway Pack were attacked yesterday.

I'm sat at a table in the far corner as Mick and Cortez divided the packs into teams.

The sound of the door opening has my heart beating faster as I turn to find out who'd joined us. But it isn't the female I was expecting. Alianna. *Shit.*

Every man in the room turns around, staring at the newcomer as she strides through the room like she owns the place. Her tight-fitting red dress leaving little to the imagination as I hear the Ridgeway Pack mutter amongst themselves. Alianna is a friend of the pack and my occasional friend-with-benefits. She's a lot like me in a way. She loves to fuck and never stays around the next day.

"Hey, handsome." She immediately comes over, sitting on my lap. "Did you miss me?" she purrs, her hand roughly gripping my shoulder.

"Always," I reply, smiling behind the searing pain her closeness inflicts. The mate bond is getting stronger.

"I hear you're on duty," she says, completely unbothered by the visiting pack's eyes on us.

"Yeah, Seth and I are headed out now."

"Well, how about we skip the foreplay, and I just put my bags in your room? You can welcome me back properly later," she whispers seductively in my ear.

"I—"

The door creaks open, and this time my eyes land upon the female I'd been waiting for. Her eyes instantly seek out mine, and I see the look of confusion and hurt on her face. I want to apologize and push Alianna off me, but it's Dani's words that stop me. *I hate you, Lautner*.

"Lautner," Alianna calls out, clasping my face between her hands and forcing me to look at her. "What's wrong?" Her head turns around to see who or what has caught my attention. I can't see her face, but I know Alianna well enough to know she is checking out the new female and her competition.

"How long are you staying?" I ask, trying to take her mind off Dani. Even as friends, if Alianna thought I was rejecting her for another female, all hell would break loose.

"A few days, maybe more. Shall I put my stuff in your room?" she asks, still looking at Dani.

I let out a sigh of relief as Seth comes into view, his face like thunder. "Alianna," Seth greets unpleasantly. "I'm surprised to see you here."

"I thought I'd drop by and see my favorite wolf." She smiles, although it doesn't quite reach her eyes. Seth and Alianna have never gotten along. He thought she was trouble and only visited when she needed help or a place to hide out. Usually, he's right. "Don't say you're coming to steal my man now, are you?" she replies possessively, loud enough for Dani to hear from across the room.

"Your man." He laughs, raising his eyebrow. "That's a new one. Thought you were the fuck-them-and-leave-them type."

"Still so serious, I see. You need to learn to relax, Seth." Gathering her dress that had ridden high up her thigh, she kisses my cheek. "I'm glad you texted me. I'll see you when you get back." She smiles before making her way into the kitchen.

I can feel Seth staring daggers at me as I glance over to where Dani had been standing only moments ago. She's gone. I search the room, only just realizing we were the last ones left.

"She stormed out of here like a bat out of hell," he states, obviously pissed at me.

"Not my problem," I pant, fighting to hold back the nausea overtaking my body from Alianna's prolonged contact. "Maybe now, she will leave me the fuck alone."

"You texted Alianna. Why?"

Because I fucked up. I want to scream. I'd stupidly believed that I would never see Dani again and that maybe, just maybe, I could withstand the pain long enough to use Alianna. But I was wrong, and now she's here, and Dani hates me. *Fuck.* Why can't I go back to being the emotionless bastard I was before I met her. Because right now, I'm hurting. Having Dani here under my roof is torture. I wanted her. I craved her. I needed her. No matter how many times I got myself off, it did nothing to cure the insatiable heat; there's only Dani.

"Does it matter," I say. I'm already pissed at myself. I didn't need Seth to confirm it.

"Not really. If anyone knows how to fuck up a good thing, it's you, Lautner," he calls out before the door shuts firmly behind him.

CHAPTER 21
DANI

"Dani," Daniel's voice calls out softly, "are you in there?"

I want to ignore him, to remain alone in my misery, but right now, Daniel's the only friend I have here, and I need him. "Just a minute." I bring Lautner's hoodie up to my face inhaling his scent one last time, letting it soothe me. It's stupid and childish, but a girl can pretend. In my haste to leave his room last night, I'd accidentally picked up his instead of my own. Hell, maybe it wasn't an accident. No matter how much Lautner hated me, I still wanted him. I quickly go over to the dresser, hiding it inside. I stop by the mirror on my way to the door, checking out my reflection. My eyes are a little red, but nothing too bad.

I open the door, hating the look of pity evident on Daniel's face.

"Nope. Forget it. You're not coming in here with that look."

"What look?" he feigns innocence.

"You know exactly what look," I scold him. "I don't need your pity, Daniel."

"It's not pity. Now, let me in."

I move back a couple of steps as he walks in, going to sit on the bed.

"Has everyone left?" I ask, going over to the window.

"Yeah, I got left behind, as usual," he mutters, shaking his head, and I notice his split lip.

"I'm sorry, Daniel. I wish things had turned out differently. I just seem to keep getting you into trouble."

"Nothing to be sorry for." He shrugs his shoulders, although his face still holds a hint of sadness that I know I'd caused involuntarily. "It wasn't meant to be," he states more to himself than me. "You're fated to be with Lautner, and despite what people say about him, he's a good man deep down."

"I-I was talking about Lautner hitting you last night," I reply, shocked at his words. I knew that Daniel liked me. I just hadn't realized it was in that way.

"Sorry." He blushes. "I thought you meant ... it's fine, really."

"No, it isn't. I should never have gone the wrong way. I can't believe he hit you," I gesture toward his busted lip.

"My own fault. I should have known better. I would do it all again though." He smiles. "It was nice to see you happy, if only for a short while."

"Yeah, up until this morning, and I come down to find Lautner's girlfriend here. I mean, how many does he have? She isn't the same one from the Warehouse." I hate how jealous I sound. I never thought I would be the jealous type, but I guess I'd never had someone to be jealous over.

"Don't take it personally. That's just Alianna being Alianna. They're not together."

His words do little to calm the raging storm I feel within. "She was on his lap, stroking his face, practically riding him in front of the entire room. If that isn't a claim, then I don't know what is."

"That was all for show. Trust me, I was there. I saw his face when she entered. He'd been watching the door all morning, waiting for you."

"Yeah, in case you haven't noticed, Lautner hates me. Oh, and this," I lift up my left hand, displaying the god-awful diamond ring. "I'm already taken. I shouldn't care, really; he's a free man, he can do what he wants." I sigh deeply, hating this unfamiliar feeling.

"Lautner's just pissed because of the mating heat, and he's too stubborn to give in and be happy. He thinks because his father was so shitty his life will follow the same path. It's sad really, he can't see that he is nothing like his father. Don't get me wrong, I never met the man, but I've heard stories about him, and Lautner is nothing like that."

"Seth mentioned yesterday that Lautner's father took him away after his mate died."

"Yeah, he should have done the decent thing and handed Lautner over to the pack. Instead, he raised him among the strays to be a cold-blooded killer."

"So, what is the mating heat?" I ask, finally ready to gain some useful information.

"Well," Daniel begins, leaning back against the bed, "from what I've heard, it's an intense heat that overtakes the body. Nothing can take it away. It continues to burn until the mating is complete or severed."

"And how long does that take?"

"A mating bond generally lasts for seventy-two hours, give or take, depending on how strong the bond is. It generally intensifies over time. If the bond is not complete, the ties begin to sever, and the mating heat subsides. Which is particularly bad for males as it only happens once. Females, however, can go on to mate again."

"Why is that?" I ask, curious.

"I have no idea."

"So, what can Lautner do to take away the heat?"

Daniel's cheeks flood a deep shade of red as he clears his throat.

"Sex?" I ask, feeling the blood rush to my own.

He nods, keeping his eyes averted. "Only with his mate. That is known to take the edge off."

"And how is the bond completed?"

"The male will mark the female somewhere on her body during sex, and the female will do the same. The marks will never heal, and the bond is complete."

"Okay, so why am I not in this mating heat like he is?"

"I don't know. That's what the whole pack is wondering."

I groan, putting my head in my hands. "The whole pack knows," I mutter.

"Relax, your pack has no idea. Luckily for you, Lautner has always been an unpredictable asshole, so no one is any the wiser. The next forty-eight hours are going to be a right bitch, especially the way Drake hangs off your shoulder. Do you want to marry Drake?"

"I don't have a choice. My father is a dangerous man. Nothing gets in the way of what he wants. The only way to break the contract is with his permission, and trust me, that's never going to happen."

"Well, you need to trust me, Dani. Lautner is far more dangerous than your father could ever be, and you both need each other. Fate bound you both for a reason; just think about that. Look, I need to go. I have some work to do for the pack, but come find me if you need anything."

I nod, watching him leave, mulling over his words. I want to believe that Daniel is right, that nothing could happen between Lautner and Alianna, but I hate she is here. It'd been obvious in their behavior they have a history, and the look Alianna had thrown my way this morning was nothing short of a challenge. She wanted him, and she's not backing down.

CHAPTER 22
LAUTNER

Drake and Alpha Cortez are already in wolf form when Seth and I arrive at the clearing. I quickly strip out of my clothes as Seth goes over to get our final instructions from Mick. I can feel Drake's eyes at my back, and my wolf within wants nothing more than to challenge him.

"We're going east," Seth replies, coming up behind me. I nod my reply, throwing Drake a look over my shoulder as he and Alpha Cortez take off to the south.

As Seth and I shift, I shake out my fur, my eyes lowering to the ground, taking in everything around me in a new light. I loved being a wolf. Everything is magnified. It's like seeing the world in a whole new way. A woman's scent lingers in the air as I let it guide me toward a discarded bullet. I raise my head, following it to where it disappears over the ridge. Snorting, I gain Seth's attention. Now a russet brown wolf, Seth heads over, catching the unfamiliar female scent in the air. I take off over the ridge, the sound of

Seth's paws hitting the wet earth echoing behind me. Suddenly, the scent in the air vanishes as I stop. Shifting back, I wait for Seth to catch up.

"Where did it go?" Seth asks, confused, looking around at the empty forest floor.

"I don't know," I reply. We were in the middle of a clearing deep in the woods. "She can't have just vanished." I take a step forward, my foot catching on something sharp. *Shit*. Fresh blood pools from a cut on the base of my foot. Bending down, I sweep away at the overgrown grass and weeds, revealing an old metal door.

I whistle to Seth. Understanding me perfectly, he quietly comes over.

"We should head back and tell the others," Seth whispers.

I shake my head. "No, let's check it out first. For all we know, it could just be an old preppers' hideout." I pull at the old, rusted handle, the hinges groaning loudly in protest, revealing a dark pit below. Even with my added wolf sight, it's hard to see what's down there. Placing my foot on the old metal ladder, I check its stability, carefully making my way down. As I touch solid ground, I run my fingers along the wall, finally feeling a switch. Light floods the small corridor as Seth comes to a stop behind me.

The bunker has two rooms. The first door I come to opens easily, revealing the largest horde of guns I'd ever seen. There's everything from AK47s to various pistols and even a grenade launcher.

The last room contains a desk and two filing cabinets. Seth goes straight over to the cabinets, testing the drawers and finding them locked.

"I'll look for the key," he says, going over to the desk.

Fuck that. Using my wolf strength, I pull the drawer hard as it opens with a loud bang.

"Shit. Now they're going to know we've been here."

"Good. They need to know we're on their asses just as much as they're on ours. I mean, look at all this shit," I say, pulling multiple files out in front of me. I flick through the documents filled with information regarding all the local packs, including charts, detailing their significant others and mates. They're thorough. I'll give them that.

I pick up the file containing my name as I open it up.

Andrews, Lautner. Age twenty-six. Stone Valley Pack Enforcer. Mother: deceased. Father: Andrews, Drew. Whereabouts: unknown. Threat status: High.

Inside there were blueprints for Micks' place and a few photos of me fighting at the Warehouse.

I continue to search through the records looking for Dani's.

Cortez, Danika. Age nineteen. Daughter to the Alpha of the Ridgeway Pack. Mother: unknown. Father: Cortez, Ryder. Threat status: low; unable to shift.

What the ... how is this even possible. She's a wolf. I felt her power.

Most females went into transition at the age of twelve when their menstrual cycle started. For males, however, the transition usually began at around sixteen. *What the hell had happened to Dani?* I quickly shove the papers back into the cabinet as Seth comes to a stop behind me.

"You find anything else?" he asks.

"Yeah, they have all our geniality here, for fuck's sake. Names, addresses, mates, marriages, kids. It's like looking at a fucked-up version of this is your life."

"How the hell do they know all this stuff?" Seth asks.

"No idea, but someone's been talking. What did you find?"

"They like to keep pictures of their kills," he motions with his head to a board on the far wall I had yet to notice. I head over for a better look. Polaroids decorated the wall, depicting numerous dead shifters, some in mid-transition, others were more grotesque.

"And people think I'm bad," I mutter, looking at the wall in distaste.

"There must be at least eighty kills here," Seth confirms.

"Come on. I think we have all we need. Let's head back."

Everybody is already back at the cars waiting, when Seth and I return. Mick waits patiently as we shift back, quickly redressing.

"Anything?" he asks.

"We found an old bunker about two miles over the ridge. They have a pretty big arsenal in there and detailed dossiers on every shifter within a two-hundred-and-fifty-mile radius," I brief him.

"They even have a kill wall. Looks like a pretty professional setup to me," Seth adds.

Mick nods. "Good work. Let's head back home and reconvene. Cortez and I will make our plans this afternoon, but I want you both back out here tonight."

I nod, happy to have a lead. *Now I just have to figure out what the hell is wrong with Dani.*

CHAPTER 23
DANI

Collecting the remote off the bed, I switch off the tv. I'd spent the full afternoon watching various old murder documentaries in my room, trying to distract myself. It'd been a good few hours now since the packs left, and as I glance over to the window, I can see the sun just starting to set. Restless, I head downstairs looking for Daniel, finding him in the kitchen, making a sandwich.

"You want one?" he asks before taking a big bite.

I shake my head, too anxious to eat. "Any word?"

"Not yet." Just then, his phone rings, and I pace the floor, waiting for him to hang up.

"That was Ryan; they're on the way back."

"Everyone okay?" I ask, although I think we both know I'm asking about Lautner in particular.

"They're fine. Lautner and Seth found an abandoned bunker not far from the attack. Looks like the hunters have been using it recently."

I let out a sigh of relief. Lautner's okay. Excusing

myself, I hurry back upstairs to my room. I can feel another migraine coming on, and the last thing I need is the threat of another seizure. Popping two pills, I lie on my bed, wishing I were normal. It's embarrassing to be a nineteen-year-old shifter that can't shift. I had no doubt that even if things were different and I wasn't promised to another, Lautner would undoubtedly reject me. I'm not a true wolf. I could never stand beside him; I would always hold him back. He's a warrior. He didn't need a defenseless broken mate by his side.

The familiar sound of cars approaching outside has me pulling out of my self-made misery and rushing over to the window. I watch as Lautner gets out of a black Camaro that I instantly know is his. He looks up, catching my eye as I scarcely breathe. The connection between us is too strong. At that moment, I didn't care that we could never be together or that he wanted to push me away. I needed to see him. I quickly don my leather jacket, racing down the stairs hoping to catch him alone.

"Where are you going in such a hurry?" Drake asks, appearing at the bottom of the stairs as if he'd been waiting for me.

"To get some air," I reply, trying to step around him as he cuts me off.

"I'll join you."

"No. I'll only be a minute," I say hurriedly, wanting to catch Lautner before he headed inside, and I lost my chance to talk to him alone.

"Looking for Lautner?" he mocks, tipping his head to the side. "You think we haven't noticed you watching him," he whispers menacingly, inching closer. "You are mine, Danika. Just because I haven't claimed your body yet makes no difference to me. I'm sure I could persuade your father to forego the 'no sex before marriage' rule." His hands reach out, gripping my arms so tight, I know there will be bruising tomorrow. "It's been a long time since I've been with a virgin. I promise I won't go easy on you. In fact, I think I'd enjoy it better seeing your pain and misery." He laughs cruelly.

I meet his gaze, refusing to show him the fear he wants to see on my face. Clearly disappointed at my lack of reaction, he lets me go. "Just remember, Danika, I'm not playing games. You're mine. Besides, Lautner has been talking nonstop about Alianna today. He's probably off fucking her right now as we speak. I mean, a female like that, why else would he have invited her. I bet she knows just how Lautner likes it," he snarls as he leans forward and licks a trail at my neck. I swallow down the revulsion building inside. "I think we both know who he'd pick." With that last remark, he walks away, pulling open the double doors that lead into the small bar and vanishing inside.

Is Drake right? Did Lautner invite Alianna here? I glance toward the door leading outside, but I don't move. *What if I catch him out there right now, kissing her?* I don't think I could face it, another rejection. Taking a deep breath, I rush toward the door before I can change my mind. His car is parked outside along with my father's, but he is nowhere to be found. Lautner is gone.

CHAPTER 24
LAUTNER

Both packs are already gathered in Mick's office as I take my seat beside Seth.

"Where did you go?" he whispers as I sit down.

"Around back in case Alianna was waiting for me." It's not a lie. She would be around here somewhere waiting for me, but as we pulled up, I'd caught sight of Dani waiting for me at the window. A haunted look on her face. I know she wants to talk to me about last night and about Alianna, but I have questions of my own. Ones that I'm hoping Mick can help me understand before I confront her.

"Right," Mick starts. "As you are aware, Lautner and Seth came across a bunker today just a few miles away from yesterday's attack. It looks like it's been used recently by the hunters. Lautner," he nods in my direction, waiting for me to speak.

All eyes turn to me as I fidget in my seat. "The bunker is filled full of dossiers about every shifter within at least a two-hundred-and-fifty-mile radius. Details included were births, deaths, arranged marriages, fated mates, etc. Basically, everything they need to know about us, including addresses old and new." I listen as the packs murmur around me, cursing under their breath.

"So how are they getting this information?" demands one of the Ridgeway Pack, Terry, I believe. "They have only just breached our borders, and already they know more about us than we do them."

"My bet is they have a few strays on their side. Somebody who knows the area and the local packs," Seth replies.

Mick nods in agreement. "Most likely, it's someone we all know or at least have interacted with before," Mick states.

"Tommy," I say aloud.

"What?" Seth asks.

"Before the fight started, Tommy was running his mouth. He mentioned something about how we didn't know what we were up against. I didn't think much of it at the time, but what if Tommy and Brandon joined them."

"Makes sense. They both hate the packs and everything we stand for," Mick agrees.

"But why would the strays team up with the hunters? It doesn't make any sense. The hunters would hate them more than us, considering what they do," Daniel jumps in.

"Maybe they're just using them for information. Keep your friends close and your enemies closer. No doubt, when the packs were finally taken care of, they would turn on them. They already know all of our weaknesses," I reply.

"We need to put a watch on the bunker starting tonight. Seth, Lautner, I want you on tonight's watch," Mick commands.

"No," Cortez replies. "I think a member of both packs should be there."

"You don't trust us?" Mick asks.

"It's not that I don't trust your pack, but we did promise the Council we would work together," Cortez sneers in return.

"Fine by me." Mick turns to Drake. "How about you? Are you volunteering?"

Drake glances my way. "Yeah, I'll be happy to keep an eye on things."

"I'll go too," Terry volunteers.

"Then it's settled." Mick looks between us. "If anyone shows up, I want them brought back here alive, understood. Daniel, any luck on the abandoned houses in the area?"

"I've looked online at satellite maps, and there are a few within driving distance we should take a look at."

"Good. If we don't have any luck tonight, we hit them tomorrow. I want a hunter within the next twenty-four hours. You have anything to add, Cortez?"

"No, you seem to have covered all bases," he replies, leaning back in his chair.

"Alright then." Mick looks at his watch. "It's six-thirty. I want you four to head out at midnight. Everyone else rest up. Meeting adjourned."

I wait as the packs start to file out, and the door closes behind them, ensuring our privacy.

"She can't shift," I tell Mick.

I watch his face furrow as he tries to understand my words.

"What do you mean, can't shift?" Ryan asks from where he stands behind Mick.

"Exactly that. It must be why she is barely displaying the mating heat. I catch glimpses of her wolf here and there if I push, but she panics and starts taking these pills. When I asked her about them, she said she suffered from seizures, and her father gets her these pills to help her control them."

"But you're not convinced," Mick asks.

I shake my head. "When we kissed, I sensed her wolf, and I could feel the mating heat start to take effect, but as soon as she took the pills, it was gone as if it never happened."

"You think the pills have something to do with it?"

"Yeah, I do. Since when have you ever known a shifter to suffer from any type of illness."

"It's certainly unheard of."

"I thought you didn't care about Dani Cortez?" Ryan asks. "Isn't that why Alianna's here?"

"I don't," I lie, "but if her father is drugging her to keep her weak, I think she has the right to know, don't you?" I wait for his reply, but he keeps quiet as I turn back to my alpha. "I want your permission to get one of the pills and take it to Thane to test. My guess is it's laced with wolfsbane or something else used as a suppressor."

"Why would a father drug his own daughter?" Ryan butts in.

"Isn't it obvious. Cortez is a control freak. He has Dani marrying a man she hates, and she can't do a damn thing to defend herself," I snap angrily.

"Okay." Mick holds up his hands. "See if you can get a hold of one of these pills, but I want it done quietly. If it is Cortez's doing, I don't want him to know that we're on to him."

I nod. "I'll be discreet."

"Good. Because if it is something like this, it's not just Dani or the Council we have to worry about. If he can physically cause a wolf not to shift, that makes him even more dangerous than we realize. As an enforcer, how powerful would it be to have a drug to stop the change during interrogation?"

"Silver works."

"Yeah, it does, but we can see that coming a mile away. If he can slip it into our drink, we would have no idea until it's too late. I'll look into it, and I'll let you know what I find out."

I nod, heading toward the door.

"Oh, one more thing, Alianna is gone for the night. I told her I needed you for the next twenty-four hours, so she made other plans. She shouldn't be here, Lautner, and you know it. I take it you can get rid of her before she finds out about Dani."

"Yeah."

"Good. We don't need any more trouble."

Closing the door to Mick's office, I can't help but feel relieved that Alianna is away for the night. I should never have texted her. I could feel the tension in her this morning. She saw Dani as a threat, and Alianna doesn't like threats. I have no idea what will happen if she finds out Dani is also my fated mate.

I make my way back through the bar, my eyes instantly searching her out. She is sitting beside Drake in the far corner, her eyes red as if she'd been crying. Drake watches me warily, pulling her closer with a sneer on his face. I instantly want to go to her and take her away from him. The invisible bond that draws me to her, demanding I make sure she is alright. Instead, I walk past her and up the stairs. I know this could be my only shot of getting the pills without her knowing. As soon as I reach her room, her scent overloads me, and I breathe in deep, wishing she were here with me. The raging inferno inside me wanting nothing more than to feel her hands on my skin and her body submitting beneath me. I push the thought aside as I rummage through her bedside drawer, finding the pill bottle. Popping the lid, I slip two pills into my pocket. It was time to get some answers.

The Warehouse is relatively quiet when I enter. I make my way down to the basement in search of Thane. My eyes instantly hit the wall where Dani and I first kissed.

"You here to fulfill your debt so soon?" Thane asks behind me as I jump. I turn around, wishing that motherfucker would start to wear a bell around his neck so that I could hear him coming.

"No. That's not why I'm here," I say, quickly composing myself. "We have a job on for the next few days, and the pack needs me at full health. Don't worry. You will have your blood when it's over."

"The time is up to Cal, not me, but I will pass on the message."

"Cal not here?" I enquire. "I thought you guys couldn't go out through the day."

"I didn't say he isn't here, just preoccupied right now."

I don't pry any further. It's none of my business what the Sun Sinners got up to. "Any news on the shooter?"

"Not yet," he replies, tapping his blue-painted nails against the wall. "But it's only a matter of time. He attacked on Sun Sinners property. Cal won't let it go."

"Well, we have reason to believe that he may be involved with a new group of hunters that the pack is looking for."

"Is that so. I take it that these hunters are responsible for the body the other night?"

I nod. "We think so. If the Club finds the shooter first, I will need to interrogate him before you kill him."

"I can't make any promises," Thane replies, "but I'll run it by Cal to consider. Now, why did you want to see me? Or is it just to ask about the shooter."

I pull one of the pills from my pocket. "I need you to test this and let me know the ingredients."

He takes the pill from my hand, bringing it up to his face for a closer inspection. "Why, what's it do?" he asks curiously.

"We don't know yet," I reply, not wanting to give anything away to the vampire.

"Don't play games, Lautner. You want me to test this shit; you've got to give me something."

I mull over his words. I needed Thane on my side, and I needed these results quickly.

"Fine. I think it has some effect over shifters being able to change at will."

"Interesting," he replies, looking at the pill with a lot more interest than before.

"I also need you to have the results by tomorrow."

"That's asking a lot, don't you think?"

"You're a vampire. It's not like you need the beauty sleep."

"Says the talking dog." He laughs. "You look like shit by the way. Alright, I'll see what I can do." He puts the pill in his pocket. "Now, if you'll excuse me, I have some business to attend." As Thane walks away, I make my way back to the stairs.

"It's not right to leave a girl hanging like you did." I turn around to find Destiny standing naked in a doorway, her arms posed on her hips. I can smell her cheap perfume as she slowly walks toward me.

"It's not going to happen, Destiny, not today."

She stands on her tiptoes as she whispers in my ear, "I promise to make you feel good, Lautner, just relax."

"No." I push her away as she falls, landing hard on her ass in the hallway.

"Big mistake, Lautner," she hisses as Thane comes around the corner.

I hold up my hands. "I didn't touch her."

He looks between the two of us before shaking his head. "Get off the floor, Destiny. Kai is looking for you." She scrambles off the floor as she storms past me, clearly pissed that Thane didn't run to her defense.

"What's the matter with you?" he asks, bewildered. "You seem different today."

"Nothing," I mutter, not wanting the vampire to start asking questions. "I've got to go." I make my way outside, heading straight over to my Camaro. By the time I make it back to Stone Valley, it would be time to leave for the stakeout. I'd successfully evaded Dani for most of the day. I should be relieved, yet I can't shake the dark pit in my stomach that something is about to go wrong.

CHAPTER 25
LAUTNER

I keep my eyes firmly on the road ahead, driving down the winding track not far from the bunker. It's damn near suicide on these roads without any lights. But I'm hoping if the hunters have any spies hiding close by, they might just mistake us for a bunch of idiotic kids with a death wish. Seth had called shotgun, sitting beside me in the passenger seat while Drake and Terry occupied the back.

"What's the deal with the female. What's her name, Arianna?" Drake calls out.

"Alianna," I correct. "What about her?"

"Is she yours?" he enquires. I can feel his eyes boring into my back as I lift my eyes to the rearview mirror, meeting his gaze head-on.

"She's a friend."

He snorts at my reply. "Yeah, I bet she is. If she's not taken, you won't mind if I fuck her then, will you?"

"You're engaged to Dani. What the hell could you possibly want with Alianna?"

"It's Danika to you," he snaps, "and I'm not married yet. Besides, after you take their virginity and break them, the fun just sort of stops, if you know what I mean. But Alianna, she looks like she could give me a run for my money."

I slam my foot on the brake, throwing us forward. Before Drake sees me coming, I'm over the back seat, grabbing him by the throat. "In my territory, we don't disrespect our mates, you piece of shit," I spit, his hands clawing at mine, where they lay firmly wrapped around his throat.

Seth clears his throat loudly. "Lautner, we've got a job to do," he reminds me, his voice stern, reminding me that no matter how much I despise the man before me, I can't kill him. Not yet. I hadn't forgotten, but I wasn't about to let this asshole talk about Dani like that. Not around me.

"You will keep your goddamn hands and dick to yourself. We clear?"

I wait for him to nod his head before slowly releasing my hands from their death grip.

"Your alpha will be hearing about this," he replies in between bouts of coughing as he rubs at his reddened throat.

I shrug my shoulders. "My alpha takes the same stand on respecting females as I do, so good luck with that." I return to my seat. No wonder Dani had been so upset last night, being forced to mate that asshole. I didn't know much about contract marriages, except that the contract is usually written and controlled by the packs alpha or the Shifter Council. Only they have the power to terminate it. Since it was all Alpha Cortez's idea in the first place, I knew he wouldn't break it, not willingly at least. But I'm betting Cortez has many dark secrets he keeps hidden. Maybe if I ask Daniel, he might be able to find something, so I can help Dani out in the process.

"Lautner," Seth calls out, pointing to the road ahead, pulling me from my thoughts. I can feel Seth's restlessness beside me. Ever since the meeting when I'd spoken of Tommy and Brandon's possible involvement with the hunters, he'd been ready. I know more than anything; he is hoping to find Brandon tonight.

Pulling over, I exit the car scanning the area for anything out of place. Satisfied we were alone, Seth and I start forward with Drake and Terry at our backs. Thankfully, Drake keeps his mouth shut the rest of the way there. If he hadn't of, he might just have had a very nasty accident. There are hunters in our territory, after all.

The door to the bunker is open as we approach. A faint light coming up from the ground as if leading the way. A car is parked close by, the engine still running, as if whoever is here is in a hurry and expects to need a quick getaway. I peer down into the bunker. Closing my eyes, I use my wolf's hearing, picking up the sound of two heartbeats below. I can instantly tell one of them is a shifter, his heart rate fast, matching that of my own. Inhaling deep, I catch his scent in the air. I can't place it, but we had definitely crossed paths before. I open my eyes, turning to Seth. I hold up two fingers. He nods his head in understanding. Seth backs up, pointing to the cover of the big oak trees behind us, urging Terry and Drake to follow. There's no point in all of us going down there looking to start trouble over two men. Besides, the bunker is too small to accommodate six of us.

Drake's hand angrily comes down on my shoulder. "What the hell are we doing?" he hisses, watching Seth's retreating form.

"Playing a game. It's called hide and seek," I grit my teeth, whispering back as I roughly force his hand away. "Now go hide." I don't wait for his response. I drop into the bunker's depths below, landing quietly.

"You heard what Alice said," I hear a man frantically explain, "we need to get all this shit moved before they come back."

"This is a stupid idea," another male responds, "leaving us to do the grunt work. I want to watch them all burn."

"You do realize with the number of shifters there is, you'll get plenty of opportunities."

Silently I creep forward, hiding behind the door that only earlier today had been filled to the brim with weapons. Now it stood empty. The hunters have been busy. I look around, wondering if they have a silent alarm. It'd only been a few hours ago that we stumbled across this place. Something or someone must have tipped them off.

"Maybe, but Lautner's the only one I want to see dead."

"Aw, poor fucking Brady. That's all you've talked about since you joined us. Get over it already and fill them boxes over there. I'm sure Brandon and Lester can handle it."

Brady motherfucking Henshaw. I should have known. Another stray. He'd tried to join our pack about five years ago. I guess that explains the wall. He was known for his flair for the dramatics. He'd tried against me for pack enforcer once and failed, humiliatingly so. I guess he never got over it. We all assumed he was dead. But Lester, I never expected this from him. We had been friends once. We had grown up together amongst the strays.

After a few minutes, the human stalks toward the stairs, a full duffel bag swung over his shoulder. I wait till he reaches the top before advancing toward Brady.

"I hear you're looking for me," I say, stepping into the nearly empty room.

Brady spins around at the sound of my voice. The bag he is holding falls from his hand, scattering papers across the floor.

"Well, well, Lautner, it's been a long time," he replies, cracking his knuckles as he composes himself.

"So, this is what it's come to," I motion with my hand to the kill wall. "Taking your revenge with a bunch of human hunters," I sneer. "I always knew you were a traitor."

"Traitor," he spits. "I'm no traitor, and neither is Brandon or Lester. We're doing the strays a favor by getting rid of you lot. Pretending to be something you're not, and you're the worst of them all. You've got more blood on your hands than anyone, even me."

He's right, and before the end of the night, I would have his. "Don't make this any harder," I start, moving toward him. "You know you've got nowhere to run."

"You'll never take me alive."

"I don't need to. I'm sure the human will give us what we need." I smile.

I watch as Brady begins to shift. My wolf growling within, approving his request, starting my own. Fully shifted, we circle one another as best we can. I'm the bigger wolf, but in a room this size, it puts me at a disadvantage.

My eyes stalk his movements as he feigns left before diving to my right, trying to catch me off guard. We dance back and forth, parrying for leverage before moving toward one another. My claws are the first to connect, tearing through the flesh of his shoulder as Brady snarls in pain. This wouldn't be a long fight. Fights to the death were always over quickly. I'd briefly considered taking Brady back alive, but we had the human hunter for information. Besides, next to Brandon and Lester, Brady was a nobody, bottom of the food chain. The human would no doubt hold more useful information. I catch the last second just before Brady's haunches leave the ground, diving toward me. His teeth clamping down on my foreleg, tearing into my flesh under the pressure of his jaw.

Growling, I use the full force of my body to throw him off me before diving for his throat. The sweet taste of blood enters my mouth as the coppery scent floods the room. Satisfied he is dead, I transition back.

Crouching down beside his body, I place my hand in his warm blood. Going over to their kill wall, I write *"Better luck next time"* in Brady's blood before smearing the walls with the rest of it. I take a step back, taking a minute to revel in my destruction.

"Lautner," Seth shouts from above, his voice panicked. I head back to the bottom of the stairs looking up through the hole.

"We need to go. Now!"

"Trouble?" I growl.

"The hunters have a new target tonight. Mick's."

I scramble up the stairs onehanded, still naked, cradling my left arm tight to my chest.

"You alright?" he asks worriedly, taking in my hand and blood-covered body.

"Not now." I stride past him, heading toward the hunter's car. "You're driving," I shout to Seth as I jump into the passenger seat, my heart banging heavy in my chest.

Dani's at Mick's, and she can't shift. I punch the dash in frustration, turning around to face the hunter in the back seat squashed between Terry and Drake. Drake is watching me closely as I scowl, wondering why he isn't as concerned for his fiancé as I am.

"You better hope that we get there in time," I say to the hunter as he looks away. *Because if anything happens to Dani, I'll slaughter you all*, I promise silently.

CHAPTER 26
DANI

Pulling Lautner's hoodie tighter around myself, I follow the steep track leading down through the woods—the light from the moon above illuminating the path ahead. I know I shouldn't be out here, but I'm sick of feeling like a prisoner cooped up in there. I'd caught my father sneaking out about an hour ago, going who knows where, and with Drake gone to the bunker, I know this is my best shot at freedom. Lautner had been a no show all afternoon, and so had Alianna. So much for the so-called mate bond. Daniel had been wrong. It wasn't just his mate's touch that he needed to fight the mating heat. After all, hadn't he been the one to invite her here.

It's all pointless in any way. This was always destined to be my life, and the worst part of it is that it isn't my life at all; it's the one my father had forced upon me. I'd often wondered if my life would have been different had I grown up with a Mom. My father told me she'd run away after my birth, but I never believed him. The older I got, the more convinced I became that he'd killed her, whoever she was. He never had any respect for women. I'd often seen whores come and go from the house, but he never had a real relationship. I don't think he was capable of it.

I turn around at the sound of a twig snapping behind me, but it's too dark to see clearly. All I can pick out is the shadows created by the moon. Bears and wolves were not uncommon in these parts, and I'm nowhere near strong enough to take on a wild animal. I break into a jog. It's probably the worst thing I can do right now, considering if it is a wild animal, they would undoubtedly chase after me. Still, my own mind wouldn't listen to common sense; it never did. I throw a glance over my shoulder as my foot hits something hard, taking me down. I cry out, falling to the ground, my knee slamming hard against a rock. Groaning, I push myself up, wincing at the pain radiating at my knee as I start moving again.

I catch a shadow to my right. I back up slowly, taking small steps, afraid to take my eyes away from the darkness in front of me. My back connects with something solid as I put my hands behind me, expecting to meet the rough bark of a tree trunk, but instead, my hands touch something else. Something smooth and warm. I jump, turning around.

"Hello Danika." The man smiles, but it isn't a friendly smile. It's all teeth like that of a predator ready to devour its dinner.

"Who are you?" I ask, backing up, wanting to put as much space as possible between myself and the naked man before me.

"Lester," he continues, his smile making me uneasy.

"What are you doing here, Lester?" I stumble once more but quickly regain my footing, refusing to take my eyes of the man in front of me.

"I was hoping to catch up with an old friend, but he hasn't shown up yet." He walks toward me until I hit another object. Only this time, I know it's a tree. I can feel the roughness of the bark where it presses against my back.

"Who's your friend?" I ask, wondering how I'm going to get away from this man. It's obvious he's a shifter. Why else would he be running around naked this time of night in the woods.

"A mutual friend by the looks of it," he says as he comes closer, scenting Lautner's hoodie. "Tell me, is he fucking you?" he asks with a sly grin.

"I don't know who you're talking about."

"Of course, you do. Why else would you be wearing his clothes? We grew up together, you know. We fought together. We killed together. We even fucked the same woman together on occasion. Then one day, he left, thinking he was better than me."

I don't speak. I don't want to encourage whatever this man is thinking. He might not be a hunter, but he is most definitely a stray, and they are just as dangerous, if not more.

"I can't help you," I reply as his hand moves to my waist, slowly traveling under Lautner's hoodie till he hits the bare skin of my stomach.

"I don't need help. Just a distraction while I wait. I'm sure Lautner won't mind me sharing you. It'll be just like old times."

His body slams into me, knocking the air from my lungs as he pins my body against the tree, catching me unaware.

I can feel his hard length against my stomach as his hands pull at the waistband of my jeans. I try to push him off me, but it's no use. It's like pushing against a brick wall. Instead, I relax, letting him believe I'd given up. His hold loosens, moving from mine, giving his hand better access at my waist. Taking a deep breath, I bring my knee up between his legs with as much force as I can. He cries out, pushing away from me as I run.

I have no idea which way to go, and I don't care. I can hear him cursing somewhere behind me, but I don't look back. I can't.

"I'm coming, Danika," he calls out maliciously before a howl breaks out, followed by that of another wolf. Fighting back my tears, I ignore the burning in my legs as I push on.

I can hear his paws hitting the ground behind me like the rolling of thunder. His howl right behind me now as my tears flow freely down my face, blinding me. I just need to make it back to my pack, to safety. I quickly glance over my shoulder as the big black wolf soars through the air, taking me down.

CHAPTER 27
LAUTNER

I should never have left tonight. I should have known it was too easy. The hunters were turning out to be far more intelligent than we gave them credit for. As Seth stops the car, I don't wait for the others as I race inside. Smoke fills every crevice of the room as I run toward the stairs. If Dani's here, I have no doubt, that's where she'll be hiding.

"Dani," I call out as I make my way through the thick choking smoke. My eyes burn as I run up the stairs. Daniel falls at my feet as a man jumps on him, brandishing a silver knife. I grab the hunter by the back of the neck, slamming his head into the wall. His knife falls to the floor as I pick it up, pulling the hunter's head back and slitting his throat.

"Where's Dani?"

"I don't know. I was on my way to find her."

"Get out of here." I push Daniel toward the stairs as I continue up to her room. Her door is already open, but there is no sign of her anywhere. The sound of bottles smashing from the bar below has me hurrying back downstairs. I enter the bar just in time to catch my alpha stab a hunter through the face with a broken bottle, shoving his lifeless body to the floor.

"Have you seen Dani?"

No," he replies, as another hunter rushes into the room, only this one is wearing a gas mask to protect himself from the smoke. As he lunges at my alpha, the sound of a female screaming has me rushing out the back door. I know my alpha can take care of himself, but Dani, wherever the hell she is, needs me.

"Where do you think you're going?" I spin around at the sound of Brandon's voice, only to be tackled to the ground. I throw my elbow behind me, catching him in the face as I scramble back to my feet. I didn't have time for this.

I turn to run, but Brandon is on me in an instant, taking me down once more. "You afraid of me, Lautner? I never thought I'd see the day when you would run from me." He chuckles. "Then again, you did just kill my brother, didn't you?" he hisses.

"Your brother should've never been in the ring, and you know it. Then again, he never told you, did he. Turns out you're not as close as you think." His fist comes down on me as I try to block, but I can't concentrate. I need to get to Dani. She is all I can think about.

"Brandon," Seth calls out. As Brandon lifts his head, I get my foot beneath his chest, kicking him away from me.

Brandon growls, "Seth, how I've missed our time together. Have you missed me; I wonder."

I grit my teeth at Brandon's words, but I don't have time to stick around.

"This fight is between you and me. I'm not going to let you back out of it." Seth launches himself at Brandon as I get back to my feet. "Find Dani," he calls out, punching Brandon in the face and taking him down.

I nod toward Seth before running for the trees.

I quickly shift, knowing I have a better chance of finding her as a wolf. As soon as all four paws hit the ground, it isn't long before the coppery scent of blood enters my nose. Rage consumes me as I push on, hearing Dani scream once more. I catch the sight of a big black wolf on top of her. *Lester.* I growl deep, drawing his attention toward me. His eyes flash red under the light of the full moon, the hate in their depths matching my amber ones.

Leaving Dani, he stalks toward me, baring his teeth. I growl, raising my hackles, steadying myself on my injured paw, hoping he doesn't notice. I crouch low on my back haunches, preparing to attack. Lester breaks into a lope toward me as I spring forward, catching his hindquarters with my claws, leaving four deep scratches in their wake. He growls, coming for me once again. This time when he attacks, I jump over his back, landing hard on my injured paw. The glint in his eye, letting me know that he noticed my injury as he circles me, trying to catch it with his teeth.

"Looks just like old times from what I hear." Brandon's voice takes me by surprise as I turn around to find Dani pressed up tight against his naked body. "Shift."

Growling, I do as he says.

"Where's Seth?" I ask, instantly concerned for my friend.

"Still alive, unfortunately. But we'll get our chance soon enough." Brandon brings his nose to Dani, inhaling at her throat. She jumps in fright as he chuckles—his hand traveling down over the mounds of her breasts, dropping further until I notice the button of her jeans undone.

I turn a murderous gaze to Lester, who laughs. "What's

the matter, don't tell me you've forgotten how to share now that your pack," he spits. "I'm disappointed in you, Lautner."

"She's not one of us."

"The hell she isn't. She felt fucking good to me. And her wolf, damn, she smells divine." Lester licks his lips, smiling wickedly.

Pushing my hatred aside, I turn back to Brandon.

"Let her go, and let's finish this."

"I don't think so. Although I might give her a little head start, make it more interesting. What do you say, sweetheart. Have you ever been fucked by the big bad wolf?" He smiles as I watch her tremble.

"Please," she begs, but it only makes it worse. Strays like Brandon and Lester feed on the fear of others.

I want to go over and snap his wrist away from her body, but I can't give the mate bond away. If they realize just how important she is to me, she's as good as dead already.

"Fine. Play your little game. We both know you're not man enough to take me on. It's two on one; the odds are in your favor," I bait, praying he will take it.

Brandon watches me as if wondering what game I'm playing. Hell, I also wondered what game I'm playing. But the sight of Dani in Brandon's arms is killing me. Mates were supposed to protect their females at all costs, and here I am, playing a game with her life.

"What do you think, Danika," he whispers in her ear loud enough for me to hear. "Shall I kill Lautner now, then fuck you, or just take you as my win tonight?"

Her eyes look at me as if in betrayal before she turns her head, looking away.

"No deal. I already earned my reward tonight."

Lester cries out, attacking me from behind. I turn at the

last minute catching him in the throat. He goes down as I stand over him. "That's always been your problem, asshole. You're too predictable. That's why you will never win against me." I raise my foot, bringing it down hard on his ribs as I hear a satisfying crack.

I leave my old friend rolling on the floor as I take off after Brandon. True to his word, Dani is no longer with him. I can hear him counting to ten, giving her a head start.

"Brandon."

He sighs as I come up behind him. "I do hope you've killed him. Saves me the trouble of doing it later."

"I made a promise to Seth that I would let him kill you, but I might just have to break that promise."

"You and I both know that Seth isn't the same man he once was. I broke him, and you know it. Eventually, I'll break all the pack, including you and your mate." He smiles. "Did you think I missed that look you gave me back there. That was raw possession, jealousy, and hate."

"It's time to leave, Brandon," Ryan cuts in. I turn around to find Seth, Terry, and Ryan standing behind me. They all looked pretty beaten up, and I know they didn't want to fight. Not now. We needed to regroup and find out just how much damage the hunters have made here tonight. Brandon looks between us as if weighing his options.

"Give my love to Danika for me." He smirks before taking off into the cover of the trees.

CHAPTER 28
DANI

"Dani," Lautner calls out.

I lower my head, unable to stop the tears streaming down my face. I didn't want Lautner to see me like this. Scared and weak. I'd spent my whole life trying to be strong, and Lester and Brandon had diminished that in a mere few seconds.

"I know you're there, Dani." I close my eyes, wanting nothing more than to go to him. I hated that I wanted him so much when all he ever does is reject me.

I place my trembling hands on the cold ground as I push myself up from behind the big oak tree. He strides toward me, taking me into his arms. I press my face against his naked chest, finally allowing myself to break. I'm safe.

"I thought I was going to lose you," he murmurs against my hair, holding me tighter. "What happened? Why were you out here?"

"I was taking a walk."

"In the woods. At night. It's not safe, Dani, especially for you," he growls angrily.

"What do you mean, especially for me?" I snap, moving away from him.

"You're here under my protection. You should have told me. I know you can't shift. Coming out here, alone at night, you're a walking liability. You don't belong here."

With me. That's what's missing in his words. He may not say it aloud, but we both know that's what he meant.

"Under your protection. I thought it was the Stone Valley Pack's protection. You've made it perfectly clear I'm nothing to you, so I don't owe you anything."

I watch the steely resolve in his eyes. I know how much he is hurting right now. I remember the look on his face when Brandon had his arms around me. He was scared, but Seth's right; he's just too damn stubborn to admit it.

"I've spent my entire life a walking disappointment to my pack, and I'm done apologizing. Go and thank my fiancé, he was the one to drag me here. You've made your feelings toward me perfectly clear. Hell, you pretty much goaded Brandon into raping me," I cry as I go to storm past him, but his hand grabs my arm, keeping me still.

"Do you really believe that? I would never have let him hurt you, but I couldn't risk him seeing the truth."

"The truth—I'm your mate, Lautner. The mate you don't want so badly, so what does it matter if he knows."

"He will kill you just to spite me. I killed his brother the other night. You were there."

"Well, maybe you should tell him Alianna is here. I've no doubt she means more to you than I do. I know you invited her here. You don't have to worry; I'm done being selfish. I'll keep my distance from you from now on," I snap, pulling my arm free from his grip and walking back toward the house.

I can feel Lautner keeping pace behind me as I storm back, but I don't turn around.

As soon as we head inside, I'm shocked by the damage within. I must have only just left before they started their attack. Going straight up to my room, I pass the body of a man with his throat slashed on the stairs. I shudder at the dead man's gaze as it bores into mine. *Had he been on the way to my room to kill me?* He's only a few doors away. I force my feet to start moving, not wanting to think about how fragile my life really is. My door is already open as I make my way over to the window, letting out some of the smoke that had traveled upstairs.

I know the pack will have a lot to discuss tonight and I should be down there helping, but let's face it, as Lautner pointed out, I would only hold them back. I was used to being a disappointment to my pack, but hearing it from the mouth of the man fate intended for me cut deeper than any knife.

Pacing the floor, I let my anger take over—the unfairness of my life. I hated my father. I hated Drake. I hated Lautner for rejecting me and inviting Alianna to take my place. Before I know what I am doing, I'm locking the door behind me, striding downstairs to Lautner's room. I try his door, relieved to find it open. It's empty as I step inside, breathing deep in relief, catching his scent still lingering in the air. I must have only just missed him. Taking a seat on the floor, I make myself comfortable. If he wanted to sleep with Alianna tonight, then so be it, but I wouldn't make it easy on him. I was done letting people walk all over me.

CHAPTER 29
LAUTNER

I hastily grab a bottle of water from behind the bar, wishing I could pick up one of the surviving whiskey bottles, but I know I can't. After what had happened outside with Dani, there's only one thing I can do to ensure her protection, and for that, I needed to be sober. I had followed her up until the second floor before heading into my own room to collect some joggers. I knew she was afraid, and I wanted nothing more than to comfort her, but I didn't know how. I'm just an asshole who doesn't know how to deal with the feelings she brings out in me. But there's one thing for certain that I do know. Seeing her out there in danger had nearly ripped me in two, and I won't let it happen again.

Ryan and Terry are busy picking up the few dead hunters and taking them out back, no doubt storing them in the deep freeze unit I had told Mick would come in handy someday. I take a seat in the far corner, waiting for my alpha to appear to update him on the bunker. Alpha Cortez appears a few minutes later, his eyes taking in the mess around him before vanishing with Drake into Mick's office. I have no idea where he had been throughout all this, but I was determined to find out. These assholes should have told us about Dani from the start. If I hadn't of stumbled across the documents in the bunker, she might very well have been dead by now.

"You alright?" Seth asks, joining me.

"What happened with Brandon?" I ask before tipping back the bottle of water to my lips and drinking deep.

"A few hunters got in the way. I had to make a choice to let him go, for now, at least. I'm sorry about that. I didn't think he would find you and Dani."

"He knows, Seth ... about Dani, being my mate."

I can hear his breathing increase beside me. Seth isn't stupid; he knew what I was trying to tell him. I didn't have a choice. If it came down to my promise to him and my need to protect Dani, she would win every time, but it wasn't just about that. It was the fact that if she left here now unprotected, Brandon and Lester would kill her.

"Don't," he starts. "If you don't plan on completing it, don't. I won't lose you." He finishes putting his head down, knowing he is fighting a losing battle. "You don't even know if it will work. Ryan just informed me that Dani can't shift."

"I have to try, Seth. I can't let her go from here unprotected. Not until they're dead. They won't stop going after her." I shake my head, hating that Brandon had found my one and only weakness. My father had been right all along. Sure, killing Seth or one of my pack would hurt me, but killing my mate, there would be no going back for anyone.

Mick comes into the room, clearing his throat loudly. Cortez and Drake are behind him, whispering closely. I watch Mick take in the damage around him. I know he is trying his best to reign in his anger. In all his time here as Alpha, no one had attacked his home. The pack's home. It was an insult, and one he would want to be rectified as soon as possible.

"You should have warned us," I turn my cold stare to Cortez, "your daughter was nearly killed tonight."

"She's a little banged up," Drake cuts in, "but nothing serious. She could do with a little toughening up if you ask me."

My eyes find Drake's. I hadn't forgotten about how he had spoken about her in the car, showing me just how little he cared for her. I had known plenty of people like him. I had grown up around the strays, thanks to my father. If Drake were right about Dani in the car, he would only abuse her and cheat until she'd finally had enough, taking her own life. I would never let that happen. If there was anything I could give her, it would be his death. I know I will have to bide my time; if anything happened to him here, it would cause a war between the two packs, and I wouldn't do that to Mick. I had to be smart about it.

"My daughter, as you point out, is none of your concern. She's alive, isn't she."

"No thanks to Lautner," Seth cuts in.

"Her failure to shift is my business, nothing to do with you. I don't know what interest you have in my daughter," he sneers, "but she is taken. I suggest you go fuck that little slut around here, Alianna, and leave my daughter to Drake. Just remember, your alpha is on very thin ice with the Council. If he gets kicked off, then he will more than likely lose his position as alpha. Is that what you want? Is my daughter worth that much to you?" He pauses, awaiting my reaction, but I remain calm. I'm not about to give this man any more ammunition than necessary. "I didn't think so." He finally smiles in victory. "Drake, go check on your fiancé. I'm sure she would just love your loving touch right about now," he continues, his eyes never leaving mine.

I can feel the very walls of my skin vibrate in anger as we stare at one another. I know what Cortez has just threatened, but it's just that, a threat. He wouldn't dare carry that out within our walls. He's just pushing me in the hopes I'll hit him, then all bets are off. I watch Drake throw me a smile as he leaves the room. Leaving me more determined than ever to concoct a plan that will help Drake meet an early demise. Before I really do something stupid, like follow his ass, and snap his neck.

"Where were you tonight?" I ask Alpha Cortez suspiciously. "It's pretty convenient that you were missing the same night the hunters attack, wouldn't you say."

"I'd be damn careful what you're implying. You don't want to go against me," he threatens.

"I'm not implying anything. I think it's a valid question. Where were you?"

"Ridgeway business. Anything else?"

"Lautner," Mick warns with a low growl, telling me to back off. He's right. I can't accuse him of anything, not yet. I need to wait for Thane to get back to me with the results of the pills, but I wanted nothing more than to take this man down before me. I just needed something useful.

"I'm good," I reply, returning my gaze back to Mick.

"So, what happened at the bunker?" Mick asks, changing the subject.

"One human hunter and Brady Henshaw," Seth answers.

"Shit, the kid that tried to join our pack?"

I nod. "He's dead now."

"I put the human in the pit for tonight," Seth explains.

"Good. He isn't going anywhere tonight. We can leave his ass till tomorrow. We've got five dead hunters here, all human. We can't underestimate them again. They attacked our home, and that takes balls. I don't think they will come back tonight, but I'm not taking any chances. I've got Daniel upping our security as we speak. We will work in shifts tonight to tidy this place up. Lautner, go meet Ryan in my office. He will check over your arm." He nods over to me.

"I'm fine," I lie.

"I'm not asking. It's an order."

"Your orders don't work on me," I remind him.

"Just do as I say."

I nod, picking up the bottle of water from the table and taking it with me.

Ryan is already waiting with his medical kit when I get there.

"What happened?" he tips his head in the direction of the chair, waiting for me to sit down.

"Just a scratch. Brady caught me at the bunker, and then I caught it again when fighting Lester." Ryan doesn't reply as he inspects the damage.

"They got you pretty good. It's deep, but it looks like it's already starting to heal since you shifted tonight. You'll live to cause us trouble another day," he replies flippantly, applying some ointment and bandages.

I don't bother replying to his sarcasm as Mick enters the office.

"You alright?"

"I'll be fine by tomorrow."

He nods. "Ryan, I need you and Drake to dispose of the

bodies. I want them off the property tonight," Mick commands.

"We'll head out now," Ryan says, leaving the room.

"Lautner, tomorrow, I want you to interrogate the hunter and find out everything they know. Until then, go get some rest. We've got a busy day tomorrow."

CHAPTER 30
LAUTNER

I draw closer to my room, catching the scent of Dani in the air. The sweetest scent of vanilla coming from the direction of my room. I growl deep, thanking whoever is on my side that I didn't have to go and find her. I hadn't wanted to risk going up to her room. If her father or Drake caught us, there's no telling what I would do. Tonight, I'm more wolf than man. That's what the mating heat did. It invoked the predator, and Dani, she is my prey.

I open the door, my eyes instantly finding hers where she sits huddled on the floor. Her cheeks are still wet, but she has a fierce look on her face as if her anger is driving her and not her tears. She quickly springs to her feet, her eyes searching behind me.

"Where is she?" she demands, crossing her arms across her chest and holding my stare. I see the slightest falter in her stance as if she sees the monster within, but she bravely stands her ground.

"Who," I reply, pretending I have no idea that she is

talking about Alianna. If this is ever going to work, I needed her riled up. I would invoke any emotion I can get from her, including her jealousy.

"You know exactly who I'm talking about," she seethes, "Alianna."

"Why? Did you come in here to watch?" I say, stalking toward her. Her face tightens, and I watch as her anger takes hold.

"Fuck you, Lautner," she seethes, but it only turns me on. Her anger, that is. I know exactly how she feels. I'd never known jealousy before now until meeting her. I wanted to kill Drake any time he put his hands anywhere near her.

"Don't touch me," she says as I get closer. She backs up before finally hitting the wall. "What are you doing?" she asks, biting her bottom lip nervously as I come to a stop before her.

I bend down, inhaling at her throat as I cup her cheek with my warm palm, holding her still. "Admit you're jealous."

"No," she says, holding her ground as I chuckle at her reply.

"So, you're telling me that if I left here right now and went to Alianna's room, you wouldn't care?" I ask, placing a delicate kiss at her throat.

"Lautner," she threatens in frustration.

"If I went to her ... and did everything I did to you last night. My hands touching her breasts. My mouth between her legs, tasting ...."

She growls as she tries to push me away, but I hold her still.

"Admit it," I say once more.

"Fine. I'm jealous." Her hands grip the taut muscles of

my arms until I feel the stinging bite of her nails on my biceps.

"Well, show me what you're going to do about it," I goad, pushing against her and letting her feel just how hard I am.

Her lips attack mine in possession as I wrap my arms around her. There's nothing nice about her kiss. It's angry and hard, a claiming, and I'd never felt so alive as I did at that moment. I'd always been a man hidden in secrets and shadows, but there would be no more hiding. I'm about to unleash the full force of my wolf upon her, demanding she answer our call and accept us. "You've got five minutes," I whisper, tearing my mouth from hers, feeling her shiver against me. "Ask me anything you want because when those five minutes are up, the only sound coming from your lips will be my name as you cum." I watch her cheeks flush at my words, and damn if it doesn't look good on her. I bend down, running my tongue over the pulse at her throat as I feel her swallow nervously. "If you don't start talking, I'm starting in anyway," I say as my hands grip her hips tighter.

"Why?" she replies huskily. "Why now?"

"Because I'm selfish, Dani. All I've wanted since meeting you is to bury myself deep inside you, and I know you want it too. You need me."

She pulls back as if needing some space, but I can't let that happen. I need her to stay in the moment, lost in the sensation of our bodies. My hands reach for the hem of my hoodie that she is wearing, and I can't help but love seeing her in it. I have no idea how she'd gotten it, and I didn't care. From now on, it's all I want to see her in. There's something about seeing this female in my clothes that just makes me feel damn proud. I know that any man that dares to go near her will catch my scent and the promise of pain if they touched her. I slip it over her head, watching her body tremble under my gaze, her nipples hardening, begging for the warmth of my mouth. I bend my head down, refusing to keep her waiting. My unbandaged hand, sliding down, unbuttoning her jeans until I'm sliding my fingers exactly where I want them to be. She's already soaked for me, and I had barely even touched her. I run my finger over her clit, catching her throaty moans with my mouth.

"Say the words, Dani," I growl as I feel my control slipping. I at least wanted to take her virginity with her permission. I had nearly lost control last night, and tonight I wouldn't stop it. Tonight, I would lose myself in the feel of her body wrapped around mine as I force her wolf to claim me.

"I want you," she moans, rubbing against the contact of my fingers, begging me for more.

"Want me to what?" I urge, fighting against the power threatening to spill out and consume her.

"To be my first," she moans. It's all I need to hear. I take her hand, entwining our fingers as I lead her over to the bed. Her blue eyes watch me intently as I kneel down in front of her. I slowly peel her jeans and panties down her legs, discarding them on the floor. Completely naked now, I run my hands up her lush body, feeling her tremble. Back on my feet, I tower over her as she backs up. The backs of her legs hit the bed as she goes down. I lie beside her, my hand going back to the sweet spot between her legs as she opens her thighs wider, inviting me. I work her over with my fingers, loosening her up as she bucks beneath me. As soon as she comes, I bring my fingers to my mouth, sucking at the sweet nectar. I stand up, removing my joggers, never taking my eyes from Dani. I watch her eyes widen as she sees me naked and hard before her.

"If you want me to stop, do it now, because I'm fighting to keep control." My words are strained as she looks at me, biting her lip.

"Do it," she whispers.

I lower myself over her body, guiding my cock to her opening. I slowly enter her, taking my time for her to get used to the intrusion. She's tight, and I'm a big guy as I try to keep it slow.

"Just breathe, Dani." I push against her barrier, feeling it give way under the pressure of my cock until I'm fully sheathed in her heat. She pants wildly beneath me, and it takes everything in me to hold still until she adjusts to the feeling of me filling her up.

"The worst's over, mate," I say, surprised at how easy the words fall from my lips. As if sensing the change, she opens her eyes. I watch her as I start to move, taking it slow, until I finally see her pain turn to pleasure. She brings her legs up, wrapping them around my waist, taking me deeper, as she moans against the new sensations taking over her.

"Lautner," she whimpers, gripping my arms tightly.

"Watch me, Dani," I growl. As our eyes connect, I let go. Lowering my barrier and letting my power rush over her just as her first release leaves her shaking beneath me.

"What the ..." I can feel her start to panic as she writhes beneath me. Taking her hands, I pin them above her head.

"Dani, I need you to trust me," I growl as she fights against the power of my wolf.

"No. Stop. What are you doing to me," she cries out.

I watch the sweat break out over her skin, and I know she's feeling the blistering heat of lava in her veins. "Don't fight it," I say as calmly as I can, but the truth is, I can't hold back much longer. Her eyes meet mine, and I hate the look of fear on her face. It's not of me, but the unfamiliar power within her.

"Trust me," I say once again.

I growl long and deep. I can feel it vibrating through my body as I lower my head down to her throat, biting down. Her wolf writhes within her as Dani cries out. Her wolf is strong as she plays me. Teasing me. Testing me. Fighting against my invasion. Making sure I'm worthy enough to claim. As Dani quietens beneath me, so does her wolf. I let go of her hands, slowly releasing my bite, making sure I hadn't broken the skin. Satisfied I haven't marked her, I start moving my hips once more, only this time she joins in. Her hips pushing back, meeting every thrust with her own. Just as I feel her walls begin to clamp down on me, I let go unleashing the full power of my wolf upon her. Her hands clutch my arms, digging her nails deep into my skin as she surges forward, her mouth biting down hard on my chest as I come hard.

She collapses back on the bed, exhausted and sated. I withdraw my power, letting it slowly drain from her body as she sleeps peacefully beside me. I watch the tiny beat of her pulse at her throat, enticing me to complete the bond, but I won't. I had everything I needed now to keep her safe. The mate bond is weak, but it's there. Closing my eyes, I pull her closer, resting my head against hers, hoping that I'd done enough. That my sacrifice, my life for hers, would be enough to save her.

CHAPTER 31
LAUTNER

Six years ago

"Lautner." I close my eyes, ignoring the desperate cries of my father wandering around the trailer park outside. It had been like this every night for the past week. Nina groans, bringing me back to the present as I grip her hips thrusting up into her heat.

"Fuck," Lester calls out as he grips Nina's shoulder, arching her back, as he plows into her ass from behind. "Looks like the old man is back up," he says as he continues to thrust in time with me.

Nina's moans turn to screams as I find my rhythm, chasing the orgasm I'm so close to achieving. Lester calls out just as I come panting hard. I kiss Nina once on the lips as she falls to the bed between us. I get up quickly, throwing my clothes back on as Lester and I leave.

It's cold as we step outside the trailer. Lester offers me the *bottle of his father's stolen whiskey as I take a sip before handing it back.*

"Your old man's becoming quite the topic of conversation around here," he says, as we make our way over to the old barn where tonight's fight would be held. The big barn door creaks open as we head over to the seats at the side of the makeshift ring. It's empty at the moment, but it wouldn't be long before it was packed.

I nod. My father was getting worse now. As the days go by, his rage is faltering, leaving him nothing but a shell of the man I once knew. He had told me that this was the curse of being mated. Being left to battle alone, only half a body and half a soul. The day she died, he had made a vow to himself to raise me differently. To make sure I never followed in his footsteps.

"You ever plan on taking a mate one day?" I ask Lester.

"Maybe. She'd have to be damn fine, though." He chuckles as we take another drink of whiskey. "What about you?"

"No, my father says it's the worst thing ever. To have a weakness. There will always be someone out there looking to take you down. Mates are nothing but trouble. That's why we fight to stay strong. The man is stronger than the wolf," I tell him.

"I heard my father say your old man's ex-pack was looking for you."

I shrug my shoulders. I had no interest in joining a pack. It was every man for himself. "You ever think about joining a pack?" I ask him.

"You kidding me, being told what I can and can't do? Fuck that. I'm a stray for life." We bring our knuckles in together as Lester passes the bottle back to me.

I take a sip, quickly handing it back. I couldn't get

drunk, no matter how much I wanted to. We were both fighting later tonight. Lester was facing an old enemy, Joe Montrose, and I was facing a newcomer from out of town. As I glance over at Lester, I can tell he is nervous. Don't get me wrong, Lester can fight, but he's too predictable.

"Remember to keep your hands up. Joe always looks for the easy opening," I say, hoping it will help Lester in his fight tonight. I knew we weren't friends, not really. There's no such thing as friends amongst the strays. It was every man for himself. But I enjoyed having someone to talk to, and I would take it however short it lasted.

"Thanks, and you too. Good luck for tonight. I hear he's quite the fighter."

I scoff. "Yeah, right. They haven't been able to find me a decent opponent for years," I say confidently.

"You'll get your ass handed to you one of these days. I just hope I'm there to see it." Lester smiles coldly.

CHAPTER 32
LAUTNER

Sighing, I quietly close Dani's door behind me, making my way down toward Mick's office. Her mark over my chest aching with every step, letting me know that I'm too far away from her. I'd slept with her by my side for as long as I could, until begrudgingly, I knew I would have to return her to her room before anyone realized she was gone.

Coming to a stop outside Mick's office, I tap my knuckles against the door.

"Come in."

Mick is sitting behind his desk with Ryan standing behind him as I enter the room. I don't speak. Lifting the hem of my t-shirt, I pull it over my head, proudly displaying Dani's mark on my skin.

"Shit," Ryan mutters, shaking his head. His eyes are black and murderous as he comes to stand near me. "Are you insane? Do you realize what you've done?"

Ignoring Ryan, I remain focused on my alpha. "Brandon knows Dani is my mate. He worked it out last night. You know as well as I do, she's their main target now. He won't let her go. He will kill her just to spite me over Tommy, whether I finish the mating or not. It's the only way to keep her safe."

"You should have at least informed us about your decision before getting her to mark you. This affects us all," Ryan snaps. "Does she even know what you've done?"

"No, and she doesn't need to. This only affects me, not her."

"Really, and what about Drake? How are you going to handle it when he puts his arm around her or kisses your mate in front of you," he snaps.

"Back off, Ryan," I seethe, clenching my fists. "It's the only way to keep her safe, or would you rather she be dead?"

"Enough, Ryan," Mick warns in a low growl, "whether you've done the right thing or not remains to be seen, but Ryan is right. This is going to affect us all. There's no going back for you."

I nod. I knew exactly what this meant. I'd essentially given it all up for Dani. I would never find peace again. If I didn't complete the bond, I would be forever cursed with the mating heat longing for a female I could never have. No other woman would be able to touch me. I would be alone until finally succumbing to the madness.

"Have you changed your mind about a full mating?" Mick asks, hopeful. "The pack," he looked directly at Ryan, "will support you. You know that, right."

"No, but I'm determined to help Dani in any way that I can. It's my fault she's in danger."

"It's not your fault, Lautner, we don't get to choose who we mate."

I stay quiet. There's nothing to say. I could think of a

hundred reasons why Dani is better off without me, but Mick's a good man and a good Alpha, and I know, unlike me, he believes in fate.

"How about some good news. I heard from Thane this morning. He said he tried to ring you first but couldn't get an answer."

"What did he say?"

"You were right. The pills were mostly Valium and Wolfsbane. Thane says the dose is high enough to comatose a wolf."

"So, what does this mean. Can we use this against Alpha Cortez and get him stripped from his position as Alpha and off the Council?" I ask, putting my shirt back on.

"Maybe, but we need more proof. Have you talked to Danika about the pills?"

"Not yet. I wanted to make sure I was right first."

"Alright, explain it to her. Tell her she needs to ask him for more. If we can somehow get his phone, I can get Daniel to place a tracker on it. If we can find out the place and time of the meet and the supplier, it might be just what we need to take him down, ending Danika's contract to Drake, once and for all."

"How's the arm?" Seth asks, coming to sit beside me.

"It's fine now. Shifting last night helped. To be honest, with everything going on, I'd almost forgotten about it. Look, I know it's none of my business, but I heard you last night. Are the nightmares back?"

"Yeah, I can't seem to hide from them. Well, the drugs helped, but I seemed to lose everything else about myself as well. Plus, it nearly got you killed."

It'd been a little over a year ago. Mick had sent us after a stray that the Council had wanted to apprehend. Seth swore he hadn't touched anything in weeks. We were supposed to lead him into a trap, but Seth never showed. I found him OD'd about a mile away. Everything was alright in the end, though. It was the night he came clean, determined to keep his pack safe.

"That's in the past. We're alright."

"I take it you went through with it?"

"I told you, I didn't have a choice," I reply sadly, although I'm not sure if that were the truth, or just a way to try and justify my actions. I wasn't sure about anything anymore. "I've never felt so connected to anyone. It scares me."

"That explains it then, why you look like shit," he explains with a laugh. "You look as bad as I felt on a comedown, and I don't wish that feeling on anyone. So why not just go see her? Drake and Cortez aren't around."

"It's not that easy. Every time we're alone, I can't seem to stop myself. I need a clear head right now. Mick wants me to take care of the hunter we've got in the pit."

"Alright then, I'm sure Daniel said he was going to check on her before, anyway."

"Shit," I mumble, getting to my feet as I hear Seth chuckle behind me.

"Where are you going?" Seth smirks, watching me head toward the door.

I don't answer with words. Instead, I raise my middle finger at him, making him laugh even harder. I can't stand the thought of any man being near her. Mated males were a force to be reckoned with. I may not be fully mated, but Dani owned me, whether she knew it or not. And Seth had just invoked the monster within.

CHAPTER 33
DANI

I spent the morning hiding out in my room. I couldn't face Lautner, not after waking up here alone. I actually thought we were getting somewhere last night. I let him take my virginity, and he didn't even have the decency to let me stay till morning. He made it so easy for me to hate him. I should be elated that I'd lost my virginity to Lautner instead of Drake. However, all I can feel is like I'd been used.

A knock sounds at my door. "Dani, it's Daniel."

"It's open," I call out.

Daniel comes through the door, looking exhausted, but I can tell something else is bothering him. "I thought you might want one of these?" he says, holding a cup of coffee in his hands but refusing to meet my gaze.

"You know, don't you?" I ask, clearly pissed at how fast the news got around.

"Of course, I know," he replies. "Why the hell didn't you tell me? When the attack happened last night, I was on my way to find you. If I'd known you couldn't shift, I would have come sooner." His eyes won't meet mine, and I know he is angry that I hadn't told him the truth.

"I didn't tell you, Daniel, because I don't like people knowing. You all assume I'm weak and that I can't defend myself. But the truth is, I wouldn't be able to forgive myself if one of you got hurt trying to protect me. Lautner's right. I'm a liability."

"You're not a liability, Dani," he replies, finally bringing his eyes up to meet mine.

"Then why does it feel that way," I say dejectedly.

"Because you're a good person, Dani Cortez. I would gladly get injured if it meant protecting you."

As I look into Daniel's eyes, I can see the truth in his words. I know his feelings toward me are more than just friends, but I also know that he's a good man. He would do anything for anyone, not just me. I smile. "Don't worry, I'm not about to sit around, feeling sorry for myself. I promise. So, what happened last night?"

"I was behind the bar clearing up, and the next thing I know, one of the windows broke. Smoke filled the room quickly as the rest of the pack started to head out. They were waiting at the door." He sighs.

"Did we get any of the hunters?"

"Yeah. Ryan and Drake disposed of five dead hunters early this morning. The rest of the packs are still tidying up the mess. The bar and kitchen took the most damage. We're just lucky we live so far out of town that no one called the sheriff. What about you? How are you feeling after what happened with Lester and Brandon?"

I fight against the tremble that his words invoke in me. If Lautner hadn't shown up when he did, the packs would have no doubt found me raped and discarded in a ditch this morning. "I'm just glad Lautner showed up when he did."

"I'm sorry I wasn't there for you, Dani. If you need anything, you only need to ask." His hand touches my arm as I flinch away, spilling the coffee down my t-shirt.

"I'm sorry."

"It's okay," I tell him, wondering what the hell is wrong with me. "Can you just go into the bathroom while I change?"

"Sure." He turns away as I quickly lift my ruined top over my head.

"Dani," the door opens as Lautner strides in.

"Can't you knock?" I shout, holding my top against my bare breasts.

His eyes flare with desire as he looks at me, and I feel the sudden rush of power that envelops me whenever he is near.

"The ... your pills," he stammers, not taking his eyes off me. "Where are they?" he asks.

"So, that's it. After everything that happened last night, that's what you come here for? No, I'm sorry, Dani. I'm an asshole for treating you like that. I didn't even bother to stick around until morning after taking your virginity."

I should feel embarrassed knowing that Daniel is in the bathroom, but I don't care. I'm too mad.

"Look, I'm sorry okay, but right now I really need those pills."

"Why?" I ask, clutching the wet t-shirt tighter against my chest, feeling my nipples harden, remembering his mouth on them last night.

"It's wolfsbane," Lautner explains. "I stole one yesterday and got Thane to test it. That's why you can't shift."

"You're lying. I have seizures. I can feel them coming on," I snap.

"No. What you feel is your wolf trying to break free.

Remember when I told you to trust me," he asks, coming further into the room until he is standing before me. His hand reaching out, gliding down the bare skin of my arm as I close my eyes at the pleasure flooding my body at his touch. "Nothing bad happened. You didn't have a seizure. I enticed your wolf to the surface, and you put your trust in me to keep you safe."

"My father wouldn't ..." I start, but we both know that's a lie. My father was more than capable of doing this to me.

"Where does he get them?" Lautner asks, taking a few steps away from me, pulling his t-shirt over his head, and offering it to me. My eyes instantly seek out the mark on his chest, and I lower my eyes in embarrassment. I've no idea what came over me. Scratch that, I do. Lautner used his power on me. Not in a bad way. His power is like a drug. It wasn't malicious like my father's. It was like he had been touching me everywhere on my body all at once, caressing me until I thought I would combust from the pleasure. Caught up in the moment, I'd bitten him like it was the most natural thing in the world. Marking his flesh for the whole world to see. I can still taste the faint metallic copper of his blood on my tongue.

"I told you before, I have no idea," I say, slipping his t-shirt over my head. I head over to the dresser, taking my last bottle of pills out of the bottom drawer. "How long will it take?" I ask as I hand over the remaining pills. "The change. Once I stop taking them. How long?"

"It depends on how much is in your system. The levels need to be low enough for your wolf to fight through. But don't mention any of this to your father. We need him to believe you have no idea and are still taking your pills."

"Why?" I enquire, wanting nothing more than to go to my father and tell him that he can't control me anymore.

"These pills are extremely dangerous in the wrong hands. We have no idea what else your father could be using them for. Ryan needs you to ask him for more pills. Tell him you're running low. Mick has set up a meet in a few minutes. He plans to get Daniel to place a tracking device on his phone. Once he contacts his supplier, we'll know, and hopefully, be able to catch him in the act."

"I'll go ask him now," I reply, getting ready to leave the room.

"I'll go down and get ready to sort out the tracker," Daniel says, coming out of the bathroom.

Lautner's eyes leave me feeling cold as they look over to Daniel.

"What the hell are you doing here?" Lautner's voice is cold as his eyes pin Daniel in place. The violence emanating from him is unmistakable, and I know I need to get Daniel out of here. I grip Lautner's arm, jumping in front of him. "How is it every time I turn around, he's here with you?" His cold stare frightens me, and I no longer recognize the man before me.

"He's my friend, Lautner," I try to explain.

"Friend. You do realize all he wants to do is fuck you?" he snaps.

"What, and you're any better. At least Daniel listens to me."

He pulls his arm free from my hold before picking the lamp up off the dresser and throwing it against the wall, storming from the room.

I don't notice my tears as I quickly try to collect the broken pieces of porcelain off the floor. "I'm sorry, Daniel, I just can't seem to stop dragging you into my mess."

Daniel remains quiet as I turn to face him. His eyes are dark as he continues to look at the door where Lautner retreated. "When did it happen?" he asks coldly, not looking at me.

"What?" I say, continuing to pick up the broken pieces of porcelain, wondering why I care so much about a damn lamp when my world is falling apart.

"The mark. When did it happen?" he asks again, only this time he turns to face me, and I can see the anger on his face.

"I really don't want to have this conversation with you," I say uncomfortably.

"It's important, Dani, please." His face softens, but I can still see he is worried about something.

"Last night. I went to see him after the attack. I was angry. He ... we had sex," I blush, although I know he'd probably just overheard our conversation from the bathroom.

"And you marked him?" he pushes me to answer.

"Not exactly. I don't really know what happened. There was a rush of power, and the next thing I know, I bit him," I snap angrily. "This is none of your business, Daniel."

"You're right. It's not my business, not anymore. I need to leave, and you need to go see him."

"No. After the way he just acted, I'm not going to see him."

"There's no going back now, Dani. Lautner, he ... he used his wolf to get you to submit and start the bond. You need to go see him; he can explain. I have to go. Until the mate bond is complete, it's not safe for me here."

"But I haven't even shifted yet. This isn't possible." I shake my head.

"Dani, Lautner is an alpha. He's more than powerful and crazy enough to do it."

"An alpha?"

"Yeah. His father, Drew, used to be the alpha to the Stone Valley Pack before he went rogue taking Lautner with him. Mick offered the position back to Lautner when he returned, but he turned it down," he replies, heading for the door.

"Wait, Daniel, you're scaring me," I say as he pauses by the door.

"Go see Lautner. He will give you the answers you need. He doesn't have a choice anymore."

CHAPTER 34
LAUTNER

I can hear Dani mumbling an apology to Daniel as I leave, pissing me off even more. He doesn't need a goddamn apology. He needs to stay the fuck away from my mate.

"What the hell was that?" Seth demands as I reach the top of the stairs.

"You stalking me now?"

"No, I was making sure no one interrupted you, jackass. I have no idea where Drake or Alpha Cortez is this morning."

"There was nothing to interrupt."

"Didn't sound like that to me. Look, I know you want her. Goddamn it. Look at you—you're acting like more of a dick than usual with this shit."

"I've told her about the pills. Her wolf will present herself soon enough, and I won't have to feel as bad that I've put a death sentence on her head," I snap.

"Is that what this is all about? You think her being with you puts her in danger."

"You know as well as I do, Seth. I have a lot of enemies."

"We all have enemies."

"Yeah, well, she doesn't deserve to have a life forever looking over her shoulder."

"But you think invoking the mate bond and driving yourself insane is the better option. You know what happens when you play with fire, Lautner."

"I'll just add it to the rest of my scars," I remark flippantly, storming past him.

"Mick's planning another raid tonight," he calls out after me. "He had Daniel check all the known locations in the area last night. If he's successful, Dani and her pack will be leaving in the next day or two. After all, your mate has a wedding to plan, doesn't she?" Seth calls out, rubbing salt in the wound.

Ignoring him, I head straight for my room, slamming the door behind me. My body like a volcano, filled to the brim with rage and desire. I was more than ready to erupt. I shrug out of my joggers, leaving them in a heap at my feet as I head over to the bed. It's getting harder having her under the same roof and not having her under me every second. Especially now that she is a part of me. I craved her touch, the way she moans and writhes under me. My father tried to teach me that we didn't have to succumb to our wolf's desire, but he was wrong. It's not just my wolf that wanted his mate. We both did. She invoked every protective instinct within me. She's gorgeous and strong, no matter what she thought about herself.

I grip my cock, closing my eyes. Her mark on my chest tingles as I search for my release. I know she'd been embarrassed when she caught sight of it this morning. Shocked that she was capable of such actions. She has no idea just how strong her wolf is. But I do, and I'm glad she accepted me. I would wear her damn mark with pride for the rest of my life. I know if I'd told her what I was doing, she would have said no. She's too selfless. If she had known her actions would eventually drive me mad, she would have run from me and never stood a chance once Brandon and Lester found her. And they would. Find her. I'd be damned before I let that happen. At least with this mark, she has a fighting chance. She has me in her corner, and I'd be damned if I let Brandon or Lester touch a single hair on her damn body.

"I see you're starting without me," Alianna purrs, exiting the bathroom. "Don't stop. I'm enjoying the show."

"What do you want, Alianna?" I snap, angry at the interruption.

"You know exactly what I want." She climbs up on the bed straddling me.

"It's not going to happen. You're wasting your time."

"Really." She lifts her eyebrow suggestively. "Because I seem to recall it happening plenty of times before."

"This hard-on isn't for you this time. Get out."

"Don't forget, Lautner, it was you that texted me, begging me to come." Her hand encircles mine around my cock as I clench my teeth at the pain her touch inflicts on me. "Don't act like this is all me."

"It was a mistake. Trust me, it won't happen again."

"Don't say it's got something to do with that fragile woman downstairs wandering around all doe-eyed. She's engaged, in case you've forgotten. Then again, you always wanted what you could never have." Her thumb slowly circles the tip of my cock as pain ravages my body.

I grab her wrist roughly. "Get out, Ali. Or I will throw you out."

Pouting, she releases my cock. I pant heavily against the pain, waiting for it to fade. I watch her lift her thumb to her mouth, slowly sucking at the precum that rested there. Her eyes glance at the bite on my chest. "It's not going to end well, Lautner. You do realize that, don't you?"

"My life has nothing to do with you, Ali." I push her off me. Standing up, I grab her wrist, pulling her toward the door to escort her out.

"Go pack your stuff and get out of here." I open the door, finding Dani on the other side, her hand raised as if she were just about to knock.

Frozen, I can't take my eyes from her. Alianna stands on her tiptoes, kissing my cheek. "Don't worry, I'm leaving. Till next time." She winks, strutting off down the hallway, leaving me standing there, hard and naked, in front of a distraught Dani.

"Dani, I ... it's not what it looks like." The unshed tears in her eyes hit me like a knife straight to my gut.

She doesn't speak. She doesn't need to. The look in her eyes tells me everything I need to know. Danika Cortez wants nothing to do with me.

For the first time ever, I felt it.

Fear.

The fear of being rejected.

The fear of truly being alone.

She turns away, my cock finally taking the hint and going down. "Shit." I slam the door. Going over to my bedside table, I pull out my emergency bottle of whiskey, taking a drink. *Isn't this what you wanted? To remain unmated. She's not going to want a damn thing to do with you now.* Slamming down the bottle, I quickly redress. Mick wanted the hunter interrogated, and I needed violence. As I leave my room, I can feel the monster within me rising to the surface, begging to be set free on the man in the pit. I should feel sorry for him. I craved destruction right now. And this man is about to get the full force of my anger.

"Where are you going?" Seth calls out behind me.

"The pit."

"So, what? You're just going to leave Dani here, not knowing what you've done. She has a right to know."

"Fuck you, Seth." The way she'd just looked at me is the only image in my mind right now, and I need to get the hell away from it. "Does it kill you that even at my worse, I still haven't stuck a needle in my arm," I say, turning around to face him. I should take it back, but honestly, I just want him to leave me alone. I was getting tired of his endless bullshit where Dani is concerned. Not all shifters wanted a mate. To love someone so completely, you would do anything for them. Whatever it fucking takes. Until one day, they die, leaving you with nothing. My father was proof of that. The man he became was the fucking devil himself, and I can't even blame him, not anymore.

"You know what, fuck you, Lautner. I'm only trying to help you, as you once helped me."

"There's one big difference though, Seth. You wanted help; I don't."

"Is it really the end of the world to take a mate?"

"It's not who I am. I'm a lone wolf. I don't need anyone. Not Dani. Not the pack. Not you."

"If you let Dani walk away, that's it. You know that, right? Cortez and Drake win, and Lautner and Dani lose."

Ignoring him, I break into a lope, heading for the back of the property and the darkness waiting to consume me.

"You know what, Lautner, you don't deserve her," Seth shouts out to my retreating form, finally saying something we can both agree on.

CHAPTER 35
DANI

I'm shaking as I make my way back upstairs to my room. *How can he do this to me? After everything that happened between us.* I refuse to cry. I wouldn't give him or Alianna the satisfaction of breaking me. As I reach for the handle to my room, a hand covers my mouth, pulling me back against a cold firm body.

"Hello, my love, did you miss me," Drake whispers in my ear, dragging me back into my father's room.

"Danika," my father greets me. He's standing, warming his hands in front of the fire.

"You can let her go now." My father dismisses Drake with a wave of his hand as he releases me, taking his usual seat by the fireplace.

"What do you want?" I mutter, irritated at being manhandled.

"Is that any way to speak to your father, Danika?"

I watch as he paces the room, wanting nothing more than to scream that I know all about the pills and his plan to keep my wolf from me, but I know I can't. Not yet. "Forgive me, I'm tired. I did almost get killed last night," I remind him.

"You will run about on your own, won't you? I hope last night was a lesson to you."

"It was. Out of everyone in this room, and our pack, the only one who came to find me was Lautner."

He scoffs at my words. "Don't think we haven't noticed his interest in you. Clearly, we need to let him know that you are taken. Collect your things. From now on, you will share Drake's room for the remainder of our stay."

I can feel Drake's eyes watching me, but I remain focused on my father. "No."

"You're not listening, Danika. It's a command, not a request. From today, you will share his room and his bed. I want every wolf in this goddamn place to smell his ownership of you, especially Lautner."

"Please," I beg. For once, hoping he sees the desperation in my eyes and shows me some compassion.

"You will do as I say."

I bite my lip, trying to think of a way out of this. The Stone Valley Pack has a plan to take my father down. I just need to play the game long enough for them to catch him in the act.

"I need more pills," I blurt out.

"So soon?" my father asks suspiciously.

"The migraines have been getting worse since we got here. I only have two left," I lie.

"Very well, I will have you some more by tomorrow. In the meantime, I suggest you go to your fiancé and make sure he knows that you only have eyes for him." The perverse look on his face tells me that he wants to see this. Reigning in my anger and disgust, I bow to my father before walking over to where Drake sits.

"I'm sorry, Drake," I manage to choke out. He pats his knee, waiting for more. Taking a deep breath, I sit down, repulsed at the feel of how hard he is beneath me.

His hand grips my chin roughly. "Is this his t-shirt that you're wearing?" he snarls, tugging at it as I look down, realizing I had forgotten to get changed.

I nod as his eyes bore into mine. "Take it off." He smiles cruelly. I look toward my father, but he is no longer paying attention to us. He is too busy tapping away at his phone. Drake laughs cruelly. "Your father won't help you." His cold hand brushes my stomach as he lifts it over my head, leaving me bare before him. He licks his lips hungrily as he stares at my breasts, his thumb and forefinger pinching my nipple hard as I cry out in pain. "Tonight, Danika, you are mine. Can you feel how hard you make me?" he whispers loudly, knowing my father can hear him, but he doesn't care. "I can't wait to slide my cock deep inside you as you beg for mercy underneath me."

I refuse to answer or look at him.

"Stay away from Lautner. I can make or break your first time. Don't push me." Drake grips my hips, pushing his erect penis against my ass before throwing me to the floor. "Go get changed," he snarls, throwing Lautner's t-shirt back at me as I slip it back over my head.

"Please, can I go now?" I ask, looking toward my father.

He nods. "Go pack your things. Drake and I have a meeting to attend."

As I exit his room, I ignore his orders, heading downstairs to the bar instead. I need some answers, and I know the only person that would give them to me now is Daniel.

"Did you know?" I demand.

"Know what?" he asks, looking at me, clueless.

"About Lautner and Alianna. Is that why you wanted me to go find him? So, I could catch them together. I know you're jealous that I was fated to him and not you, but do you really hate me that much."

He shakes his head, looking confused. "Dani, slow down. I would never do that to you. What happened?"

"You lied to me. You told me that during the mating heat, he wouldn't want anyone but me. You lied," I cry loudly, grateful that we are the only two people in the room.

"Did you talk to him?" he asks.

"I just caught him having sex with Alianna. Do you really think I'm going to stick around and talk after that."

"Follow me." Daniel opens the hatch to the cellar, leading me downstairs. He pulls on a small cord hanging from the ceiling, casting the area in a dim white light. "Nothing would have happened with Alianna. It can't."

"I know what I saw, Daniel. I'm not an idiot. I caught her coming out of his room, he was naked, and she kissed him."

"Alianna is a bitch, but trust me, whatever you think happened, didn't. You marked Lautner. You staked your claim, starting the mate bond. There is no going back for him. No other woman other than yourself will ever be able to touch him sexually without causing him unendurable pain."

"Something tells me his stupid ass could deal with the pain," I bark.

"Maybe so, but he wouldn't do that to you."

"Why? Why would he do this without telling me?" I snap.

He sighs, pushing his wavy brown hair back from his face. "To protect you. Lester and Brandon, they know you're his fated mate. They won't stop coming after you. It's the only way to keep you safe. Now that you've marked him, he will be able to sense whenever you are near or in pain."

"What about the contract and my father?"

"It doesn't matter. This only affects him, not you. If he doesn't mark you within the next day or two, then you will go on as normal, and he... well, he will eventually go mad," he says with a shake of his head.

"I don't understand. Why would he give up his life to keep me safe?"

"Because you mean more to him than anyone. He may not say the words, but his actions prove otherwise."

"I won't allow him to put this on me, Daniel. I wouldn't be able to go on, knowing he'd damned himself for me. I will make him mark me," I say, determined.

He nods in understanding. "Don't worry, we'll deal with your father," he promises me. "Mick has set up a meet in a few minutes. I will place the tracker in your father's phone. Did you ask him for more pills?"

"Yeah, he said he will have them by tomorrow."

"Good. Once we catch him in the act, my pack can present the evidence to the Council. Your father will be stripped of his alpha position, and your contract to Drake will be over. You will be free to be with Lautner without the threat of war between the packs. We just need a little more time. In the meantime, stay away from Drake. Lautner won't be able to control himself now as he did before, and we can't tip your father off when we are so close."

"It's too late. My father has already commanded me to move into Drake's room tonight. He knows something is going on."

"You have to try. You need to speak to Lautner and

explain it to him. He finds you in Drake's room, that's it, game over."

"Would it really come to that?" I ask worriedly. "A war between the two packs?"

"Yeah, it would. Lautner will do anything to protect you. You're on Stone Valley Pack territory and fated mate to a pack member. In the eyes of my pack, that means you are protected by us, not your father. My father will stand by you. We all would."

"I'll go talk to him now."

"He's not here," Seth calls out behind us, startling me. "He's in the pit."

"Take me to him."

"I can't," Seth says. "You don't want to go down there, trust me. When he gets like that, it's not safe to be around him."

"Take me to him, Seth, or I'll find him by myself somehow. I don't think Lautner will be too happy when he finds out you let me wander outside alone." I go to walk past him.

"Shit, he's totally going to kick my ass for this," he grumbles, moving ahead of me. "Follow me. But don't say I didn't warn you."

CHAPTER 36
LAUTNER

I plunge the knife deeper into the hunter's thigh as he screams, begging for me to stop. Ignoring him, I take another, piercing his other thigh. I don't know who I'm more pissed at. The hunter before me, who had spilled every secret he knew, trying to escape with as little damage to himself as possible. Or the fact that no matter what I did, I can't get Dani out of my mind. *I was a monster. I didn't deserve her.* Yet she unleashes something inside me I have never felt before. The fact that she lets me touch her still confuses me. The way her body responds to mine, always ready for me, just like I was for her. Even now, in the midst of violence, I'm rock-hard. Her mark on my chest caressing my skin as if taming the usual rage that takes over. I had been raised to believe that my mate would be nothing to me but my downfall. Still, I can't get her from my mind. Dani had burrowed her way inside of me, and she wasn't going anywhere.

"Please," Jaxson begs. "I've told you everything, I swear. Please let me go."

"You're pathetic," I snap at the weak man before me.

"I don't want to die," he whimpers.

"You should have thought about that before trying to kill my mate," I seethe, picking up a hammer and forcing his hand onto the small makeshift table beside him.

"Please," he cries. I don't listen. I bring the hammer down hard on one of his fingers, hearing the satisfying crunch of bone. I wait for the numbness to take over. To get rid of everything Dani had been making me feel. But it's still there. The man whimpers as I raise the hammer again.

"Lautner." Her voice is like a soothing caress pulling me from the darkness I seek. I turn around, waiting for her to freak out, to panic. To tell me she never wants me to touch her again. Yet her face is calm as she wanders further into the room.

Jaxson's eyes flick toward Dani, and I can feel the anger inside me begin to rise. It's what I've been waiting for, and having this man's eyes on her finally triggers it.

"Don't look at her," I growl, dropping the hammer and pulling the knife from his thigh. I stand behind him, forcing his head back. I look over to Dani as she watches me. Without breaking our connection, I drag the blade across his throat. The man gasps, choking on his own blood, but I have no interest in watching the hunter die. Dani is looking directly at the monster within me. The man who can kill without question. Without remorse. And she doesn't turn away.

"You shouldn't be here, Dani." I let the knife drop to the floor at my feet, advancing toward her, waiting for her to run. I see a faint tremble in her shoulders, but she stands her ground as I circle behind her. I grip her arms roughly, pulling her flush against my body as she gasps.

"Welcome to the pit," I whisper in her ear. "Why are you here?" I place a kiss on her throat as she moans before turning her around to face me.

"I know you didn't sleep with Alianna," she says, "and I know what you did. I know about the mark." Her eyes travel down to my chest, and I swear it's as if I can feel her touching me. "You made me mark you, knowing damn well what it meant. You're risking your life, your sanity for mine. You're not selfish at all. You're just pig-headed."

Oh, I'm selfish, alright. But fuck if I wouldn't do anything for her.

My hands roughly push her shoulders as I guide her away from the dead man in the room, pinning her against the far wall.

"You care about me." Her hands grip my cheeks roughly, forcing our eyes to meet, and I swear I'm looking into her soul. "All my life, no one has really cared about me, except for you. Only you cared enough to question my seizures and the pills. You risked your life to protect me from Lester and Brandon. You want the truth, Lautner. I may not feel the mating heat like you. I may not know what you're going through, but I was dead until I met you. The first night we met, it's like I took my first breath, and it's all because of you. You say you're a monster, and you're selfish. Well then, I'm those exact same things. I know the risks, and I don't care. I'm selfish. I would die for you, because without you, I'm already dead."

Fuck. Her words hurt as they slice through me, but damn it if they aren't the best words I'd ever heard. They unlock something inside me I'd never even known was there. The fear of not being accepted, of being too tainted to be loved. If she can take a chance and be selfish, then so can I. My father was wrong. Dani is not my weakness. She is my motherfucking strength.

I smash my lips against hers. I know I'm being rough, but I can't help it. Starting the mate bond and not completing it was sending me over the edge. Her body instantly responds just as it always does when I'm near. I love that about her. Her little whimpers against my lips, sending me into overdrive.

My fingers hungrily pull at her jeans as she breaks the contact, helping me discard them. I'm acting like a sex-starved teen, and I can't hold back my groan as my fingers slide beneath her silk panties, finally connecting with her heat. She's already soaked as I rub my fingers between her folds, making her gasp.

I shouldn't be doing this here. Dani deserved better than this place. I'm covered in blood, and I should stop. But I can't. She's just accepted the man, the wolf, the monster, and she would get them all. I would be whichever one she needed, whenever she needed it.

"Do you have any idea what you're getting yourself into, Dani? If you're mine, you're mine," I state between bruising kisses.

"I'm yours," she replies, kissing me back with just as much fervor. "I hate my father for keeping my wolf from me. I want to be consumed with the mating heat. I want to feel everything," she murmurs against my lips.

I know what she is asking for, and my wolf gladly accepts. I lower my shields, letting my power consume her once more. I watch as she moans, this time embracing the heat instead of fighting it. My mouth finds her nipple, and I take it into the warmth of my mouth, using my teeth and tongue to tease her. She arches her back as I switch to the other. She is a fucking goddess, and I want nothing more than to worship her.

I reach down between us, shoving my joggers down my legs, freeing my cock. I lift her hips as she wraps her legs tight around my waist. I can feel her heat where my cock touches her. "Fuck." I bring my hand between us, snapping the panties at her waist. "I want to go slow, but I can't. I need you," I pant. She bites her lip, and with one quick thrust, I enter her. This female was made for me, taking everything I throw at her. I know I should go slow, and goddammit, I want to, but now isn't the time. There would be plenty of time for that once we got her father and Drake out of the way and the bond was complete.

"I love you, Lautner, my alpha," she whispers, her fingers brushing against her mark on my chest. That's all it takes. I thrust harder, deeper. It's a primal claiming as I lose myself in her body, completely under her spell. Her moans increase, and I know she's close. This is my promise to her. That I will claim her and take her as my mate. My lips find their way back to hers as she sucks my tongue deep into her mouth like she never wants to let me go. She needn't worry. From this day forward, she will never be rid of me. I would give her anything and everything she wanted.

"Come for me, Dani," I groan, feeling my own orgasm rise. My teeth find her throat as I bite down carefully. Her legs tighten around me, and I feel her muscles spasm around my cock like a vice. With a final thrust, I empty myself deep inside her.

As we pant together against the wall, I silently promise myself that there would be no more secrets between us, not after this.

"I'm supposed to move into Drake's room tonight," she says, watching me carefully for a reaction. "I have to," she begins, "but I promise nothing will happen. I will never betray you."

"I once told you that I would never start a war over you. I was lying. I would start ten wars and kill anyone that tried to take you from me. Nobody touches my mate but me. Just say the words, Dani, and I'll do it. I'll kill them both for you." I kiss her again, making sure she understands that I mean every word. Mick would understand. If he didn't, I would gladly leave if it meant keeping Dani safe.

"Lautner," Seth shouts from above, his voice echoing in the room, interrupting our moment.

"What," I snap, my eyes never leaving Dani. Imagining, we were back in my room and not deep in the confines of the pit surrounded by my destruction.

"Mick wants to know if it's done?"

I sigh, knowing anything else will have to wait until after the briefing. I hated waiting, but Dani deserved better than this place.

"I'm coming up now," I say, waiting to hear the door close behind him. I watch as she closes her eyes, disappointment marring her perfect face. I know she wanted me to claim her just now. Hell, I wanted to, but I'm trying my best to do the right thing by her. If all goes to plan, her father and Drake will be out of the way soon, and I can spend the rest of forever marking that sweet body and making it mine.

"Come on, let's go get cleaned up." I pull up my joggers as I wait for her to get ready. Taking her hand, I lead her back up the stairs and out of the hatch. Seth and Ryan are waiting for us as we emerge. As soon as Ryan sees Dani behind me, he launches himself at me, but I see it coming, pulling Dani safely behind me.

"What the hell is she doing down there? Have you lost your damn mind?" Ryan shouts, clearly frustrated. I can feel Seth's eyes watching me, wondering why the hell I let her stay down there, instead of bringing her back up here. They would never understand. They never did. I can pretend all I want to that my childhood didn't fuck me up, but it's a lie, and they both know it. They just never wanted to accept it, unlike Dani. She loved the monster just as much as the man. She had just proved it.

"What I do with my mate has nothing to do with you, Ryan," I state.

"Your mate?" he spits.

"Yeah, my mate." I pull Dani tight to my side, placing my arm over her shoulder.

"You realize she is still engaged to Drake, right. And Dani, don't take this the wrong way, but his scent is all over you. You can't have your father or Drake see you tonight." He talks to her, but his eyes stay on me. He's smart.

"I need to go wash up, anyway," she says as if just noticing the fresh blood that covers her clothes. She goes to leave my side, but I hold on, not wanting to let her go. It was always natural for fated mates to want to be near. The trouble is, I hadn't even marked her yet, and I was this bad. I have no idea what will happen when I finally do.

"It's alright, Lautner." She places her hand against my heart as if sensing my unease. "Ryan's right. We need to be sensible about this. We've come too close now not to see this through to the end." I know she's right, but it doesn't make it any easier. I nod before tipping her head back and kissing her, claiming her before my pack. As we slowly part, I watch her walk away, her mark on my chest burning with every step that takes her away from me.

I turn back to face Ryan, waiting for him to say whatever the hell he needs to before heading back for the meet. I can see the play of emotions across his face as if he wants nothing more than to drag me back into the pit and kill me himself. He could try. Ryan may be my Beta, but he knows just as well as I do that I am an alpha. His alpha if I chose it, and in a fight, I would always win.

He turns around, storming back to the house.

"You got anything to say?" I ask Seth, wondering what my next move is when it comes to her father and Drake. I know they are going to be in that room waiting when I enter.

"We're good."

I nod. "I'm still pissed that you brought her down here. It's too dangerous for her right now. I won't lose her, Seth."

"I know, but trust me, if I hadn't of taken her, she would have found a way. She's just as stubborn as you are. It all worked out for the best, though, didn't it?" He smiles.

"Yeah, it did." I smile back. "Now we just need to catch Cortez in the act so I can make it official."

"That's the other thing Mick wanted me to tell you. The plan worked. Cortez sent out a message just a few minutes ago. Looks like he's meeting with the supplier tomorrow morning."

I nod, just wanting this whole thing to be over, so I can finally have Dani all to myself.

"So, what are you going to do. In there?" Seth motions with his head toward the house.

I run my blood-coated fingers through my hair, wondering if I should shower first. I know I looked like shit. My clothes soaked in my enemy's blood, like a predator wearing his trophy. I turn to Seth. "Let's go."

"You not showering first." He wrinkles his nose at my appearance.

I don't reply. I continue walking past him toward the house. It was time for Drake and Cortez to see the real me.

Cortez had threatened Dani with killing me, but I'm betting neither his nor Drake's hands have ever been so encrusted with blood, it took days to clean out from under your fingernails. It's time they realize exactly who they're dealing with because I'm done messing around. Danika Cortez is mine.

CHAPTER 37
LAUTNER

Mick is waiting for me by the front door as I approach. No doubt, Ryan had run straight to him, letting him know of the latest problem I'd caused.

"A word," he calls out as I follow behind him. I can't help but glance toward the stairs as I pass, catching the faint scent of Dani in the air.

He leads me straight into his office, closing the door behind me.

"I told you before that the pack will support you no matter what your decision; that still stands," Mick says, taking his seat.

"Yeah, everyone but Ryan."

"Give him time. He'll come around. His job is to protect me, and the pressure from the Council isn't helping. My pack will always come first. You do what you have to, within reason," he warns. "So, I spoke to the Council about Cortez. I told them about the pills and Dani's inability to shift."

"What did they say?"

"As long as we have proof and can hand over the details of his supplier, he will be stripped from his position as alpha and off the Council."

"Seth mentioned the meet is planned for tomorrow."

"Yeah, near the abandoned power plant. It's got to be for the pills. Ryan and Daniel are going to surprise him."

"Does that mean the contract will be annulled?" I ask.

"Because of the circumstances, you should be free to claim your mate without causing a war between the two packs. In the meantime, I need you to stay away from her. I want this done without bloodshed if I can help it."

"Cortez has ordered Dani into Drake's room tonight. I won't let that happen."

"Trust me, it's not. Daniel's already got a lead on a few places, and whatever information you have, we have a chance to at least take a stand against them. They attacked our home. It's time we repaid the favor. Tonight, we take care of business, and tomorrow, we hand Cortez over to the Council."

The bar goes quiet as Mick and I enter. My eyes scan the room, instantly landing on Drake and Cortez.

"His name was Jaxson, twenty-five, from Ohio," I say, taking a seat beside Seth.

"He's a long way from home," Mick steps in. "So, who exactly are these hunters? What do they want? And who do they work for?"

"He doesn't know."

"Bullshit," Drake says snidely. "You're telling me you couldn't even find out the necessary information."

"I'm telling you, he told me everything he knew. He's a nobody, bottom of the food chain, a bit like you," I sneer.

"How dare you." Drake jumps up, coming around the table and getting in my face. "I'm Beta to the Ridgeway Pack, and you will show me some respect."

"My respect lies with my Alpha, not you." I stand up, meeting him head-on.

"Enough," Mick shouts as Ryan comes to stand beside me.

"Not here, not now," Ryan says, placing his hand on my arm.

"How dare you," Cortez shouts in my direction. "That is a blatant show of disrespect to one of my men." He turns to Mick. "I want him punished."

"He will be punished after our assignment. Right now, we need him."

"Need him. He has done nothing but cause trouble for Drake and my daughter since we got here."

"Lautner, sit down," Mick orders. I do as I'm told, biding my time. "Continue."

"They have a few safe houses in the area, mostly abandoned farms and another bunker ten-mile south of the Warehouse. There is a whole online movement for the extinction of shifters. They are offering money to strays and ex-pack members as a way to gather information. That's how they know our weaknesses. He has no idea who runs the program. He answered to a female called Alice."

"Daniel, where was the activity you located yesterday?" Mick asks.

"The old Duvall farm and the bunker that Lautner just mentioned south of the Warehouse but—"

"Well, that's settled. We go tomorrow night," Alpha Cortez interrupts.

"Hell no," Seth jumps in. "It's the first good lead we have. I'm not waiting for Brandon to slip through the net again."

"They will still be there tomorrow," Cortez confirms.

"How do we know that. They will know by now that Brady is dead and Jaxson is missing. What if they run?" Seth continues.

"I agree with Seth. We end this tonight," I say, "with our Alpha's permission, of course."

"I agree," Mick confirms. "It's time we fight back."

"No, we must be wise about this," Cortez tries again.

"If the Ridgeway Pack would rather stay here and let us deal with the hunters, that's fine by me. But I think the Council will be displeased when they hear about this." I smile, knowing that I have just forced his hand. He wouldn't be able to refuse, not without losing the respect of his pack and the Shifter Council.

I can feel Drake's eyes on me as I turn to face him, throwing him a smile. Hoping he knows exactly what I'm doing. *Nobody shares a bed with my mate but me, asshole.*

"Daniel, I want both coordinates sent to all of our phones now," Mick commands.

"I'm on it," Daniel replies, heading out of the room to his computer.

"We meet outside in twenty minutes," Mick says, dismissing us.

I watch Cortez and Drake as they whisper to each other, glancing my way. They were up to something. I just wasn't sure what cards they had left to play.

As everyone files out of the room, I follow Drake outside.

"I should have known you'd follow me out."

"I'm just wondering if you've got the balls to complete

this mission tonight. After all, it would be a shame if your incompetence got you killed."

"Oh, don't you worry about me. I plan to keep myself safe. I have an extra bed partner tonight. I need to be in full working order, if you know what I mean," he says, clutching at his crotch.

I grab him by the collar, slamming him against the wall.

"You can't do shit to me, and you know it." He laughs. "To think your pack has to put up with your bullshit day in and day out, just because you can't help your temper and daddy issues."

I tighten my hold as I slam him back against the wall once more, cutting his laughter short. I have no idea how this asshole knows about my past, but it just pisses me off more that he is trying to use it against me. "I may not be able to kill you yet, Drake, but I will. That's a promise."

"You can't stop this, Lautner. I can smell her scent all over you, and yet do I look worried. In the end, you have no idea what you're up against. Dani belongs to me. She always has." He smirks.

Drake is playing a dangerous game, and I have a feeling that whatever it is, I was playing right into his trap. I let him go, heading back indoors, needing to find Seth.

"What's up?" he asks as I find him heading back to his room.

"Drake and Cortez. I need you to stay with them tonight. Do not let them out of your sight."

"Why?" Seth asks instantly on alert.

"I have a bad feeling that they're planning something, and I have no idea what it is."

"Relax, Lautner. There's not much left they can do. The mission should take up most of the night, and the meet with the supplier is at nine. All we have to do is ride out the next few hours, then Dani is safe."

At the mention of her name, I immediately want to go upstairs and see her, but there's no time. I need a quick shower, and I have to make sure that Drake and Cortez make it out on this mission tonight, and as far away from her as possible. That's the problem with being a predator. You can always sense danger, and I was starting to worry that maybe, I'd underestimated Drake and Cortez all along.

CHAPTER 38
LAUTNER

"Come on, Daniel," I growl as the phone continues to ring. "Where the fuck is he?" I ask, turning to look out the window.

"He's probably getting a drink. Will you relax. Everything's fine," Ryan grumbles, keeping his eyes on the road ahead, driving us toward the bunker by the Warehouse.

I try Daniel again.

"What is it?" he finally answers.

"Where the hell have you been?" I demand.

"Relax, I was only getting a drink. All this talking makes me thirsty, you know."

Ryan looks over to me smugly as I flip him off.

"Have you checked on Dani?"

"No. Is this what this is about. Since you started the bond, I'm keeping my distance from your mate."

"Will you just shut up, Daniel. I need you to go check on her. I need to know she's alright. I've got a bad feeling about tonight."

"Is it the mark? Did something happen?"

"No, the mark's fine. It's just a feeling."

"Look, if she wanted company, she would be down here. It's been a pretty hectic day for her. She probably just needs some time alone. I mean, she's stuck with you now forever. That's enough for anyone to deal with." He chuckles as Ryan and Mick join in. "The security on this place is tight. Nothing's been breached, and Seth checked in over an hour ago. Drake and Cortez were with him. Nothing's going to happen." I close my eyes, wishing I could go back and be with her. "Alright," I reply, "but anything happens, I want to be the first to know."

"Yeah, I got it," he says, ending the call.

"See, you can stop worrying now," Ryan replies irritably beside me. I don't bother to answer. He has no idea what I'm going through; none of them do. Just wait till they find their mates. I'll be sure to remind them of this moment.

As Ryan pulls over near the bunker, I bolt from the car. We'd devised our plan on the way over. I was to head in first and scope the place out before calling Ryan and Mick to join me. Pulling my phone from my pocket, I quickly check the coordinates as I make my way through the quiet cornfield toward where the bunker is located. Within a few minutes, I find the hatch. It's dark as I peer down into the hole. Lowering my shields, I use my wolf to listen for any signs of life within. After a few minutes, I'm sure the place is empty, calling Ryan.

"This place is a bust. No one's home. Do you want me to keep searching?" I ask.

I can hear him talking with Mick before he answers. "Go down there and see if you can find anything useful. But be careful. I wouldn't be surprised if they'd started booby-trapping the place. Call us at the first sign of trouble."

I end the call, shoving my phone into my back pocket, carefully ascending into the darkness below. It's cold down here as my feet finally reach the bottom. Keeping my hands on the wall, I inch forward, listening for the sound of anything that might give away a trap springing into action.

I find the switch located to my left as I pull the cord. It's empty. Not a damn thing.

My phone rings as I pull it from my pocket, Daniel's name flashing on the screen.

"Get to the old farmhouse, now," he shouts as I answer.

"Daniel, what is it?"

"It's an ambush. I've got a drone overhead. It looks like about thirty people are ascending there. Seth and the others are inside."

"Shit, we're on the way." I run back up the stairs sprinting back to the car.

"The old Duvall farm," I shout.

"Why?" Mick asks worriedly.

"It's an ambush."

"Shit," Ryan curses.

CHAPTER 39
DANI

I'd received a text from Daniel about an hour ago. He informed me that the packs were out on a mission tonight, and my father was meeting his supplier first thing in the morning. All I had to do is stay out of Drake's way till morning, and hopefully, if all went to plan, my father would be arrested, and my contract would be over.

Picking up my phone, I try ringing Lacey. It's late, and I have no doubt she will be sleeping, but I'm too excited. I want to tell her that she'd been right all along about Lautner, and that in just a few hours, my father would no longer be able to control me. I listen to the phone ring continuously before switching to voicemail.

Snuggled in Lautner's hoodie, I leave my room, heading downstairs toward the bar. I'm restless tonight, and I know I won't be able to sleep. There's too much going on. I just wanted for this all to be over, so I can be with Lautner without having to hide.

I could go see Daniel. But I know he is working hard to keep the packs safe on their mission tonight, and I don't want to distract him. Instead, I grab a bottle of Lautner's favorite whiskey from behind the bar, pouring myself a shot. I scrunch up my face as I take a sip, wondering how the hell he drinks this stuff all the time. I pour myself another—anything to help me feel closer to him. I hated not seeing him properly before he left. I'd watched him go from my window, his eyes glancing up to meet mine for the briefest second. I know it's for the best. We need to keep a low profile until tomorrow, but it doesn't stop me from missing him. In just a few days, he'd become my everything.

Finishing my drink, I head back upstairs. I hadn't taken two steps back into my room before a hand covers my mouth, cutting off my scream.

"Didn't I give you a direct order for tonight?" my father growls as he uncovers my mouth, pulling me tighter into the cold of his body. I feel a sharp prick at the side of my neck as my father pulls away a syringe.

"What are you ... I-I thought the packs were out tonight," I stutter, clutching my neck, terrified to think of what he'd just injected me with.

"They are. But Drake and I had other business to attend. Now, sit down," my father orders, walking away from me. I look around the room, but the only place to sit is the bed, where Drake is now patting the empty spot beside him.

"We haven't got all night, Danika," my father warns.

I go sit at the far end of the bed, away from Drake.

"Did you really think I wouldn't know. After all, didn't I warn you not to do anything stupid. You should have listened to me, Danika. Everything that happens now, you have brought it on yourself."

"I don't know what you're talking about," I say as I feel the first stab of fear starting to take hold.

"I think you do." His hand goes into his pockets as he pulls out some photos. My hands shake as I reach out, taking them from him. The pictures are of Lautner and me on the first night we met at the Warehouse. As I look through them, a cold shiver works its way up my spine.

I look between Drake and my father, their cold eyes assessing me. "You knew all along, didn't you?" I hiss. "You knew Lautner was my mate. That's why you brought me here. You knew this would happen."

My father laughs. "Of course, I did. You both thought you could play me for a fool. Lautner almost surprised me for a minute. I really thought he might keep rejecting you, but then you had to wander off and get yourself into trouble. If you hadn't of, Lautner might never have given in, and that would have messed up my plans."

"I won't do it. I won't betray him," I say, knowing where this conversation is heading.

"You don't have a choice," my father replies coldly. "Tomorrow morning in front of the packs, you will inform everyone that you and Drake are to be married as soon as possible. That you just can't wait." He smiles wickedly.

"He wears my mark. The mate bond has already begun. I wouldn't be surprised if he is already on the way here." I smile, praying that he could feel my fear right now.

"I don't think so," my father replies, pointing toward the injection. "You think I didn't know all about your plans. It only works when your wolf is awake, and trust me, with the amount of valium I've just hit you up with, that's not going to happen for a very long time."

"Just think, Lautner will end up insane, just like his father. Everything he has ever feared. I think we both know he would end his own life before that happens. That's all thanks to you." Drake smiles in victory.

I close my eyes, praying this is all a nightmare. *How could I not have known that my father had been playing me all along? But he hadn't mentioned anything about the pills. If he didn't know, then there's still a chance to catch my father out tomorrow.* "What if I say no. You have nothing here to hold over me," I say, determined to keep believing that their plan could work.

"That was my other business tonight. Tell me, when was the last time you spoke to Lacey?"

"What have you done?" I ask, overcome with worry for my friend.

"Only what I needed to, to keep you in line," he replies, heading toward my bedroom door.

"Don't do this," I beg. Standing up, I go to meet him across the room, wishing I'd told Lautner to kill him earlier when I had the chance.

"It's too late. It's already done. She's alive, for now. But for her to stay that way, you will do as I say."

"He will know I'm lying. He won't give me up easily," I say with determination.

"For Lacey's sake, you better hope he does. And by the way, you won't be needing any more pills tomorrow. It's just no fun now that you've figured it all out." He smirks, hitting the final nail into my coffin. "She's all yours, Drake," he calls out as he leaves the room, closing the door behind us.

The sound of Drake's boots coming to a stop behind me is my only warning before he pulls me flush against his body. His fingers sliding down the front of my jeans and touching my bare flesh. I ram my elbow hard into his ribs, trying to break free. He grunts in pain but doesn't let go.

Instead, he brings his free hand up to cover my mouth. "You let that fucking bastard touch what is mine," he says forcibly, ramming two fingers inside of me. I'm still sore from earlier today, and the pain it causes has tears streaming down my face.

"This is how I always pictured it, Dani," he whispers. "You, crying while I take whatever I want from you. I don't care if that is him I can feel you wet with up there. It will always be me that touches you last. You will never escape me, no matter how hard you try." His hips pound against my ass as he continues to assault me with his fingers. After a few more thrusts, I feel him sigh against my neck, and I don't need to turn around to know that he has released in his pants.

"That's just a little preview of our future together." His hands let me go as I fall to the floor. "I'm saving the actual fun for tomorrow after I watch Lautner's face at your rejection."

"He will kill you, Drake," I promise.

"Maybe, he will." He smiles. "But Lautner's not going to want a damn thing to do with you now, Dani. You're tainted. For just a minute, you had it all—everything you ever wanted. Everything fate ever wanted for you. And now, you have nothing."

As I hear the door slam behind him, my throat burns as I quickly scramble off the floor and make it to the bathroom in time before throwing up. After a few minutes, I start the shower, needing to rid my body of Drake's touch. I pick up my phone, dialing Lacey's number one last time, needing to hear her voice.

"Hi, you've reached Lacey—"

I end the call, closing my eyes. My father didn't make

idle threats. If I wanted to keep Lacey alive, I've no other choice. I would have to break every promise to Lautner I'd just made, inevitably damning us both.

CHAPTER 40
LAUTNER

I try Seth's phone, but there's no answer.

"Lautner," Mick calls out from the backseat. "When we get there, I want you to head straight for the house, you hear me. Find Seth. We'll patrol the outside. If they're cornered, I need you to flush them out, where we'll be waiting." I nod at my alpha's instructions. It's our best plan. There's only the three of us, and we can't leave our alpha unprotected. That's our beta's job.

Ryan slows down as I leap out, keeping close to the fence line. I spot a few humans as they scurry about, holding their AK47s close to their chest, barking out orders. I look up toward the shattered windows catching a glimpse of movement as I ring Daniel.

"Is Seth still in the house?"

"Yeah, Seth and Terry are holed up on the second floor. They've killed a few hunters inside, but they just keep coming."

"What about Cortez and Drake?"

"I don't know. Their signal went down about thirty minutes ago, and I haven't been able to get it back."

"Shit."

"I'll keep trying, and I'll let you know as soon as I find anything," Daniel replies as I hear his fingers tapping furiously at the keyboard.

"Get word to Seth. I'm going to find a way in. Keep searching for Drake and Cortez," I demand, ending the call. *Fuck.* I knew they had something planned, but I can't think about that yet. Dani is back home, and she's safe for now. I need to focus on getting Seth and the rest of Ridgeway out of there.

Sneaking around the back, I head toward the old barn, finding their vehicles hidden inside. I quickly rummage through their bags before finding what I needed. I pick up two hand grenades as I make my way toward the door, carefully taking out one of the pins. As soon as I hit the door, I throw it behind me, running as fast as I can. The explosion deafens me as I watch the hunters racing toward the fire. A couple of men stay behind as I advance up behind them. Within minutes, I have three dead hunters at my feet, without breaking a sweat.

The door creaks open as I ease my way in. The air inside is thick with the coppery scent of blood, as I find a young woman on the floor with her throat ripped out. Her face, watching me, forever frozen in a mask of fear.

"Motherfucker," a man calls out behind me. I turn around just in time to catch a bat that is aimed at my head. Growling, I snatch the bat from his hand, returning the favor as I hear the satisfying snap of his neck at my swing.

Shit. This is bad. I creep forward, heading for the stairs, keeping the wall at my back. I turn the corner to find bloody handprints lining the walls as if leading the way.

There are six doors up here, each one shut tight. I start forward, my feet gliding across the old wood, barely making a sound. I can hear the erratic heartbeat of a man, and I can instantly tell he is human. I kick the door with as much force as I can, hearing a satisfying grunt and the sound of metal hitting the floor. I catch the man by his neck, slamming him against the wall.

"Where's Seth?" I growl. The man struggles against my hold, kicking out with his feet. I punch him twice in the face as blood runs from the corner of his eye and his nose.

"I'm not telling you anything, motherfucker."

I start to shift. The man's eyes stare wildly as the hand that holds him spurts fur, and my sharp claws pierce his neck.

"Lautner," I hear Seth panting heavily from another room close by.

"Looks like I don't need you after all," I say to the shocked man. I slash my claw across his jugular, letting him fall into a pool of his own blood.

I walk into the next room, finding Seth on the floor, a silver spear protruding from his thigh.

"What happened?" I ask.

"Some fucker hit me with a spear gun," he groans as I look at the damage. The thing went clear through to the other side. There's no way to remove it, not yet. He would bleed out before we ever got back home.

"It's nothing. Come on, we've got to get you out of here." I pull his arm over my shoulders as I help him to his feet, calling out to Terry. "Where are the others?"

He shakes his head. "I have no idea. As soon as we entered, they were waiting for us. Logan and Sid were downstairs with us, but when Seth got hit, I dragged him up here."

"You did the right thing. Go ahead and clear a path. The car is parked about a mile up the road. We need to get him back, fast."

He nods, taking off before me.

Another explosion erupts outside as we reach the front door. I peer out first, looking for any signs of an attack before making a break for it.

"I'm sorry, Lautner. It was too late. They were waiting for us," he grunts.

"It's alright, you did good."

I half carry, half drag Seth as we hobble down the road to safety. "It's all clear," Terry calls out, catching up to us and taking Seth's other side. "Most of them are heading toward the trees. Your alpha and beta are right behind them."

"I tried to keep an eye on them," Seth spits out as I help him into the back seat, "but I don't know where they went."

"Don't worry, we'll find them."

"Stay here," I say to Terry as I swiftly move past him, going in search of Mick and Ryan. I'm not halfway back to the house before they find me with Logan and Sid in tow. All of them are naked and bleeding as we make our way back to the escalade.

"Where's Drake and Cortez?" I demand to Sid and Logan, who only shake their heads.

"We don't know. They left before the rest of the hunters got here," Sid replies.

"Shit." I ring Daniel. "Where the fuck are Drake and Cortez?" I shout down the phone.

"I don't know," he replies, and I can hear the worry in his voice.

"What do you mean you don't know?" I seethe.

"I can't find them."

"We're on the way home now. Go find Dani, and do not leave her side until I get there. You got that?"

"I got it," he snaps as the line goes dead.

"Seth's hurt," I say to Ryan just as we reach the car.

He nods as he gets in the back. I wait for everyone to get in the car before jumping behind the wheel.

Seth screams from the back seat as Ryan pulls the silver spear from his thigh before applying a makeshift tourniquet.

Slamming my hand against the wheel, I hit my foot on the gas, careening us forward.

"Hang on, Seth," I call out as I race down the old dirt tracks, trying my best not to kill us all. *I'm coming, Dani.*

CHAPTER 41
LAUTNER

As soon as we get back, she's waiting in the bar, but something isn't right. I stride toward her, the heavy clunk of my boots the only sound in the room.

"Dani," I call out. She sits ramrod straight wedged between her father and Drake.

"Don't come any closer," Drake warns, standing up, blocking her from my view.

"Dani, are you alright?" I ignore Drake, looking around him as she finally turns, and I see the glassy look in her eyes.

"What have they done to you?" I growl.

"I'm fine, Lautner," she replies, turning away quickly. "It's no business of yours."

"What happened?" I demand, wondering why she won't even look at me. It'd only been a few hours ago that she'd sworn to be mine, and now, I feel like she is a million miles away. My hand automatically goes to her mark, but there's nothing there. It's like the connection we had is gone, and once again, I'm alone. I look between the three of them before once again resting my gaze on Dani. "Remember what I told you. You only need to say the word, I promise."

"It's nothing, please, leave me alone. I'm not yours. I never was. I'm Drake's."

Drake smiles coldly at her words, pulling her into a tight embrace, yet she does nothing. She won't even look at me.

"Get your hands off my mate," I threaten, but he only smiles wider. "Dani," I try again, hating the almost pleading tone of my voice. I'd never been so weak, so unsure of what to do. The alpha in me wanted nothing more than to kill Drake and drag Dani kicking and screaming from this room. I would force her into submission with long hard strokes of my cock until she finally relents, telling me the truth.

Finally, she lifts her head, and I feel like I don't recognize the woman staring back at me. "Yesterday was a mistake. I used you, Lautner. It was always Drake. I choose Drake," she replies coldly.

"You're fucking lying, Dani. Just tell me the truth. I promise I will keep you safe."

"Keep her safe," Cortez snarls. "All you've done since we got here is put her in danger. Is it any wonder she wants nothing to do with you. You're just like your father. Pathetic."

I clench my fists at my side. "You know fuck all about my father," I growl.

"I know when your mom died, he dragged you away to live amongst the strays before going mad. Now, you get to do the same. You might as well do your pack a favor and end it now before you end up hurting them. You heard her. She wants nothing to do with you. I suggest you leave her and her fiancé alone from now on. Are you really going to start a war over someone who clearly thinks you're a monster?"

"Fuck this, you've done something to her," I demand,

rushing at Cortez. But it's Mick's hand that holds me back. I'm suddenly aware of the rest of my pack in the room. I can hear Seth grunting in pain as Ryan lays him down across the seats, attending to his wounds, but none of it matters.

"Dani, whatever they have said to you, tell me," I plead. "I won't let them take you from me. I promised you that."

"This is my decision, not theirs. And I choose him." Her words are steady, her breathing even, as I seek out any indication that she is lying. She's made up her mind. I stumble back, unsure of what to do. Usually, I would hit something, but the pain radiating inside me is excruciating. I feel like I'm about to break in two.

"Fuck you, Dani," I finally spit. "I was right all along about trying to keep my distance from you; I just wish I could have fucking listened. After everything, I hope he enjoys that tight little cunt of yours, because like you told me once before, this is it for you." I watch her flinch, finally getting a reaction.

I don't turn back as I leave the room, heading for the front door, needing as far away from this place as possible.

I climb on my bike, gunning the throttle as I take off, heading straight for the Warehouse.

CHAPTER 42
DANI

Drake pulls me close, grabbing my ass with a smile as Lautner storms past.

I choose Drake. The biggest lie I had ever told in my life had just passed my lips, taking everything I had ever wanted away with it. The look in his eyes would haunt me forever. He had sacrificed his entire future for me, and I'd just stomped on his heart in front of his pack as if it were nothing.

"You did good," Drake whispers in my ear. I look away. I didn't want his approval. I wanted nothing from him, but to be as far away from him as possible. I look around the room at the remaining members of the Stone Valley Pack. They looked at me in disbelief, as if they couldn't quite understand what had happened and why I'd just damned their brother. Tearing my eyes away, I fight back my tears, determined to try and hold myself together. There's nothing I can do. The hatred they feel toward me would never match the hatred I feel for myself.

"Excuse me," I say as I run from the room. My tears falling fast. It's not until I stop that I realize I'd run straight to Lautner's room. I couldn't face my own room and the memories of Drake's assault. Going over to the bed, I pick up his discarded shirt, bringing it to my nose. I inhale his scent, instantly feeling a sense of safety, which is just another lie. I would never be safe again.

"Isn't this sweet," my father comments from the doorway.

"Just leave me alone. I did what you asked. Lautner is gone."

"Go pack your things. Drake is taking you back home. You're of no more use to me here."

I wait for him to leave, before taking one final look around. I drag my feet back upstairs, each step feeling harder than the last. As I enter my room, it's still in darkness. The drapes are closed, and I have no desire to open them. The darkness fits my mood perfectly. I quickly empty my dresser, shoving everything into my bag. My phone beeps, signaling a text, but I ignore it. I didn't want to see whatever Daniel wanted to tell me. It was obvious what the rest of the Stone Valley Pack thought of me. I didn't need to read about it as well.

"You ready?" Drake asks, smiling as he enters the room.

"Yeah," I murmur, tossing my bag over my shoulder. We manage to make our way down the stairs and out of the building without running into anybody. I climb into the car, taking one last look behind me at the place I'd hoped would be my new home with Lautner.

We don't speak as Drake starts the car. I'm exhausted, but I know there will be no rest for me. Instead, I watch the scenery passing by, wondering if I would ever see this place again.

We must have been on the road for about twenty minutes when I feel the car start to slow down. I look out the windscreen to find a lone figure lying in the middle of the road.

"What the ... pull over," I call out to Drake, "he might still be alive." Drake pulls over as I quickly exit the car.

"Are you alright?" I ask as I lean down. The man is lying on his stomach, his face hidden from my view.

"Call an ambulance," I shout to Drake.

The man grumbles on the ground as he turns around. "I'm alright, now. Remember me." Lester smiles.

I try to scramble back to my feet, but he's too fast, catching my arm in his steel grip. In the past few hours, I'd forgotten all about Lester and Brandon. Lautner had warned me they would never stop coming. It looks like he'd been right.

"What's the hurry, darling. We've got plenty of time."

I look toward the car, shocked to find Drake just sitting there watching me. Lester smiles as he starts to drag me away.

"Thanks, Drake, we'll take it from here," he shouts over his shoulder as I watch Drake nod, putting the car into reverse.

"Drake," I scream, wondering why I'm even surprised as I drop my shoulders in defeat.

"Shhh, don't worry," Lester mumbles, pulling me close. "We've got a very special treat lined up for you."

"You're wasting your time," I say. "It's over between us. Lautner won't come for me."

"That's where you're wrong. You know just as well as I do, he won't leave you behind. Now, let's go." He drags me roughly toward the trees where Brandon waits, next to a pair of Harley-Davidsons.

"Hey, sweetheart." He winks. "Any trouble?" he asks Lester.

"No. We're good."

Brandon pulls a large hunting knife from a sheath around his waist. "You ready to be famous, Danika. We've got a couple of home movies we need to make, and ... well, you're going to be the star."

CHAPTER 43
LAUTNER

Thane spots me as soon as I barge through the door of the Warehouse. "What's up with you?"

"Take my blood," I demand, striding past him and heading down toward the Sun Sinners' living quarters.

"What, no. We don't need any yet." He follows behind me.

"Take it, or I will fucking bleed out on the floor, right here, right now," I growl. I let my canines elongate, bringing my wrist up to my mouth. "What's it to be?" I say, turning around to face him.

"Shit," he mutters. "Follow me." He strides past me, leading the way downstairs and ushering me into a small sterile room at the end of the hall.

"Over there." He tilts his head to the gurney in the middle of the floor. I shrug off my coat, lying down.

"Hold out your arm." His blood-red nails grasp my arm, applying the tourniquet and pulling it tightly. "What the fuck's gotten into you?" he asks harshly, swiping my arm with a sterile wipe before lining up the needle with my vein.

I don't reply. I wait, glancing at the sterile bag that would soon hold my blood, hoping it takes away even a fraction of the pain that I'm feeling, even if only for a short while. It would never be long enough.

Cortez was right. I might as well end it. I wouldn't be able to handle it. Wanting Dani for the rest of my life and never being able to have her. To know somewhere out there, Drake would be sliding into her warm heat while I remained cold and alone, unable to stand the touch of another.

"I'm done," Thane replies. I close my eyes waiting to be dragged under, but it's not enough. The pain is still there. I can still see her when I close my eyes. "More," I demand, opening my eyes as I stare at Thane.

"No, you're talking about losing a severe amount of blood here."

I didn't care. I needed something to take away the memories. "Do it," I growl, gripping his cold hand in mine.

"It's your fucking funeral," Thane replies coldly. I nod, closing my eyes, waiting to be taken under.

"I'm going to kill him." Seth's voice breaks through the cloudy haze that engulfs my mind. I can't move, no matter how hard I try.

"What's everyone doing in here?" Cal commands loudly, making my head spin.

"What the hell did you do to him?" Ryan demands as I open my eyes to find my pack surrounding me.

"Only what he promised in return for breaking the rules. His blood," Thane replies, entering the room.

"Shit. This can't be happening right now," I hear Mick call out. "Seth, get him up."

"I wouldn't do that if I were you; he's lost a lot of blood," Thane reminds him.

"Really, did you think this was necessary? After all the money he brings in for you with the cage fights, did you really need to take so much?" Seth demands.

"No, but he did request it," Thane replies. "Why do you think I called you? Your dog here clearly has a death wish."

"Lautner, you're a fucking asshole," Seth all but screams at me now as I try to move. "Dani's in trouble. Do you hear me? She needs her mate. She needs you," he continues.

Dani. It seemed like a distant memory since I'd seen her last, and yet I know it can't have been more than a few hours ago.

"Where's Dani?" I croak, trying to speak, although my tongue feels like sandpaper in my mouth.

"Seth, get him a drink of water." Ryan holds my head up as I take a sip.

"Where's Dani?" I ask again.

"We're not sure exactly," Ryan confirms. "Drake was taking her back home when they found a man lying in the middle of the road. Dani got out to check on him, but he took her and ran."

Shit. This is all my fault. I should never have left. Whether she wanted to be with me or not, I should never have abandoned her. I've no doubt that Lester or Brandon would be behind this. If anything happens to her, it would be all my fault. Straining, I try to force my body to move. *Damn it.* "Seth, help me up."

"Lautner, you can't do anything, not like this." Mick pushes at my shoulders, keeping me down.

"Get me up," I croak as my phone rings. *Please be Dani,* my mind roars. Seth limps over toward my leather jacket. I'd nearly forgotten about his injury. "Unknown," he murmurs before answering the call and putting it on speaker.

"Lautner," Lester's cheery voice greets us. "Say hi, Dani." I can hear his voice fading into the background. A scream sounds down the line that has me fighting against my weakened state.

"Lautner," I hear her call out faintly over Lester's laughing in the background. "Go on, tell him how much fun we're having," Lester urges.

"I'm sorry," she whispers. I can almost picture her in my mind as I hear her soft pleas. The echo of a slap rings out, and I hear what sounds like Dani grunting in pain.

"I'm going to kill you, Lester," I growl.

"I don't think you will." The voice belongs to Brandon now. "You took my brother from me, and now I get your mate. We'll call it even." The call ends as I fight against the panic, threatening to consume me.

"Fix this," I demand, turning to Thane.

"I can't," he replies, clearly agitated.

"Can't you just give him a transfusion?" Mick asks.

"The blood has already been sent out."

"Well, what about one of us? Ryan, you're the same blood type," Seth demands.

I turn to Ryan. I know he despises me, but I know he wouldn't let Dani suffer just to spite me. Ryan nods. "Alright." He goes to sit in the empty chair beside me, rolling up his sleeve. "You will owe me for this," he growls as Thane inserts the needle.

Grateful, I nod. "How long will this take?" I ask Thane, needing to get out of here and find my mate.

"A few hours, you've lost a lot of blood."

"We don't have that kind of time." I rip the needle out of my arm, panic overtaking me.

"Hold him down," Mick calls out. "We need to knock him out."

"Don't you dare." I threaten everyone in the room, including my alpha.

"We don't have a choice. You go out there now; you're going to get yourself killed."

I use what little adrenaline I have left to knock his arm away from me as I roll to the floor.

As my pack surrounds me, I try to fight, but it's useless. Their hands pin me down and I curse them all. Thane stalks toward me, holding a syringe. I try to kick out, but I can no longer feel my legs. I watch the needle pierce my skin. "If anything happens to Dani, I swear, I will kill you all," I warn before everything around me goes black.

CHAPTER 44
LAUTNER

It's dark by the time I wake up back in my room. For a moment, I don't remember anything until the faint hint of vanilla on my sheets hit my nose. *Dani. Lester and Brandon have her.* As my memory returns, I groan as I get out of bed. Whatever Thane had given me is still raging in my system. My body groans in protest as I pull on some clothes, determined not to let Dani down.

Everyone goes quiet when I eventually make my way down into the bar.

"How long have I been out?" I seethe, my eyes dancing over everyone in the room who dared hold me down.

"Twelve hours," Mick confirms.

"You let me sleep for twelve hours when Dani is out there," I demand. "What the hell is the matter with you." I head over to where Drake and Cortez sit. "And you, how could you let him take her?"

"I tried to fight him off," Drake replies, "but he got the

jump on me. Besides, it's all your fault anyway, isn't it. Don't blame me. You're the one he wants to hurt, and my mate is paying the price."

I grit my teeth at his words.

I hear my phone beep on the counter and Mick instantly goes toward it. "It's another video from Lester," Mick says, his eyes dark as he glances at me. "You don't need to see this."

I pick up the phone, pressing play. The room on the screen is dark, except for a single beam of light shining down on Dani from above. She is bound and gagged. Her face a mixture of bruises and blood. "Look at the camera, Dani," Lester demands. "Don't make me hurt you again." Her vacant eyes stare into the camera before the video ends abruptly.

"He will accept the deal. It's just a matter of time," Cortez speaks calmly.

"Deal. What deal?" I snap, looking at him.

"Money, in exchange for her life."

"You think that's what this is all about, money. He will kill her. He doesn't care about the money. This is your daughter," I shout, thrusting my phone in front of his face. "Why aren't you worried?"

"Son of a bitch." I hear Terry behind me. I turn around, but he isn't looking at me. His eyes are on Cortez. "It was you, wasn't it? You did this."

"How dare you accuse me. I'm your Alpha, and she is my daughter."

"Your daughter has been missing for nearly a full day. Yet you haven't once joined us in the search for her," Terry says.

Seth clears his throat. "You never did explain to us what

happened the night of the mission. When you and Drake ran off, leaving us all behind."

"The mission was a bust, so Drake and I came back here."

"That's a lie. I overheard you and Drake talking before we left. You were planning on meeting someone that night," Terry pushes.

"I don't have to tell you anything of my whereabouts," Cortez demands.

"Maybe not to him," Mick interjects, "but to me, you do. You're on my territory. Now answer the damn question. Where did you go?"

"This is outrageous," he demands, getting up to leave. Ryan places his hand on Cortez's shoulder, pushing him back down.

"Answer the question," Ryan hisses.

"You met Lester, didn't you?" I ask.

"I did what was necessary for Danika," Cortez replies.

"You think this is necessary for your daughter," I demand, pressing play on my phone. "Is this for her own good? Lester and Brandon will kill her."

"No, they won't. We have a deal."

"A deal. A fucking deal. You think they care about a deal. Brandon wants to hurt me, and your daughter will pay the fucking price. She's my mate."

A look of pure hatred distorts his face as he sneers at me. "Your mate. Rather she be dead than mated to the likes of you."

"Motherfucker," I shout as I launch myself across the room, grabbing Cortez by the throat. "Why. Tell me why?"

"Simple. She needed to be punished for defying me. I've been one step ahead of you all this time. I knew all about the mate bond," he spits. "You may wear her mark on your chest, but you know as well as I do that only buys you so much time. This is my insurance. Lester and Brandon keep her long enough for the mate bond to sever, and you follow in the footsteps of your father. I always win, Lautner. Always."

"You may think you know everything," I sneer, "but you got one piece of information wrong. My father didn't kill himself. I killed him, and I promise you, your days are numbered."

"Take them both to the pit," Mick calls out as I drop my hands away from Cortez's throat.

As Daniel takes hold of Drake, Drake's eyes turn to me. "You want to know why we came back here last night. If you hadn't taken her yesterday, I might have been gentle with her. She cried as I touched her. I wanted her to call out for you, knowing damn well you couldn't save her. You will never find her, Lautner. Even if you do, do you really think Lester or Brandon's going to pass up on taking her as well. They hate you even more than I do."

Mick holds me back as if anticipating my next move. "Take them away," he orders. "We have more than enough evidence to present to the Council. They will both be dealt with."

"You're dead, Drake. Do you hear me. You and your alpha. I will find her and bring her home, and you're going to wish you'd never met me." I can't stop myself as I pull my arm free from my alpha's hold and slam Drake to the ground. I straddle his hips, every punch I throw connecting hard with his face. Even as his blood coats my hands, I continue. I ram his head hard into the ground before I feel hands at my back, pulling me off him. In my weakened state, I fight against them, but I'm not strong enough. Someone grips my wrists, forcing them together in front of me as I feel the burning pain of silver. "Fuck," I cry out as I'm pushed, handcuffed back into a chair. "I love her. You hear me. I love her, and I will save her," I shout as I watch Drake sneer before being dragged bleeding from the room.

CHAPTER 45
LAUTNER

Six years ago

I'm an alpha. The rightful heir to the Stone Valley Pack. That was my father's big secret. With his inevitable death looming before him, he had finally told me the truth. He had once been a respected alpha. A powerful alpha with a fated mate by his side. It had all been perfect until one night, my mom stumbled upon my father's enemy. He had watched helplessly as the alpha killed her before his very eyes. Broken by his grief, he abandoned his pack in the middle of the night, taking me with him.

We had traveled aimlessly, until eventually, my father found some peace amongst the strays. Their need for destruction and violence helping him deal with his own demons, and that's how I would be raised. To grow up fearing nothing and no one. To know that I was strong enough to deal with the world around me. Strong enough to reject my wolf's need for a mate. He believed he could do it, and as I look down at his lifeless body before me, I knew he was right. After watching him succumb to his mate's loss, I would never fall victim to the same fate.

Standing over his prone body, I wait. For what, I'm not sure. Maybe for remorse to finally take hold or the anger to simmer inside me. But I feel nothing. I had just murdered my father in cold blood. Not out of love, but out of pity. He had known all along the monster he created would eventually kill him. Perhaps that had been his intention all along.

Picking up his body from the ground, I carry it over to the grave I had just dug, dropping him inside and taking one last look at the man that had raised me. The hole is deep, and it takes me a while to cover him, the sky growing dark around me. Satisfied at a job well done, I place a small stone etched with his initials D.A atop his grave.

It was time for me to leave. To walk away and start anew. I knew Lester would be pissed at me. After all, he was my only friend here, but I couldn't stay. Not now. This had been my father's life, and I was done living in a world he created. Maybe I would search out the pack my father had been so desperate to keep me away from. To see what life had awaited me if things had turned out differently. Turning away, I walk straight ahead, and I don't look back.

CHAPTER 46
LAUTNER

I'm losing my mind, afraid to close my eyes. All I can see is her calling my name, and I can't move. I can't help her. Clutching my phone, I stare at the blank screen, just waiting for the next video to show me that Dani is still alive, no matter what state she is in. I had watched the videos Lester had sent over when I was comatose upstairs. Each video more violent than the last. I had watched him cut her, beat her, and there wasn't a damn thing I could do about it.

I scream in frustration at the empty room around me, unable to control myself. My wrists burn from the silver cuffs where I had tried to remove them. Is this how my father had felt all those years before. Watching as his mate was killed before him, not being able to do a damn thing but blame himself and the choices he made. But there is one difference between my father and me. If Dani died, if I couldn't save her, then it's all over. I would gladly take my own life because I can no longer imagine my life without her.

Seth limps into the room, looking around wildly as if expecting danger. As his eyes track over to me, he comes over, sitting beside me.

"Get these cuffs off me, Seth," I say coldly.

He shakes his head. "I can't do that."

"I'm not just going to wait around. This is what you wanted, right. Me to mate. Well, she's out there, and if I don't get to her soon, it will all have been for nothing."

It's the truth, and he knows it. In just a few hours, the mate bond would be over. It was all I had ever wanted at first, but now the thought of losing it, of losing her, is sending me into a panic.

"Once we get another call from Brandon, we'll sort something out. We won't abandon her, but you need to be smart about this. If you go now, you're dead."

I hate that he's right. I'm in no goddamn state to face-off against Brandon and Lester, but I'll fucking do it, and I'll win. For her.

"His plan is to hurt you. Not her."

"Yeah, don't remind me. This is all my fault."

"You can't blame yourself."

"Who else can I blame. I played Brandon for a fool, toying with him over Tommy's death, and look where it's gotten me. Dani's paying for it."

"He won't kill her, not until he gets you."

"That doesn't help, Seth, and you damn well know it. You know just as well as I do the damage that can be inflicted in such a short amount of time. Not just physically but mentally," I say, remembering how Seth was when he returned from Brandon and Tommy's clutches.

Seth pauses as if just realizing that Dani could be suffering the same fate as he once did. "I've been where Dani is. It's not easy, but she has you, and she is stronger than you know. She loves you," he says with a wince as he grips his thigh.

"What's the deal," I nod toward his thigh.

"I'll be fine. The silver was in for quite some time. Ryan's scared there maybe some left-over muscle damage."

Mick calls out for Seth and he gets up, heading toward the office. I know they are having a meeting right now, one in which I'm being purposefully left out of. I know Mick doesn't trust me right now, and he has every right not to. I don't give a shit about the shifter Council or the damn treaty. I just want her back.

I jump as my phone rings, instantly answering. It's Brandon. "If you want your bitch back, meet me alone down at the old cabin by the creek. You know the one."

"Let me talk to her."

"She can't come to the phone right now, I'm afraid. Lester is keeping her entertained."

"This is between us. It always has been. Just let her go."

"It was, but then, you went and took something of mine. It's only fair."

"She's not like us."

"I wouldn't be too sure about that. In the past couple of hours, Dani and Lester have come to know each other rather intimately." He laughs. "Come alone, or Dani dies." Brandon ends the call as I glance toward Mick's office. I know I should tell them about the call, but I'm done playing the Council's games. If I turn up with the pack in tow, it's all over. I watch the door open, catching sight of Daniel coming out.

"Daniel." With hunched shoulders, he slumps over. His eyes are red, and I know he hasn't slept in a while. "I need you to take these cuffs off."

"I can't. My father will kill me."

"Daniel, I know you care about Dani. You're the only one that can help me get her back. Just take the cuffs off," I demand.

He stares at me, and I can see he's confused. He would never willingly betray his father, but he cares for Dani. I might not like it, but I know she doesn't think of him in that way. To her, she is his friend.

"Shit." Daniel goes over to the bar. Opening the safe, he takes out the key.

"You promise to bring her back?" he asks as he slides the key into the lock.

"I promise." Satisfied at my answer, he turns the key freeing me from the cuffs. I rub my wrists. "Go back in there and act like nothing has happened. I need a head start."

He nods and retreats from the room. Grabbing my leather jacket off the chair, I head out toward my car. It would probably be quicker to shift, but I know Dani's injured, and I may need to move her fast.

As I start the ignition, I hit the accelerator, my tires kicking up the gravel in their wake. I catch a glimpse of my home in the rearview mirror, and I can't help but wonder if I would ever see it or my pack brothers again.

CHAPTER 47
DANI

"I think I might keep you." Lester grins, coming back into the room. I have no idea how long I've been here for. I'm so tired, and my body feels like it's been run over by a train. "What do you think? Do you want to stay with me? We make quite the cute couple."

I peer at him from between my swollen eyelids, wondering if this is what awaited me with Drake. *Is this just my fate? To be abused at the hands of unworthy men.* I wanted to think about Lautner and the tenderness he had shown me, but it seemed out of place here. A cruel reminder of a life not meant to be.

"Hey, I'm talking to you, Dani. Do I need to cut you again?" he asks, moving toward me, twirling the blade already saturated with my blood in his hand. "It seems to be the only way of keeping your attention. Well, that, or I know you like it when I bite you." His hand roughly pushes against his most recent bite on my collar bone as I cry out in pain. "Did it turn you on as much as it did me? Hmm.

Maybe I should do it again and see for myself." He chuckles at my ear before pacing the room once more. "Man, I wish I could have seen the look on Lautner's face when he watched me do this. I bet he was pissed. God, I'm getting hard just thinking about it. He always thought he was better than me growing up. Better at fighting and fucking. It was always a competition, and now, I'm really going to get one over him by claiming his precious mate."

My eyes glance down, noticing the bulge in his pants before quickly turning away. I didn't want to add fuel to whatever fire is brewing inside him. In the last twenty-four hours, I'd lost my virginity to Lautner, been sexually assaulted by Drake, kidnapped, and tortured. I didn't want to have to add rape to my ever-growing list of firsts. "I'm listening." I hate the way my voice sounds in an almost pleading tone.

"Yeah, darling. It won't be long now till he gets here. Then once he's dead, we can be together." He smiles, his eyes watching me closely.

I had come to realize that his sinister smile is my warning that he is ready for more.

"Please, can I have a glass of water?" I beg. Anything to try and take his mind off whatever he'd been planning to do next.

"Water?"

I nod. "I'm losing my voice," I croak for added effect.

"It's all that screaming in pleasure you've been doing, isn't it?" He smiles as if expecting me to agree.

I could play this game. "If you want me to scream for you, then I need some water."

"Alright, stay there." He laughs at his own joke, pointing to the binds at my wrists and ankles. "I'll be right back."

I close my eyes, forcing myself to remain strong. I'm not

sure how long it will take Lautner to get here, wherever here is. I have no idea how far out they took me. All I know is that I have to bide my time and pray that Lester wouldn't hurt me any more than he already had. Brandon made it clear that I was expendable. He didn't care about me in the slightest. I was bait, pure and simple. Lautner is his target. On the other hand, Lester seems to think we are lovers, and all this ... is just some sort of twisted foreplay to the start of our happily ever after.

"You know, Dani," he starts as he brings a glass of water to my lips. "Once Lautner is dead, I'm going to mark every inch of your body, claiming you for myself. I know what you're thinking," he smiles, "why bother. My mark won't last once you finally shift. But it will ... if I use this."

"You're sick," I spit, staring at the bottle of draino in his hand.

"Oh, now come on, it's genius." He comes closer as he tries to unscrew the lid. "Now, which one of my bites should we try it on first, I wonder. Or shall I make a new one," he snaps his teeth.

"For God's sake," Brandon mutters, coming into the room. "Are you still at it?"

"What, she's going to be my mate. It's only right."

"Has anyone ever told you that you're psychotic and not in a useful way," Brandon sneers. "If you're going to do it, do it now. It shouldn't be long before Lautner gets here, and I want everything to go according to plan."

"What's the big deal, anyway. He's not getting out of here alive. You honestly think he can take the both of us?"

"No, but unlike you, I don't leave things to chance. I can't have you committing yourself to our prisoner. She may very well die yet, depending on how things go."

"Well, we will always have this time together," he replies, kissing my cheek.

"Touching," Brandon replies, looking somewhat bored. "Now, go out front and keep an eye out."

I watch as Lester places the draino down, leaving the room.

I breathe a sigh of relief now that it's just Brandon I have to contend with. I'm not an idiot. Out of the two of them, Brandon is the most dangerous. He might act calm and in control, but he's a cold-blooded killer on the inside, and I'm nothing more than a pawn to play in his twisted game. But he has shown no interest in raping or torturing me just yet. All his plans are focused on Lautner. I know he would only touch me if it proved to be in his interest.

"You do realize your father paid me a lot of money to keep you safe."

"I'll be sure to tell him what a great job you're doing," I reply sarcastically.

"Tell me, Dani. Do you know why the contract to marry Drake is so important that your father has made your life hell?" he asks.

I shake my head. I'd always wondered what my price was, but my father would only lie. He didn't see me worthy of the truth, even if it is my life that pays for it.

"Let me give you a quick history lesson while we wait. Your father murdered Drake's father in cold blood. There was no challenge. He knew he could never beat him for alpha in a fair fight, so he cheated. Your father never counted on Drake witnessing it and catching it all on video. He used that video to blackmail your father. Forcing him into signing a contract to take your hand in marriage, ensuring that he would take his rightful place as alpha when the time comes."

"Why didn't he just use the video to show the pack? They would never have accepted him as alpha."

"Because where's the fun in blackmail if you can't use it to your full advantage. Did you never wonder why Drake and your father are tied at the hip? Cortez is good at getting information, and Drake uses that to his full advantage. Plus, they both despise you."

"Why, why do they hate me so much?"

"Do you remember when you were twelve, you had your first shift. Turns out, you aren't just another typical wolf. You're a luna—an alpha female. You threaten them with your power. They needed to keep you weak. A little toy they can control."

"No, you're wrong. I've never shifted."

"That's where you're wrong. When your father beat you, you shifted and nearly killed him."

"That's impossible. Lacey was there. She saw everything."

"Lacey passed out. She never could handle the sight of blood, could she," he enquires. "That's why your father made up the lies about your seizures. He couldn't risk you shifting again."

"Why are you telling me this?"

"Your father and Drake have fed you enough wolfsbane that you're not shifting any time soon. Also, unlike Lester here, I don't think you will survive the night."

"How do you know all this?" I shake my head, struggling to accept everything that I'm hearing.

"Drake isn't just your Beta and soon-to-be mate. He's also my cousin. Although we don't really get along, he can be useful now and again."

"Lautner will kill you," I say, still reeling from the recent news.

"He will try, but the fact remains, you would have been perfect together. Two strong alphas capable of many things, and I can't let that happen. I won't." He stands as if getting ready to leave the room. "I have one more gift for you before I leave." He smiles, coming closer as he pulls the hunting knife from the sheath at his waist. "Just to be sure you don't try anything." He thrusts the blade forward as I cry out, the blade puncturing through my skin like butter. "When I remove this knife, you'll have about thirty minutes before you bleed to death. Even if somehow Lautner spoils my plans and I die, just know, I will distract him long enough to know that I have taken my revenge." He pulls the knife out as I scream.

CHAPTER 48
LAUTNER

I drag my eyes away from the road ahead of me as I stare at my phone—Seth's name flashing on the screen. Damn it. I pick it up, hurtling it out of the window. I'd only been on the road for the past twenty minutes. I was hoping I would've had more time before they realized I was gone. I wasn't far now, but I have no idea what awaits me when I get there. Lester is your typical stray; he doesn't plan ahead, but Brandon, he's cunning, and I have no doubt that whatever lies in wait for me is all his doing. I could very well be walking into a trap with the hunters, not that it mattered. I'd do anything to get Dani back.

The roof of the cabin between the trees comes into view as I drive the last few feet.

Lester is waiting outside for me. He smirks when he sees me, cracking his knuckles as if I should be afraid. He knows me better than that. Out of everyone here, he's the only one I'd actually called a friend growing up.

I exit the car, slowly looking around. It's quiet. Looks

like Brandon wanted to keep this between us, instead of involving the rest of the hunters.

"Glad you could make it." Lester heads toward me like a long-lost friend instead of the man who had my heart and soul trapped in the basement behind him.

"Where is she?" I get up in his face, nose to nose, instantly smelling Dani's blood on his skin.

"I smell good, don't I." He grins wider as we face off. "Don't worry, she's alive for now." I watch him warily, forcing myself to stay in control. No matter how much I want to punch him in the face right now, I know I have to be patient. For all I know, Dani may not even be here. It might just be a trap to lure me out. Once I saw Dani for myself, then I would make my move.

"Follow me." We enter through the crumpling front door, and I feel like I've stepped back in time. It looks the same as it did two years ago, except for a few more broken windows and a lot more dust. The house is dark as I follow Lester into the kitchen and through the old wooden door leading down into the basement. The wooden steps creaking under my feet as I tentatively make my way down. A lone bulb is swinging precariously overhead, casting the room in dangerous shadows. Dani is slumped in the same chair I found Seth in two years ago. I didn't know much about PTSD, but I'm pretty sure that's what Brandon is hoping for. Something to throw me off my game. He's going to be disappointed. I square my shoulders, instantly on alert. I know Brandon is down here somewhere, hidden in the shadows.

"Dani," I call out, but she remains still. The scent of her blood permeating the small room.

"Glad you could finally join us," Brandon calls out,

emerging from behind Dani, swirling his brother's beloved knife in his hand.

My foot finally hits the bottom of the stairs as Lester comes behind me, pushing me forwards.

"Is he alone?" Brandon asks Lester, never taking his eyes off me.

"Yeah, you were right. He actually does give a shit about the female, after all. Your father would be so disappointed in you." Lester laughs. "I always knew you were weak." I turn around to glare at him as Brandon comes toward me, his heavy boots making a loud clunking sound on the concrete beneath our feet.

"It must bring back some memories, being back here—Seth, bound to the same chair as your mate. I always had a soft spot for him. Even now, I miss his company. The times we shared down here." He smiles. "The thought of bringing him back here, well, it's what keeps me going. Once you're out of the way, I'll find him again. Although, I did hear he's injured. I do hope he recovers again before we meet. It would be a shame to find him broken. That's my job, after all." I can feel the sharp tip of the blade as it hits my chest, nicking my skin. He pushes it deeper, slowly dragging it down as it cuts through the fabric of my wifebeater, tearing at my skin below. It's not deep, but my chest burns from the silver blade, and I grit my teeth, determined not to give him anything.

"Lester, get the chains." I watch Lester pull on a pair of leather gloves so as not to burn himself.

"You think I'm just going to stand here and let you chain me up. Let Dani go. You've got me now."

Brandon laughs. "Did you really think it was going to be that easy? No. What you did is unforgivable. You killed my brother," he seethes. "I didn't even get the chance to say goodbye. I don't have a body to bury. I have nothing left of my brother except for this knife. So, this," he thrusts the blade toward me, "is how you die. You and your mate."

I can hear the chains rattling together behind me. I'm running out of time.

"Let her go, and I'll come willingly."

"Again, you're not listening," he shouts. "You don't have a say in anything that happens now."

I can feel Lester standing behind me, and I know if he gets the chains on me, it's game over. I'm still recovering from the transfusion, and nowhere near at my full strength. I throw my hand out, knocking the blade from Brandon's hand as I smash my head against his. Spinning around, I grab Lester's shoulders. Using my surprise attack to my full advantage, I pull him down as my knee repeatedly connects with his midsection until he drops the chains. Brandon growls behind me, advancing as I push Lester away, his head hitting the wall.

I catch Brandon with a hard right as he stumbles. I follow his movements, continuing to hit him with everything I have left in me. I watch as he goes down hard, dropping the knife. I bend down, ready to pick it up and end this once and for all. A weight lands on my back as I fall to the ground with Lester on top of me. I try to roll him off, but he straddles over me, pinning me beneath his weight. Lester has his own knife now as he swings it wildly at me. The blade catches me a few times, but Lester was never into weapons. The cuts he lands are superficial at best. Frustrated at his sloppiness, I knock his hand, the knife slipping easily through his leather gloves to land beside me. His fist comes down, but I tip my head to the side as he barely grazes my cheek. I buck my hips off the floor, dislodging him and throwing him off me. I snatch the knife up off the floor as I dive toward Dani. Her head hangs low on her chest as I put my hand against her forehead. She's cold and clammy. Fear claws its way inside me, and I fear I'm too late. I've failed her.

"Dani." She doesn't move. My eyes roam down to the blood pooling at her waist, and I know she's been stabbed.

I can hear Lester and Brandon getting back to their feet behind me. Using the knife I'd taken off Lester, I cut the ties off her wrists and ankles.

"This is it, Lautner," Brandon calls out, but I don't turn around. I carefully run my fingers down Dani's cheek, memorizing her face. It might be the last thing I ever see. "I'm sorry, Dani." I take her hand off the armrest as I bring it toward my mouth. I strike fast, biting her arm, tasting her blood. I call my wolf forward, sending her every bit of power inside me, praying it's enough to keep her alive in the hope the pack will find her.

Empty, I fall to the floor at her feet. Brandon looms above me, Tommy's knife aimed at my throat.

CHAPTER 49
DANI

It's quiet. Too quiet. I have no idea whether I'm awake or asleep. Perhaps I'm dead. I remember the pain of the knife as it penetrated my stomach. The blood. So much blood as it coated my clothes. But now, I feel nothing. No pain. No fear. Just an eerie silence. I thought I had heard Lautner at one point, but I can't be sure. He's the one person I want right now. I must be dead. Isn't that what's supposed to happen when you die? You hear and see your life pass before your eyes. In five short days, that's what he'd become, my life.

Mate. The word sounds strange. A calling from deep within my chest awakening me. The pain comes back tenfold as my blood boils, racing through my veins. I cry out, but it's no use. Panting, I try and control my breathing as my insides quake. The breaking and crushing of my bones now pierce the peaceful silence. I fall to the floor, having no idea why I'm no longer bound to the cold wooden chair. I feel the hardness of the concrete as I collapse under the pain. Surely, I would pass out soon. The pain is too much. I try to open my eyes, but I'm instantly blinded, closing them quickly. I fight to remain in control, but it's pointless. Perhaps if I accept death, it will pass soon. Accepting my fate, I let go, allowing the pain to run its course as everything goes black.

🐾

I carefully open my eyes. It's strange. My sight is different now, sharper. I go to speak, a howl breaking from my lips. I look down, noticing the white paws on the ground in front of me. I take a step back, and it follows my movements. I gasp in shock, but it comes out as a whimper from my elongated jaw. I shake my head, disorientated at the newfound power within me. *I'd done it. I'd finally shifted.* I can feel the blood still dripping at my side from my stab wound, but I no longer feel the pain of it crushing me.

I test my paws against the concrete, expecting to fall flat on my face, but I remain steady. Looking around the room, I realize I'm still in the dark cellar they had brought me to. I scent the air, catching the smell of the woods on a rainy fall day, and I know Lautner has been here recently. Panic consumes me as I notice the blood on the floor, and I instantly know it is his. I let out a howl filled with all the rage and sorrow brewing inside of me.

I creep toward the door leading upstairs, my paws silent as if I know the exact path that I'm taking. My mind focused on the only thing I need. *Lautner.*

It's cold and dark outside, the full moon overhead my only source of light illuminating the darkness ahead of me. I can scent them all now. Wherever Lautner is, they are also with him. I put my nose to the ground, greedily tracking them.

The sound of a fist connecting hard against flesh,

followed by a grunt, has my ears twitching. *Lautner*. I break into a lope, coming to a sudden stop as Lautner's body hits the floor. Brandon and Lester turning their cold eyes toward me.

"Looks like our little luna isn't dead after all," Brandon says, a smile cracking his face. His eyes look at me hungrily as he licks his lips, and I instantly take a step back.

"Move again, and I slit his throat," Brandon warns, crouching down beside Lautner and pulling his head back. I instantly stop.

"Good girl," Brandon says as I snarl in reply.

Lautner's eyes find mine. I can see the instant relief on his face at seeing me alive before quickly turning to panic.

"I'm starting to see the appeal Dani holds for you. Her power is quite something, don't you think?"

"Pity you're not going to live long enough to experience it for yourself," Lautner spits, but Brandon only laughs.

"Can you feel her power? I think you had the right idea after all, Lester." Brandon pushes Lautner forward as he falls to the ground. His eyes watch me greedily as he slowly strips off his clothes, letting me see just how much my power is affecting him. He is rock-hard as he stands there naked before me, watching me.

Lester is also naked now, and I can't help but notice he's just as hard as Brandon. I quickly avert my gaze.

"Dani, run," Lautner calls out.

Something tells me that Lautner is right. I need to go right now because if I don't, I won't get another chance. But I came to find my mate, and I wouldn't leave without him. I stand my ground.

"No," Brandon calls out as Lester positions to shift. "She's mine."

"The hell she is," Lester snaps. "You promised her to me if she survived."

Brandon sneers. "You haven't got it in you to claim a luna. You're weak. She would be taken from you instantly."

Lester ignores Brandon as I watch him shift, and I'm left facing his black wolf once more. I tremble, remembering him pinning me to the ground as his teeth snapped at my throat. Lester growls, advancing toward me before a brown wolf intercepts him taking him down. I look over to Brandon, but he is no longer there, and I realize he must be the other wolf. I hurry over to Lautner.

"Dani," he mumbles. I lick his face, confirming it's me. His hand lifts from the ground as he touches my fur, a weak smile on his face. "You're fucking beautiful, do you know that. My beautiful white luna."

The sound of a wolf yelping behind me has me turning around, trying to shield Lautner behind me. Brandon is on top of Lester, his teeth biting anywhere he can land. Lester howls in pain as Brandon continues his vicious attack. There really is no loyalty amongst strays, not like packs. It's every man for himself, and I'm the prize. I quickly turn back to Lautner, praying he can move. I have no idea what I'm doing. I don't even know how to shift back. It won't be long before Brandon comes for me.

Lautner groans as he stands up, his face a mask of pain. His eyes focused on the wolves fighting behind me.

His fingers grip the fur at my neck as he looks down. "I need you to run, Dani. I need you to get as far away from here as possible."

I shake my head. I wouldn't leave him.

"You have to, and you need to go now. If Brandon catches you, that's it. You will be mated to him. It's a full moon tonight. You're a luna, Dani. You're special. Brandon can take you from me. I promise to explain everything later, but for now, you need to run. Go. Don't look back."

I watch the determination on his face as Brandon growls low behind me. I turn to find him watching me. The black wolf that had once been Lester dead beneath him.

"Run," Lautner shouts as he comes to stand in front of me. I watch Brandon as he breaks into a run, his body slamming into Lautner and taking him down. I'm frozen. I want to take Lautner's advice, but I can't. I won't leave him to die. I'd made him a promise. If he died, I died, and I'm not changing my mind. I break into a run as I lunge for Brandon, catching his hind legs. The move is sloppy and uncontrolled, but it works as Brandon rolls off Lautner. I growl as I start forward. Brandon tips his head to the side as if trying to work out my next move. He won't be able to. I don't even know it myself.

"Dani," Lautner shouts, and I know he's pissed. He doesn't want me here. He's just told me what happens if we lose. I'll no longer be his.

Brandon takes a few steps toward me, his eyes shining bright, and I know he's smirking at me underneath his wolf's exterior.

I back up, but it's no good. Brandon is ready. He crashes into my side as I'm thrown to the ground, landing instantly on top of me. I writhe beneath him, trying to get my back legs up high enough to kick him off, but he's better at this than I am. He has my entire body trapped beneath his. I close my eyes, bracing myself for the feel of his teeth at my throat.

It doesn't come. I hear him grunt above me before I feel his weight pulled from my body. Suddenly free, I roll back on all four paws, panting for breath. Growling, I turn to watch Lautner and Brandon as they circle one another. You can feel the aura of their power in the air, and I can instantly pick out Lautner's. The power of the alpha. They both attack simultaneously, but Lautner takes control as if Brandon is nothing beneath him. He dominates him, attacking over and over until the scent of Brandon's blood is heavy in the air. Lautner lifts his head as if sensing me watching him. The connection between us is undeniable as he leaves Brandon crumpled and broken at his feet, stalking toward me.

Brandon groans as I glance toward him. I watch as he shifts back, trying to climb to his feet. He's covered in blood, and I know he's hurt, his eyes blazing fury as he turns to meet my gaze. It's over for now. He knows he's lost tonight, but he won't give up. He's nowhere near finished with me yet. With a nod of his head, he skulks toward the cover of the trees before vanishing from sight.

Lautner growls low, demanding my attention. The look in his eyes screams possession and dominance as he pounces, catching my legs out from under me. We land hard as he rolls me under him. His beautiful amber eyes burning brighter than I'd ever seen. He growls a warning before his teeth nip at my throat. I thrash beneath him, trying to dislodge him, but he holds firm. His growl vibrating through me until I yield. I instantly feel the power inside me weaken as my bones once again break inside my body. I cry out, riding out the pain until I'm human once more.

I open my eyes, surprised to find Lautner already shifted back before me. His eyes look down at me, filled with awe and desire. There's no doubt in my mind that this man is my alpha. His mouth comes down hard and fast, taking mine, claiming me in a promise of forever. His hand finds its way between my legs as if testing my readiness for him. I am. I'm more than ready. This close to death, my body welcomes the warmth of life he breathes back into me. He lifts my leg, positioning himself at my entrance before sliding deep inside me. I moan in relief, gripping his shoulders as he relentlessly takes my body higher and higher.

"You're mine, mate." His words are raw, animalistic, powerful. Every thrust of his hips pushing me to the edge. A promise that there would never be anyone else. He would consume every part of me relentlessly. Always.

"Say it," he demands. He doesn't stop as he pounds inside of me deep into the earth, gripping my hips. I'm aching and hurt, but I don't care. I need this. He needs this.

"I'm yours." Tipping my head to the side, he doesn't leave me waiting. His mouth strikes fast—my orgasm tearing through me as I feel the sharp pain of his bite. The pain is over quickly, replaced by the gentle caress of his power combining with my own. Seducing me as if it were the most natural thing in the world. I feel Lautner tense up beneath me as he releases inside me. We stay there, locked together, regaining our breath until finally, Lautner pulls back.

"I'm sorry," he murmurs, his eyes roaming over every crevice of my body, taking in my injuries.

"I'm not," I say truthfully, hoping he can hear just how much I needed this.

"We need to get you back to Ryan." Unable to move, I nod as he picks me up in his arms. I must pass out once or twice because the next thing I know, we're in the car.

"Hold on, mate." His hand clasps mine, taking us home.

CHAPTER 50
LAUTNER

A knock sounds at my door as I rest on my bed—Dani wrapped around me.

"Come in," I call out, adjusting the comforter up over her.

"How is she?" Mick asks, entering the room.

My alpha looks like he has aged a few years in the past twenty-four hours, and I know I'm partly to blame for all the stress the pack has been through.

"Lester and Brandon have put her through hell, but she's tough. She'll heal."

As soon as I'd brought her home, Ryan attended to her wounds while I sat there feeling helpless. Once he'd finished, I'd taken her straight up to my room, determined to check her over for myself. Every mark on her body leaving me shaking in anger. It was only at her words that I finally calmed down.

"I'm okay," she repeated over and over. Even in pain,

she was soothing me. I'd wanted her to tell me everything that happened, but I knew she needed time to heal.

"I'm sorry I ran out on the pack before, but I couldn't take the risk, not with her," I explain.

"I know. You're a good man, Lautner. I just hope you're finally starting to heal yourself. I know you feel guilty about what happened to her, but that was her father and Drake's doing, not yours."

"Maybe," I reply with a shake of my head. "I just added fuel to the fire. Her father may have planned the kidnapping, but if it hadn't been Lester and Brandon's hatred for me, then maybe they wouldn't have hurt her so badly."

"Her father was already deranged. Nothing would have stopped him. And Lester and Brandon, they're just as bad. She's safe with you now."

I think over his words. He's right. She is safe here with me. I would never let anyone get their hands on her again. All these years, I had honestly believed I could never love another more than myself, and yet here she lay beside me. I would never be able to go on living without her. In just a few days, she'd taken me apart and remade me. Taming the monster within.

"She's my mate. I would go to the ends of hell for her, and as crazy as it sounds, she was prepared to die for me, even after the way I'd treated her. She knew before I did that fate wouldn't take no for an answer."

He nods. "I'll leave you to it. If you need anything, just message down." He closes the door, and I return to watching Dani as she sleeps. She looks so peaceful, even with the bruises that covered her face. She looked content. Happy even. Her hands wrap tighter around my waist, pulling herself closer to my body as if she can sense my thoughts. Maybe she could. She's a luna, after all. Her power is pure. Undeniable.

I leave the room as Dani goes to take a bath, determined to find Daniel.

"Hey man, how is she?" he asks tiredly. Just a few days ago, I would have been pissed at his affection for Dani, but now, I knew that she loved me, not him.

"She's good. Just needs a little time. Look, I need a favor, or well, Dani does."

"Anything."

"I need you to trace this number. Dani's father threatened her friend Lacey if she didn't marry Drake. Dani can't get a hold of her, and she's worried her father has done something."

"I'll look into it now," he says. "We already have Cortez's phone. I should be able to find something."

"Thanks. Look, I'm sorry about how I acted. She's lucky to have a friend like you." He nods, accepting my weak-ass apology. Now I just have one more thing to sort out.

I knock at Mick's office door.

"Yeah," he calls out. "Everything alright?" he asks as soon as he sees me.

"Yeah, she told me everything. Where do we stand with the Council? I'm prepared to leave if need be."

"We know the supplier. We managed to get it off his phone. We have more than enough evidence to support that he had his own daughter tortured and kidnapped. Plus, Drake is singing, trying to save his own skin, although it won't do him any good. The Council has everything. I'm just waiting on word back. Did you really mean what you said before to Cortez. Did you kill Drew?"

"Yeah, I did. I put him out of his misery."

He nods in understanding. Sometimes words weren't needed.

"Congratulations on being the first of us to mate. Dani is a great addition to the pack."

"She's a luna," I say, watching the shocked expression on his face. "That's why her father and Drake were so threatened by her. Once she shifts again, others will find out, and they will come for her."

"A luna. Does she know what this means?" he asks.

"Not yet, but I will tell her everything. I won't keep secrets from her."

"Lunas are rare," Mick agrees, "but she will be safe with you and the pack. If you ever change your mind about the alpha position, you know I would step down. You proved yourself over the past few days. Heck, even Ryan is impressed, although he'll never admit it."

"I have no intention of taking over. I never wanted this, and I still don't. You are my alpha, and Dani is my mate. My family."

He nods, accepting my words. "It's over, Lautner. Now go see your mate."

CHAPTER 51
DANI

"Hey, how are you feeling?" Lautner asks as he comes through the door of his room, or should I say, our room. I still can't believe that he's mine. After everything that happened between us, it seemed like all the odds were stacked against us. Yet here we stood, together. Victorious. It's far from over. The hunters and Brandon are still out there. But for now, I have a mate by my side and a father that can no longer control me. It's perfect.

"Better," I say. I'm still a little sore, especially around the stab wound to my stomach, but I would survive. Ryan had told me that I was extremely lucky. Had Brandon stabbed me just an inch to the right, I would have been dead by now.

"I have a little surprise for you if you're up to it," he says, coming to sit beside me on the bed.

I moan, pulling him closer. "I like your surprises." I wrap my arms around his neck, pulling his face down to mine. He kisses me with a scorching hot mouth, pouring everything I need into the kiss, before pulling away with a sigh, and resting his head against mine.

"I know you do, but you're not healed enough for that, just yet." He winks, pulling away from me and adjusting his hard length I can clearly see through his joggers. I fan at my heated skin, his mark at my neck tingling at his words. He always had this effect on me, and I hoped it would never go away. "But I think you will like my other surprise. Wait here," he says, going over to the door.

"It's about time," I hear Lacey call out as she walks through the door.

"Lacey," I say excitedly. "How ... what?"

She comes over to the bed, throwing her arms around me. "I'm so glad you're safe," she murmurs, hugging me tightly.

"Ow, Lacey, you're pulling my stitches," I say with a grimace.

"Oh my God, sorry. I'm just so happy to see you."

"I'll leave you two alone. Just be careful with my mate," Lautner grumbles as he heads toward the door.

"Thank you," I say as he turns back around.

He shrugs. "It wasn't just me. Daniel helped."

"Yeah, but I bet you're the one that thought of it. Thought of me. Thank you," I say again.

I can see him begin to blush at my appreciation as he hurries out the door, and I turn my attention back to my friend.

"Lacey, I'm so sorry. What did my father do to you?"

"Don't worry, I'm fine. I lost my phone, although now I know what happened, I'm sure your father must have had one of the pack take it. I was never in any danger. Anyway, forget about me, look at you," she says, concerned. "Lautner filled me in on everything. Didn't I warn you that your father would be the death of you one day."

"And you were nearly right. Luckily, I have Lautner on my side, so it worked out for the best," I assure her.

"So, tell me, are you guys mated?"

Blushing, I lift my neck, proudly displaying Lautner's bite.

"I told you," she screams excitedly. "I knew all along he was your fated mate. Now I just need to find mine. I hope it's that sexy male downstairs, the one with the wavy brown hair and killer dimples."

I smile at her description. "That's Daniel. The one you thought was a serial killer," I remind her with a laugh.

"Damn, he could totally murder me." She laughs as I join her. "Promise to introduce me before I leave?" she asks.

I nod. "How long can you stay?" I ask, not wanting to let her go just yet.

"As long as I want, now that Terry is Alpha."

"Terry." I smile, pleased to hear this. Although young, he has a good heart, and I know the pack respects him.

"I'm just glad you're alright, and everything worked out for the best in the end."

"It did," I say with a smile. "Now, how about we go for a drink, and I'll introduce you to Daniel."

"Are you sure you should be out of bed?"

"You're starting to sound like Lautner," I groan, pulling myself out of bed. "I need to get out of this room, if only for a few hours."

"Here, I'll help you," she replies, coming to take my arm. "So, is Daniel single?" she asks as we head toward the door.

CHAPTER 52
LAUTNER

I awake to the sound of a blood-curdling scream disrupting the quiet of the night. Dani is fast asleep beside me as I quietly slip out of bed, pulling on yesterday's joggers and leaving the room. I pad down the hall, rapping my knuckles against Seth's door before I enter.

"Shit," Seth whispers as he sees me. He's panting heavily. His skin glowing in the moonlight, coated in sweat. "I'm sorry I woke you," he mutters, reaching over to the nightstand, and grabbing his cigarettes, lighting one up.

"They're getting bad again," I say, although I didn't need to. It'd been happening too frequently lately.

"Yeah. I had him. I had him, Lautner, and he got away, again," he spits angrily. "It's the same nightmare every night. I have him before me and ...."

"It's just a dream."

He nods in agreement, but I see his shoulders tense up. "What if ... what if I can't do it. All I've ever wanted is his death to move forward, yet I freeze every chance I get. It's like he still has this power over me." He shudders.

"He didn't break you, Seth. You're one of the strongest men I know."

"Then why do I feel it ... broken." His eyes drop down to his leg. He'd shifted a few times over the past few days, yet still he walks with a slight limp, and I catch the odd glimpse of pain on his face when he thinks no one is looking. "How's Dani?" he asks, clearly trying to change the subject, and I let him.

"She's good. Her stitches are healing. Luckily, he hit her liver. If it'd been anywhere else, she mightn't have been so lucky."

"You've got a good female there, Lautner. I'm glad you didn't blow it." He smiles, and I can't help but join him.

"I know, but finding out she's a luna brings its own set of problems."

"If any two people were meant to be together, it's you guys. Now, go back to your mate. I'm good now."

"You sure?"

"Yeah. Thanks, though. For checking up on me."

※

As I slip quietly back into my room, Dani is awake in bed.

"Is everything alright?" she asks.

"Yeah, just Seth having one of his nightmares," I assure her.

She nods, but I can see how worried she is about him. "Will he be alright?"

"I don't know," I reply honestly, climbing into bed and taking her into my arms.

"Do you think Brandon is still around?" she asks as her hand strokes intricate circles on my chest.

I can't lie to her, but I don't want to scare her either. "He won't have gone far. The hunters are no doubt still around. I'm sure when we find them, he will also be there."

We sit in silence as the minutes pass. My fingers gently stroking her arm as she relaxes against me.

"Lautner," she whispers in the dark, "make love to me."

"I don't want to hurt you, Dani," I say, my hand automatically going to her stitches.

"You won't hurt me," she whispers. "You could never hurt me."

Her fingers trail down to my already hard cock. I just needed to be in the same room with her, and I was ready.

"But first, I want to do something." She sits up in bed as she brings her knees on either side of my hips. She watches me closely, biting her lip, and I know she's nervous.

"You don't have to do anything you don't want to," I tell her as she smiles, determination shining in her blue eyes.

She brings her lips down, pressing firm kisses to my abdomen, before continuing down and taking my cock into her mouth. I moan at the contact of her lips around me. I'd dreamed of this moment since we met. I can feel the trepidation of her mouth as my hand automatically strokes the back of her head, encouraging her. Her mouth and tongue work together until I'm putty in her hands.

"Come here, Dani," I growl as she smiles, obviously proud of her work, shimmying up the bed.

"Now, it's my turn." I flip her onto the bed, gentle of her stitches as I spread her legs. I growl approvingly, nipping the inside of her thigh. "Two can play that game, mate." I run my tongue up her slit in one long movement. She moans as I pay special attention to her clit, nibbling and sucking it into my mouth.

"Lautner," she breathes huskily, and I know from this day on I'm a willing slave to her. My fingers play teasing circles at her entrance before sliding in, sucking her clit at the same time. I feel her orgasm tighten around me, drawing me in. Removing my fingers, I bring them to my mouth, savoring every last drop of her.

"I love you, Dani. I was born to love you," I say, laying on top of her, resting my weight on my elbows so as not to hurt her.

"I love you too, Lautner." She lifts her body from the bed, meeting my lips with her own. I wanted to wait for her to heal before we made love again, but I know there is no going back now, not after a taste. I lie down beside her, carefully pulling her on top of me. I grip her hips, guiding her down until my cock is fully seated in her heat. "It's always been you, Lautner," she whispers as she starts to move above me. I'm lost in the feeling of her as she trails her nails over my hardened nipples. I thrust harder, taking control. Her nails rake my chest, leaving a trail of red marks as she smiles wickedly, knowing I love every mark she makes on my body. I sit up quickly, capturing her face in my hands.

"You're mine, Dani, always and forever." I tip her head back as she continues to move above me, driving me wild. I bite her mark once more at her throat, reclaiming her with everything I have.

CHAPTER 53
DANI

It had been two weeks since the kidnapping, and for the past few days, Lautner had taken me out to the woods, trying to help me shift. But every day, nothing happened. He could entice my power to the surface whenever we were intimate, but still, she remains dormant. I know he's worried, but he never lets on.

"I hate this," I grumble, kicking at the leaves under my feet. "It's never going to happen."

"It will," Lautner says, pulling me to a stop and taking me into his arms. "One day, it will just happen, but until then, I will protect you with everything I have. You're mine, remember that," he says before claiming my lips possessively. I melt into his kiss, letting him take away all of my insecurities until there is nothing but him and me. He pulls away, his hand trailing down my cheek as his amber eyes burn their way into my soul. "I believe in you, mate."

A small shudder of pleasure runs through me. *Mate*. I loved it when he called me that. He had fought against it for so long, but now it rolled off his tongue with ease. I know he's right about my wolf. I shouldn't worry too much about this. We've already overcome so much. I'm sure she will come out when she's ready.

Last night after we'd made love, Lautner explained a bit more about lunas. Apparently, we were extremely rare. Lunas were capable of producing powerful alphas, and with the right mate by their side, their power is a force to be reckoned with. Unfortunately, there is a downside to being a luna as well. According to ancient lore, a luna could be remated on the night of the full moon. It didn't have to be by choice either. If I were captured and taken by another and forced into submission, I could be reclaimed. That thought terrified me more than I cared to admit. I would never submit to another. There is only Lautner. No matter how much I promised him, I could still see the worry in his eyes. Until my wolf presented herself and I learned how to control her, I would always be a burden. Even if he never said the words aloud, I know he can't protect me forever. Eventually, I would have to be able to do it myself.

"Have you decided about your father and Drake?" he asks as I close my eyes, leaning into the warmth of his chest.

"Not really. I have no idea what to do."

The Council had responded with their decision a few days ago, and my father and Drake's punishment lies with me. I know I should kill them. That's what the whole pack is waiting for, and yet I just can't say the words. I hated them. After everything they did to me, it should be easy. Yet having that power scares me.

"What should I do?" I ask him, needing his reassurance, if nothing else.

"That decision is not for me to make. I'll stand by you,

no matter what. He can't control you anymore. You're free. Only you can decide how this ends."

"Death just seems too easy," I say. "I want them to suffer, just as they made me."

"Death doesn't have to be easy. That's up to you."

"Why did you kill your father?" I ask, hugging him tighter as he rubs my back.

"Pity, I guess. He wasn't strong enough to do it himself. At first, I hated him. I'd spent my whole life fighting at his request. He beat me until I was strong enough to defend myself. Then it became a sport to him. The strays have their own way of bringing up their children, and none of it is pretty. I guess that's what makes me understand Lester and Brandon. I'm just like them, or at least I was."

"Why did you come back to the pack?" I ask.

"After I killed him, I was alone. I knew the pack was looking for me, but we moved around so much they would never find me. So, after I buried him, I made my way here. Mick's father had taken over at the time; apparently, I looked just like my father, so there was no doubt about who I was. He accepted me with open arms. The pack knew I was different, but they never shunned me for it, and for that, I was grateful. I've spent most of my life hating my father, but now, I think I kind of understand. When Lester and Brandon took you, I was so scared. I'd never known fear before in my life, not until that moment. Maybe that's what my father had tried to protect me from all along—the pain of losing my soul. I never knew that I needed you, Dani, not until you took my heart. I thought I was happy alone. I didn't care about anything or anyone. I was emotionless, but knowing I could have lost you, I never want to feel that way again. I know now that I'm strong enough. If you'd died, I wouldn't have thought twice about it. My life and death lie with you. Always."

I close my eyes, loving the words he spoke. His feelings reciprocated my own perfectly. I had been dead myself, emotionless until he lit a fire inside of me when we met. Two people destined to help repair one another.

"If I choose their death, I need to be the one to do it. Will you stay with me?"

"Of course, I'm never leaving your side again, Dani." His head bends down, his mouth claiming mine in a promise of forever.

SETH COMING SOON

THE STONE VALLEY PACK BOOK TWO

Kyla: I shouldn't be here. When Brandon found me and my sick brother living on the streets, his offer seemed too good to be true. The plan was simple. Find Seth Michaelson, drug him, and wait for the hunters to arrive. That was it. My initiation into the hunters would be complete, and my brother would be safe.

Wrong.

Seth is far more dangerous than I imagined, and now, I'm his. His captive. His prisoner. The war has only just begun, and my family is caught in the middle. I need to escape, but the more time I spend with him, the more I'm not so sure I want him to let me go. He's supposed to be my enemy, and yet when his dark eyes meet mine, I can almost feel his pain as if it were my own. His beast calls to me, and I want nothing more than to submit. Will he let me tame the raging beast within? Or will his need for vengeance destroy us both.

Seth: For the past two years, I've been haunted by my past. I tried to move on, tried to forget, but the night Tommy showed back up in the Valley, it all came back. The beatings, the torture, the rape. Tommy is dead, but his brother Brandon is still out there.

When an attack at the Warehouse leaves Daniel for dead and a pretty redhead trying to stick a needle in my arm, it's time for me to face my demons head-on. I'm the best tracker in the Valley, and this time, the hunter will become the hunted. I will use everything I can to my advantage, including my prisoner, the feisty redhead, Kyla. She's a complication that I don't need.

She's human and my enemy, but my wolf calls her Mate.

War has come to Stone Valley, and this time, I'm planning on ending it.

Seth is Book Two in The Stone Valley Pack series.
This book is recommended for readers 18+
Warning: This book contains scenes that some readers may find triggering, including flashbacks of rape, scenes of violence and torture, strong language, and steamy sex scenes.

Thank you for reading Lautner and Dani's story. I hope you enjoyed it. There will be another book coming your way later this year titled Dani, continuing their story.
Book Two of the Stone Valley Pack will be available soon on Amazon and KU in 2021.

ABOUT THE AUTHOR

Elizabeth Jones lives in Newcastle Upon Tyne in the UK with her husband Lee, two kids, four cats, one dog, and two chickens. Life is generally hectic, and she copes by drinking copious amounts of coffee and relaxing with a good book.
Deciding to fulfill her lifelong dream of becoming an author, she sat down at the laptop and let her imagination run wild with the Stone Valley Pack. Lautner is her debut novel, and she hopes it's the first of many more. You can contact Elizabeth on Facebook or by email. She would love to hear any feedback you may have as she tries to navigate the crazy world of writing novels, which she hopes you will enjoy.

Printed in Great Britain
by Amazon